MURDER ON THE BRIGHTON EXPRESS

CLEOPATRA FOX MYSTERY, BOOK 9

C.J. ARCHER

WWW.CJARCHER.COM

CHAPTER 1

BRIGHTON, AUGUST 1900

The annual summer exodus from London was a boon for seaside towns like Brighton, but it made for a rather crowded experience for those of us holidaying there. I didn't mind. I'd never been to Brighton, and the excitement of visiting a new place outweighed the negatives. It was also my first seaside holiday since I was a child, and the salty tang of the fresh air and the carnival-like atmosphere brought back fond memories of happy times with my parents.

Despite the crowds and the busy attractions, most of the holidaymakers were relaxed. The lazy pace of the passing days meant our two weeks were over too soon. Although I missed my London-based friends and I looked forward to seeing them again, I didn't want to return to the bustle of city life yet.

My cousin, Flossy, felt the same way, but Aunt Lilian did not. She was keen to go home, and expressed it by finding fault with everything. The weather was too warm, it was too windy, the bedsheets were either too crisp or not crisp enough, the other guests too loud, and the hotel itself lacked in every department. She'd become so ill-tempered, and her headaches so frequent, that Flossy and I had gone out alone the last few days and stayed out all day to avoid her.

It was no hardship. There was plenty to do in the seaside leisure capital of England. With the Bainbridge family holidaying in Brighton every year for as long as Flossy could remember, my cousin had seen all the sights many times, but she took great delight in visiting them again with me. We toured the Royal Pavilion, had picnics in Preston Park, shopped for hats and bathing costumes, attended concerts and dance halls, and walked until our feet hurt. She particularly liked promenading along the Palace Pier, since it only opened the year before, making it all rather new for her, too.

The pier provided visitors with all manner of opportunities to part with their money, from games in the amusement arcade to live concerts, dances and carousel rides, and enough refreshment stands and shops to satisfy even my spendthrift cousin. By the second week of our holiday, I had to forbid her from slotting more coins into the fortune-telling machine. She'd already spent far too much in an unsuccessful attempt to discover where she'd meet the man she would marry.

On the final day of our holiday, Flossy wanted to return to the Palace Pier again, but I insisted on visiting the West Pier. It lacked the flashy amusements of its newer rival—and its popularity had dwindled since the Palace Pier opened, according to Flossy—but I liked its old-world charm. Flossy agreed to spend our last afternoon on the West Pier, but only after I promised to buy her ice cream.

We paid our entrance fee at the kiosk then began the long amble to the pavilion at the other end. Flags on the kiosk roofs flapped in the sea breeze, but it wasn't so strong that we needed to hang onto our hats or lower our parasols. Seagulls coasted high above, or perched on the railing, waiting to swoop on morsels of fish and chips that fell out of paper wrappings.

We listened to the band performing a lively tune on the bandstand as we marveled at the view back to the promenade and Kings Road. The creamy stone facade of the Grand Brighton Hotel where we were staying gleamed in the sunshine. Perhaps Aunt Lilian sat on the balcony outside her room, gazing out to the sea and the pier, but I doubted it. We'd left her lying on the sofa with a damp cloth over her forehead, the electric fan whirring soothingly in the corner.

We purchased our ice creams and enjoyed them while seated on a bench in the shade with several other holiday-makers. Just as we were about to walk back, a trio of guests staying at the same hotel as us arrived. We greeted Lord and Lady Pridhurst and their daughter, Odette. Lord Pridhurst introduced the handsome young gentleman with them as an associate, Mr. Holland. Judging by the way Odette batted her eyelashes at him, she hoped he would become more than an associate.

"Mr. Holland works at his father's canned goods business," she said enthusiastically. "He's very dedicated to it. He came down to Brighton just to discuss some particulars with my father."

That explained Mr. Holland's attire. He was rather over-dressed for a warm day at the seaside. Where Lord Pridhurst wore a white straw boater and light gray lounge suit, Mr. Holland looked as though he was going to the office in London with his black suit and high, stiff collar that must make it impossible for him to inspect his own footwear of polished black shoes.

"I came to see you, too, Odette," Mr. Holland said with a smile for her and a flick of his gaze to her father.

She blushed and nibbled on her lower lip. Lord Pridhurst seemed pleased with their flirtation, although his face was partly obscured by the handkerchief he dabbed across his sweaty forehead. Even though he was the more appropriately attired of the two men, he looked more uncomfortable in the heat.

Odette took Flossy's hand. "It's such a pity to be leaving tomorrow. I was just saying how much I will miss the friends I made in Brighton this summer, and that I hoped to see you again in London when next I visit with Mama."

Flossy didn't miss the opportunity to promote her family's business. "You must stay at the Mayfair Hotel when you do. My parents would be pleased to have you as our guests."

Odette flushed with embarrassment. "Oh. We always stay at the Coburg Hotel when we come to the city. Papa will be there all next week, as it happens, but Mama and I must return home." At Flossy's downcast face, Odette appealed to her parents. "Perhaps we could consider staying at the Mayfair next time."

Lady Pridhurst smiled benignly. "We shall indeed

consider it. It would be a delight to see your mother again, Miss Bainbridge."

I knew a noncommittal answer when I heard one. They had no intention of switching their allegiance to the Mayfair. My suspicion was confirmed by Lord Pridhurst's flat refusal.

"Unfortunately, the Mayfair is not conveniently located," he said in a tone that invited no argument.

I failed to see how the Coburg's position was better. Situated near Grosvenor Square, it nevertheless did not overlook it. Nor did it overlook any kind of park, unlike the Mayfair Hotel. Neither Flossy nor I mentioned that both were well situated in the best part of London. Wisely, she changed the topic of conversation altogether.

"Which flavor of ice cream is your favorite, Odette? I'm rather partial to chocolate, but Cleo prefers lemon sorbet on a hot day."

Odette proceeded to list her favorites in order from most to least with an enthusiasm that rivaled my cousin's.

In many ways, Odette reminded me of Flossy. They were both aged about nineteen, with an innocence that could be either endearing or immature, depending on the situation. At their core, they were sweet-natured, with a romantic sensibility that left them open to either heartbreak or a grand love.

I wasn't sure yet which category Mr. Holland fell into. It wasn't fair to judge a man on a first encounter. After all, I'd found Harry Armitage—the former assistant manager at the Mayfair and now a private investigator—to be somewhat arrogant and far too charming on our first meeting. While I still found him charming, he was so much more. It was why I'd decided to keep my distance from him.

A glint of metal in the sun caught my eye as a woman lounging against a lamppost lifted a pair of opera glasses and peered through them at us. I quickly looked away so as not to let her know I'd noticed, but I continued to watch out of the corner of my eye as Flossy and Odette chatted.

Mr. Holland cleared his throat to gain our attention. "All this talk of ice cream means you must want one, Miss Pridhurst. May I have the honor of purchasing the flavor of your choosing for you? And for Miss Bainbridge and Miss Fox, too, of course."

Odette dipped her head coyly. "That would be lovely. Thank you."

Flossy and I declined, given we'd just finished ours, and Lord and Lady Pridhurst also declined, although Lord Pridhurst insisted that *he* be the one to buy his daughter an ice cream. He marched off toward the ice cream shop before Mr. Holland could say another word.

Odette batted her lashes at Mr. Holland while her mother stared out to sea, her gaze distant. She gave no sign she'd been listening to the exchange.

I watched the woman who was observing us through her opera glasses. She'd watched Lord Pridhurst as he walked to the shop, before focusing her glasses on us once more.

An awkward silence threatened to descend. Flossy seemed unsure what to say or do, so I suggested we return to our hotel to pack.

"Are you leaving tomorrow, too?" Odette asked. "We're catching the ten-thirty express to London, where Papa will leave us. Mama and I will continue home to Wellingborough."

"We're taking the ten-thirty as well," Flossy said. "Perhaps we'll see you checking out in the morning."

Lady Pridhurst and Odette asked us to give Aunt Lilian their regards, then we went on our way, while they waited for Lord Pridhurst to return with Odette's ice cream.

We passed the woman with the opera glasses. She looked out to sea, or pretended to, the opera glasses clasped tightly in her gloved hand. Like Mr. Holland, she seemed out of place in a seaside town with her dark clothing and a narrow-brimmed hat that didn't keep the sun off her face. She was no older than me, with light brown hair arranged in a simple style at the nape of her neck. Her dress was plain, her shoes sensible, and she wore no jewelry. A pair of spectacles on her freckled nose made her seem bookish, and the brown leather satchel at her feet added to the cliché. A brass name plaque was attached to the satchel's smooth leather, just below the clasp. I couldn't read the inscription.

She did a terrible job of feigning interest in the sea. Her gaze flicked to us as we passed, only to return to the water after it connected with mine.

When Flossy and I reached the kiosks at either side of the pier's entrance, I looked behind me, but the woman was no longer there.

The beach was busy. Holidaymakers sat on the chairs provided or on the sand, while children made castles and dug holes. Several of the bathing machines were already in the water, their female occupants hidden from view for the sake of their modesty. The male bathers required no machines, but were relegated to a spot further along the beach away from the public.

"Are you sure you don't want to have a dip?" I teased Flossy. "It'll be our last opportunity." It was a conversation we'd had almost every day since our arrival. I'd enjoyed getting in the water numerous times from the safety of one of the horse-drawn bathing machines, but she'd refused without giving it even a moment's consideration. No amount of pleading had encouraged her to join me, so I'd ended up going alone.

She didn't even bother to refuse this time. She lowered her parasol with a snap and strode off. I caught up to her and we entered the hotel together.

The Grand Brighton Hotel lived up to its name in both size and opulence. The entrance foyer oozed elegance from every marble column and gold-leaf ceiling rose glinting in the light cast by the crystal chandeliers. Like the Mayfair, the building was powered by electricity and had a comfortable lift, coincidentally also operated by a man named John. The manager and assistant manager both greeted us and inquired about Lady Bainbridge's health. Their attention to detail and friendly service reminded me of the Mayfair's extremely capable Mr. Hobart and Peter, and Harry before him.

When I pointed out the similarities to Flossy, she merely sniffed and said the Mayfair had a more welcoming, homely feel. I did not remind her that it *was* her home. I suspected she was missing it and her life in London, and at that moment, even a royal palace would fall short of her expectations.

As Flossy inserted the key to the room we shared, I caught her elbow. "Let's collect our costumes and head back to the beach. You don't want to go this entire holiday without going for a swim, do you? It would be a shame for the costume you bought to go unused."

"I think I should sit with Mother for a while. You go."

Instead of entering our suite, she headed to the next room where Aunt Lilian would be resting alone. Uncle Ronald had stayed in Brighton for only a week before returning to London. He'd claimed something at the Mayfair needed his attention, but I suspected that was a ruse. For one thing, he wouldn't tell us what it was, and Mr. Hobart was very capable of handling any issues. Secondly, Uncle Ronald had been restless the entire week. Like Aunt Lilian, he found fault with the Grand Brighton Hotel at every turn. Nothing was good enough. But *his* restlessness seemed to stem from the fact he was bored. He grumbled every time we suggested going for a walk or picnic. He behaved like a child when we sat on the beach, asking every five minutes if we were ready to leave. The only time he seemed to enjoy himself was when we met other guests in the foyer or at dances or the theater. He took those opportunities to make new friends and suggest they stay at the Mayfair Hotel next time they were in London.

Flossy said her father had always been like that on holidays. The Mayfair Hotel was his life and he was incapable of relaxing when not there. Neither Flossy nor I minded when he decided to leave. We breathed a sigh of relief when we waved him goodbye.

My other cousin, Floyd, had elected to remain in London. Since he was planning the Hessing-Liddicoat wedding reception, his presence at the hotel was necessary. Although Harmony would do most of the work, Floyd needed to be visible. The bride-to-be's mother expected a Bainbridge to be at her beck and call, and she was too important to disappoint.

Harmony would have come to Brighton as maid to Flossy and me, but her temporary promotion to Floyd's assistant meant she had to miss out. Her replacement, a maid named Jane, was in our suite, arranging clothes on the bed to pack. She bobbed a curtsy when I greeted her and offered to order me tea from the kitchen through the speaking tube.

"I think I'll take a dip," I told her. "The packing can wait."

She curtsied again. "I'll gather your costume and towel, Miss Fox."

"Will you enter the water with me? It's our last day here, and it really is quite invigorating. You can borrow Miss Bainbridge's costume if you don't have one."

"No, thank you."

I'd asked Jane every time I went into the water, and she'd declined every time. She accompanied me to help me change into and out of my bathing costume, but she always refused to get in. She was afraid of being washed out to sea or eaten by a shark. Both reasons were illogical, given the shallow depth, and I'd told her as much on our first day, but she still refused. Perhaps a similar fear stopped Flossy, too.

* * *

ALTHOUGH I'D NEVER LEARNED to swim, I managed to move through the water by kicking my legs and making circular motions with my arms, although my heavy wet costume didn't make it easy. I spent some time in the water while Jane watched on from the safety of the bathing machine. Or so I thought. When I paddled back to her, her attention was focused on the hut next to us, and she failed to notice me until I cleared my throat.

She jumped up and helped me up the steps. "Sorry, Miss Fox! I'll get your towel." She threw it around me and rubbed my arms to warm them. "Come inside and dry off quickly. The clouds have come over and it's a little cool now. You don't want to catch your death, all wet as you are."

"I don't think a little cool weather will harm me, but thank you."

She closed the hut's door for privacy, but not before she glanced again at the bathing machine alongside ours. A woman's giggle drifted on the breeze, followed by a gentleman's deeper voice. I couldn't make out his words, but merely hearing it piqued my interest as much as it had Jane's. The bathing machines were supposed to be for women only.

Jane pulled the cord to raise the flag on the hut's roof, signaling to the operator on the beach that we were finished, then she joined me inside. By the time she'd helped me out of my wet flannel costume and into my dry clothes, the horse had brought us back to the shore. We alighted from the hut onto the sand and headed up the beach to the promenade. Once on higher ground, Jane and I both had the same idea, and turned to face the water. The bathing machine that had been beside ours was still out. Someone appeared to be swimming away from it.

When Jane saw me also watching, she leaned closer and whispered. "He swam up to it while you were paddling. It's quite shocking, isn't it?"

"I'm sure it happens all the time. Those carriages provide the perfect cover for a tryst. Besides, we don't know if those two are a married couple."

"He is married. I recognized him, and he's a well-known philanderer, so I doubt she's his wife."

"Who is he?"

"Clement Beecroft."

I'd heard of him. Indeed, most people would have known his name. He produced some of the most notable plays in London, and usually took the lead role himself. He was also famous for bedding his leading ladies, if the gossip columns could be believed.

"He's always in the society pages," Jane went on. "I'd know his face anywhere. He's extraordinarily handsome, and cuts a very fine figure, too. It's a pity you didn't see him climbing up the carriage steps in his bathing costume, with water sliding off his bare arms and legs." She suddenly blushed and mumbled an apology.

"I'm sorry I missed it," I said with a smile to ease her embarrassment.

She giggled behind her hand.

We parted ways near the hotel. I used the main door while Jane took the servants' entrance. The doorman greeted me, followed by the hotel manager who asked if I'd enjoyed my swim. The assistant manager joined us and informed me there was a letter for me at the post desk. Assuming it was from London, I was surprised to find it had no stamp or postmark, and no return address. It must have been hand delivered.

I tore open the envelope and read the note then and there. It was brief and to the point, brutally so.

I know what you are, the message said. *Meet me at 6PM at the entrance to West Pier or I will tell the columnist from The Evening Bulletin that the niece of hotelier Sir Ronald Bainbridge is a private detective.*

There was no signature or any indication who I was supposed to meet. I glanced at the clock on the wall behind the post clerk's head. "Who delivered this?" I asked him.

"I didn't see, Miss Fox, sorry."

I tucked the letter back into the envelope and exited the hotel. I had five minutes to reach the meeting point. There was no question whether I should go. I could not afford for my occupation to be splashed over the pages of *The Evening Bulletin*, the most notorious of all the gutter dailies. Uncle Ronald would have a fit, right before he disowned me. He'd made it very clear that if I were to continue my investigative enterprise while living under his roof, no one must find out.

It wasn't simply that concern that propelled me toward the West Pier, however. I was also terribly curious. The author of the note had not asked for money. So, what did he or she want from me?

CHAPTER 2

The young woman clutched the handle of her brown leather satchel with both hands and watched me approach with a steady, almost defiant, gaze. She was prepared for battle.

She wasn't the only one.

When I'd seen her on the pier earlier that afternoon, I'd fallen for the cliché that a plainly dressed woman with spectacles meant she was shy and bookish. Now that I was closer, I dismissed that assessment. This woman didn't seem at all wary, even though my first words to her were unfriendly.

"Who are you and what do you want?"

Her fingers adjusted their grip on the bag's handle. "I am someone who can ruin your reputation with a telephone call, something I won't hesitate to do unless you help me."

"Usually when someone asks for my help, they don't threaten me first."

"I can't pay you."

"So, you're blackmailing me instead?" When she didn't respond, I added, "I assume you want me to investigate something or someone, since you think I'm a private detective."

"I don't think, I know, and I'm quite capable of conducting my own investigations. I just need a little assistance with a certain matter." She coupled her snippy response with a lift of her chin.

"Are *you* a private detective, Miss…?"

The woman lowered her gaze. It was the first sign of uncertainty she'd shown. I assumed it was because she couldn't decide whether to reveal her name, but it turned out that she didn't want to answer my question. "In a manner of speaking," she finally said. "Well? Will you assist me?"

It was my turn to hesitate. Should I admit she was right, that I was a private detective? Or should I pretend she'd made a mistake?

Considering I'd answered her summons by meeting her, there was no point denying it now. "That depends on what you want me to do."

"Why does it matter? You don't have a choice."

"There is always a choice, and there are some things I refuse to do for the sake of protecting my reputation. Reputations can be salvaged. A good conscience cannot."

Our gazes locked, neither of us looking away. The battle of wills lasted until something behind me caught her attention. She quickly put her hand to her hat brim, hiding her face.

I turned around and searched the sea of faces belonging to the men and women promenading along the foreshore. I didn't recognize any, but one man did appear to be watching us over the top of his newspaper. With his hat pulled down and the newspaper obscuring the lower part of his face, I could only see his eyes.

My blackmailer was rattled. "I-I'll contact you again in London and we'll discuss this further."

She went to move off, but I blocked her path. "Why not discuss it now?"

"I have to be somewhere now."

"Tomorrow then, before I leave Brighton."

"I'm also leaving tomorrow. I'll contact you at the Mayfair Hotel." She tried to step around me, but I moved to block her again.

"Why *The Evening Bulletin?*" I asked.

"Pardon?"

"In your message, you specifically mentioned that newspaper. There are many newspapers that stoop to spreading gossip, so I'm curious as to why you wrote that particular one."

The woman glanced behind me again, then, when I followed her gaze, she slipped away. With a hand to her hat, she hurried off. I let her go. She wasn't going to offer any answers while someone watched her.

The entire encounter had been strange and left me with more questions. I'd not had the opportunity to ask her how she knew I was a private detective or that I lived at the Mayfair Hotel. Also, why was she watching the Pridhursts on West Pier earlier? Or had she been watching Flossy and me? Lastly, why was someone watching us just now, if indeed he had been? The man with the newspaper had disappeared into the crowd while I wasn't looking, so I couldn't question him.

The only information I'd gained from the encounter was her initials—R.P. At least, those were the initials etched on the brass plaque attached to her bag.

Patience not being my strong suit, I was frustrated that I had to wait to find out more, but I comforted myself with the knowledge that I would be sharper in London, and more focused. Here, I was in a holiday frame of mind.

Back at the Grand Brighton Hotel, none of the staff could tell me about the woman. No one had seen her leave the note at the post desk. It was growing late, however, and while the manager, assistant manager and front desk clerks were the same, the porters and doorman were different from those working earlier.

* * *

THE CHECKING-OUT PROCEDURE the following morning was thrown into chaos when one of the clerks failed to arrive at work. With several guests leaving that day, the foyer of the Grand Brighton Hotel quickly became crowded as a queue formed at the desk. My aunt's irritable mood didn't help matters. Flossy and I tried telling her we wouldn't be late for the train, but it did no good. She complained nonstop for the entire twenty-minute wait, albeit under her breath so that no one else heard. Thankfully, she didn't take out her frustrations on the harried staff. As if she'd flipped a switch, she was all sympathetic smiles.

The brown and gold train was already waiting at the

station when we arrived. Jane and Aunt Lilian's maid headed to the second-class carriage while Flossy and Aunt Lilian climbed on board the first-class one. I told them I'd join them soon. I wanted a few moments of peace, before sitting in a confined space with my aunt for the next hour.

The platform bustled with activity as holidaymakers headed to their carriages and perspiring porters pushed trolleys laden with trunks. I spoke to the Pridhursts before they boarded and received a hug goodbye from Odette. A woman bumped into me, mumbled an apology then climbed aboard behind the Pridhursts. It was no wonder she didn't see me, with her head down and a large hat decorated with wine-red feathers and flowers obscuring most of her face. She refused to accept the guard's offered hand to assist her up the steps, leaving him blinking at her disappearing back in disappointment at the snub.

He planted a cheery smile on his face when another passenger approached. The passenger looked a little familiar, but it wasn't until the guard greeted him by name that I realized he was Clement Beecroft, the actor and impresario Jane had seen swimming away from the bathing machine yesterday. He showed the guard his ticket, chatting amiably with him, before placing a foot on the step. He paused there, as if suddenly undecided if he should continue, before he made up his mind and entered.

I checked the clock jutting out on iron supports from the ticket booth. It was time to board. I approached the guard, but someone carrying a leather bag in both arms rushed past me. It was R.P., my blackmailer. If she saw me, she gave no indication.

The guard reached for her bag. "Allow me, ma'am."

She jerked it out of his reach, and climbed aboard unaided.

I accepted the guard's assistance and followed her. By the time I passed her, she'd already settled in the first compartment. She clutched the bag on her lap, even though the rack above was empty. She sat alone.

I joined Flossy and Aunt Lilian in a compartment further along, just as the guard called out to a passenger to hurry up and board, before his voice was drowned out by the hiss of steam. The guard blew his whistle, and we lurched forward.

After the conductor checked our tickets, Aunt Lilian removed her gloves and closed her eyes. The constant fidgeting with the lace gloves proved she wasn't asleep, however. I relaxed into the soft velvet-covered seat and read a book while Flossy flipped through the pages of a fashion magazine. At one point, she asked me what I thought about one of the dresses in the magazine, but her mother shushed her. We stayed silent for the remainder of the journey.

The train sped through the picturesque countryside, until finally slowing when we reached London. The two stops before we arrived at Victoria Station were a welcome distraction from the taut silence in our compartment. Both times, I lowered the window and stuck my head out to watch the comings and goings, before raising it and settling back in my seat.

Eager to alight, Aunt Lilian stood before the train completely stopped at its final destination. She led the way out of the compartment and along the narrow corridor to the exit at the front of the carriage. I looked in at each of the compartments as we passed. Lord and Lady Pridhurst smiled and wished us a good day, but Odette continued to stare out of the window beside her, a handkerchief scrunched in her hand. I'd not met the other passengers in the next two compartments, although I did recognize Mr. Beecroft. The actor drummed his fingers on his thigh and tried to peer past me.

The man seated opposite him offered him a cigarette, but Mr. Beecroft declined with a shake of his head. The man looked out of place in the first-class carriage, dressed in a workingman's clothes and cap. He had a rather distinctive face with a flat nose, as if it had been the target of too many fists. He must have been the fellow who'd almost missed the train in Brighton.

The lady with the large hat occupied the next compartment with another woman wearing an equally large hat. Neither looked out from beneath their brims as we passed, so I had no idea what they looked like.

The compartment where R.P. had sat was empty. I expected to see her ahead of us, eager to be first off the train, but the only person waiting at the door was the conductor. He opened it for us when the train came to a stop at the platform and touched the brim of his cap in farewell. A guard on the platform assisted Aunt Lilian down the steps, then offered a hand to Flossy then me.

I didn't follow them as they walked to the gate. I looked around, frowning. If R.P. hadn't been in her compartment or any of the others I'd passed, nor had she been waiting to get off, where was she? Our carriage was first, behind the locomotive and the tender carrying coal and water, so if she'd changed carriages on the journey, she could only have gone to the second one, and to do that, she had to pass our compartment. But I'd not seen her, and I was quite sure I would have noticed, as the top half of the compartment door was glass. Nor had she joined the other passengers in the compartments between hers and ours.

I returned to the conductor. "Excuse me, may I have a word?"

"Did you leave something behind, Miss?"

"No, nothing like that. There was a woman carrying a brown leather bag traveling alone in the first compartment of the first-class car. Have you seen her?"

He scratched his thick beard as he thought. "Young woman with spectacles?"

"Yes, that's her. She didn't get off and her compartment was empty just now, but I'm sure she didn't alight at the other two stops."

"She must have changed carriages on the journey and got off from there." He waved in the general direction of the rest of the train behind our first-class carriage.

I shook my head. "I would have seen her pass our compartment." Although I had looked out of the window at one point.

The conductor shrugged. "I'm sure there's an explanation, miss." He didn't offer one, however.

"Cleo," Flossy whined. "Mother wants to go. Please don't upset her. She has a raging headache."

"Just a moment." I turned back to the conductor, but he'd

disappeared inside. With a sigh, I followed Flossy through the gate and along the concourse to the vehicles queuing up to take passengers to their final destination.

We found Aunt Lilian already ensconced in one of the two waiting carriages emblazoned with the Mayfair Hotel's emblem of an M inside a circle. Once the groom closed our door, Cobbit the coachman instructed the horses to pull the vehicle away from the curb. The second carriage would wait to take our luggage and the two maids.

"Did either of you notice the young woman with the brown leather bag?" I asked.

"No," Flossy said.

"Did you see anyone at all pass our compartment to change carriages?"

Flossy shook her head. "Why?"

"That young woman didn't get off the train. Not at Victoria Station or the other two stops. Aunt?" I prompted. "Did you see her?"

Aunt Lilian had been staring out of the window, but she now turned to me. She looked like she hadn't slept for days, and her cheeks looked even more sunken than usual. I'd not thought it possible, but she was also thinner than the day we left London, two weeks ago. "Why would I notice the other passengers?" she snapped.

I abandoned my questions and, once again, Flossy and I sat in silence. Aunt Lilian returned to staring out of the window. At one point, she closed her eyes and rubbed her temples, before opening them again when the traffic on Piccadilly slowed our progress.

The Mayfair Hotel was a welcome sight. Frank the doorman greeted us with more warmth in his voice than I'd ever heard. It was most likely for my aunt and cousin's benefit rather than mine, but I didn't care. I'd missed his familiar grumpiness.

Goliath and the other porter greeted us before rushing to collect our luggage as the second carriage with the maids pulled up. Peter, the assistant manager, bowed and inquired how our holiday had been, and the manager, Mr. Hobart, said he was pleased to see us looking so refreshed.

"It must be the seaside air," he said, smiling. When Mr.

Hobart smiled, his entire face lifted, and I couldn't help smiling back and giving him an enthusiastic response about how much I enjoyed it.

Flossy did, too. Aunt Lilian, however, smiled tightly as if it pained her to move the muscles in her face. I knew she genuinely liked Mr. Hobart, but the cocaine addiction that controlled her had not only altered her mood, it had also broken her spirit. The times when she didn't take the substance, when she tried to go without, the fight to regain control required all her energy.

I touched her elbow, wanting her to know that I knew she was fighting, and that I supported her. But she jerked away and hurried to catch the lift before John closed the door.

"How has everything been here?" I asked Mr. Hobart.

"All is well, Miss Fox. Thank you for asking." Even if the hotel was in turmoil, he would give the same answer in front of Flossy.

She was distracted by one of the hotel guests, however, and hadn't heard.

"Actually, Miss Fox," Mr. Hobart went on, "I have a message that needs delivering to the mews. Would you mind taking it?"

Why was he asking me to run errands? He'd never asked before, and the mews was out of the way.

Sensing he'd made a rare *faux pas*, he quickly apologized. "Goliath can take the message. I'm sure you want to rest before afternoon tea."

As Flossy and I headed to the lift, I asked her why she couldn't stop staring at the blond gentleman with the gold-topped walking stick, reading his mail at the post desk.

"Well, just *look* at him, Cleo."

I looked. "He's quite handsome, I suppose."

"A 'golden gentleman with a limp.'"

"Pardon?"

"Don't you remember? And you call yourself a detective." She hooked her arm through mine and glanced over her shoulder. A 'golden gentleman with a limp' is the description of the man I'll marry, according to the fortune-telling machine in the Palace Pier's arcade."

I resisted the urge to roll my eyes. "I'm not sure blond hair and a gold-topped walking stick match the description."

"It's either that or a crown." She gasped. "Perhaps I'll marry a prince!"

I laughed softly. "Perhaps you will."

* * *

"IT'S WONDERFUL TO BE HOME," I said to Harmony. She'd come to my suite soon after I'd entered it, having heard we were back.

"You didn't enjoy the holiday?" she asked.

We sat on the sofa, our shoes off and the top buttons of our dresses undone. It was warm on the fourth floor and the fan did little to cool the air. Usually doing maid's work at this time of day, Harmony had more freedom now that she was Floyd's assistant for the duration of the wedding reception preparations. While she was busier than ever, her schedule wasn't quite as regimented.

"I did, very much." I sipped my lemonade. "But I missed you."

"Just me?" She sounded serious, but the wicked gleam in her eyes gave her away.

I wasn't going to give her the satisfaction of walking into her trap. "I missed all of my friends here."

"Just here? Or the ones from, say, Soho?"

I gulped down the rest of my lemonade, then set the empty glass aside. "How are plans for the reception coming along?"

"That was a cumbersome change of topic, but very well. The plans are progressing, put it that way."

"Is something the matter? Is Floyd being hopeless?"

"No more than usual." It was testament to how comfortable she felt with me that she could say that about my cousin to my face. She knew I'd not pass on her words or be offended. "He leaves me to manage things alone most of the time, which is all well and good. I prefer it, actually."

"Then is it Mr. Chapman again?"

The hotel steward managed the restaurant and its staff.

He'd been upset when Uncle Ronald had given the task of preparing the wedding reception to Floyd and Harmony, but he only had himself to blame. The Hessing-Liddicoat engagement dinner had been a near-disaster. On the back of it, the bride-to-be's mother, Mrs. Hessing, had almost taken the wedding reception to our competitor. Fortunately, she'd been convinced to keep it at the Mayfair, but she'd insisted Floyd be the one to manage the event.

Mr. Chapman's nose had been put out of joint, but he'd been somewhat placated when Floyd tasked him with preparing the old restaurant for the reception. The steward was given free rein to organize the waiters, and had input into the decorations, but Harmony would be the one to liaise with suppliers while Floyd passed on the requirements of the woman paying for it all. I wasn't sure what the snobby steward would abhor more—having to answer to a maid, or having to decorate the room in Mrs. Hessing's ostentatious style.

"It's not Mr. Chapman," Harmony said. "It's Mrs. Hessing. She wants the world, but she doesn't want to pay for it."

"But she's wealthy!"

"That doesn't mean she likes parting with her money." Harmony picked up the jug of lemonade and refilled both our glasses. "Every time I get a quote from a supplier, she tells me it's too much and I must find a way to lower it. When I asked how, she said people like me should know how to haggle."

I groaned. "What did you say to that?"

"I asked her if she meant people from the East End."

Harmony had been born and raised in a London slum. Despite enduring prejudice for her darker skin, she'd gained employment as a maid at the hotel, and was now the occasional assistant to the owner's son. Those of us who knew her weren't surprised. She was intelligent, efficient, and had a strong work ethic. She deserved the promotion. Yet prejudice from some quarters persisted.

"Mrs. Hessing thought I was being rude and complained to Mr. Bainbridge. He defended me, but things haven't been the same since."

"Do you think she'll cause more trouble?"

Harmony paused, the glass halfway to her lips. "She can't

change her mind and have another hotel host the reception now. It's too late for that. Nor will she want to jeopardize the success of the event. It's important to her. She wants it to be remembered for all the right reasons, not the wrong ones, hence the spectacular nature of her requests. What she might do is not pay the bills."

"If she doesn't, then the suppliers won't supply things. It'll be a disaster."

Harmony didn't think so. "The reception is important to them, too. Having their name associated with it will be a boon for their business. Also, with her rumored wealth, they will happily deliver on the day, expecting payment afterward."

"But?"

"But I think she'll pay what she wants and leave Sir Ronald to pay the rest. He'd agree to it, to maintain a good relationship with suppliers and to keep one of his best guests happy."

Indeed he might. Mrs. Hessing could certainly afford a lavish affair, so that wasn't the reason for her reluctance to pay the quoted prices. I suspected she was testing us. Or, rather, testing my uncle's loyalty to her. Would he prefer to displease our suppliers or Mrs. Hessing?

Harmony checked the time on the watch Floyd had loaned her, but didn't get up. She tucked it back into her pocket. "Tell me all about the holiday. Did anything nibble your toes while you were sea bathing? Is the Royal Pavilion as peculiar as they say? What was the hotel like?"

I gave brief answers to all her questions. By the end, she sensed there was something else on my mind. After she glanced at her watch again, I knew I had to get to the point or my opportunity to discuss it with her would vanish. "A woman disappeared on the journey home. She tried to black-mail me in Brighton, threatening to tell *The Evening Bulletin* that I was a private detective if I didn't help her. She didn't say how she knew I was a private detective or how she'd learned where I lived, or even how I could help her. She told me she would contact me here at the Mayfair to discuss it further. But I'm concerned she may not have made it back to London. I saw her get on the carriage, but not get off. Oh, and either she, or I, was being watched. I think."

Harmony's eyebrows rose higher and higher with every sentence. It did sound rather extraordinary when I laid it out like that. Most people would dismiss my concern for R.P., just as the conductor had, but not Harmony. She suggested I contact the police immediately.

"Your instincts are usually good, Cleo." She checked the time again. "I have to get back to work. Let me know what the police say."

I followed her out of my suite and headed downstairs. There were only two telephones on the ground floor, one on the front desk and one in Mr. Hobart's office. My call required privacy, so I asked the manager if I could use his.

Instead of telephoning the local police station, I put in a call to Detective Sergeant Forrester at Scotland Yard. I'd dealt with him before, and as a trusted former colleague of the now retired D.I. Hobart, I knew he'd take me seriously.

Even so, there was nothing he could do. "Unless she's reported missing, or a body is discovered, there's no case."

"I understand, but perhaps you could find out if any luggage from that train wasn't collected."

"I could do that for you, Cleo. But are you sure she didn't pass your compartment on her way to the next carriage?"

"Quite sure, Monty." I felt awkward calling him by his first name, as we'd agreed to do on our last encounter, but he'd already used mine, so I had to follow suit.

The telephone line crackled, and I couldn't hear what he said, so asked him to repeat it. "Are you suspecting foul play?" he said in a louder voice.

"I suppose I am, yes. There's nowhere to hide in the car, so we can dismiss that idea. If she fell out of the window, or was pushed out, we would have heard her scream."

"It wouldn't be easy to push someone out of a train window, particularly if they were struggling."

"Precisely. So, I think she was murdered in her compartment, or silenced in some way, then bundled out."

Someone on the line gasped. I doubted it was Monty. The operator must be listening in.

We quickly ended the call.

The hotel foyer was busy with ladies arriving to experience the Mayfair's famous afternoon tea. I had no plans myself, but I remained in the foyer to welcome those I recognized. Many were guests currently staying with us, but quite a number were London residents who regularly enjoyed the experience with friends.

Mr. Hobart and Peter had also taken up positions to welcome the ladies and direct newcomers to the sitting room. It was a sunny day, so there were no coats to deposit at the luggage room, which doubled as a cloakroom, but several checked in their parasols.

When the gaggle of ladies began to thin, Peter joined me. "Is it just me or are the hats bigger this summer?"

I laughed. "Definitely bigger, and more elaborately decorated. A woman bumped into me at Brighton Station because she couldn't see where she was going from underneath her enormous brim. She did look exceedingly elegant, though. Her outfit wouldn't have been out of place in a fashion magazine."

"I'd wager it cost a small fortune."

"More than you or I could afford, Peter."

A crease connected his eyebrows, and I was reminded that most people thought I was wealthy. While my uncle gave me an allowance, it wasn't enough to live independently outside of the hotel, and certainly wasn't enough to buy new outfits every year. My mother—Aunt Lilian's sister—had been cut off by their parents when she married my father, a man not of their choosing. It meant I'd grown up not knowing her family, until I was forced to move in with them last December. After my parents died when I was ten, my paternal grandparents had taken me in, but on my grandmother's death, I'd found myself utterly alone and facing poverty. I was fortunate indeed that my aunt and uncle invited me to live with them. I shuddered to think where I'd be now if I'd not swallowed my pride and accepted their offer.

Mr. Hobart approached and asked Peter to look over the next day's guest arrivals. Once he was out of earshot, the manager smiled at me. "Did you know Lord Dunmere checked in a few days ago?"

"Did he bring his automobile?" Last time, his motorized vehicle caused unrest among the mews staff where it was stabled. Cobbit and the other coachman and grooms had gone on strike, afraid they'd be out of a job if the hotel decided to switch to using horseless carriages instead of horse-drawn ones. If Harry Armitage hadn't suggested a compromise, the unrest could still be going on.

"He did," Mr. Hobart said. "That's actually what I want to talk to you about. Would you mind going to the mews and speaking to Cobbit to gauge his feelings? If he's going to go on strike again, I'd like advance warning."

"Of course, but why me? Wouldn't it be better if a member of staff spoke to him? He might confide in Peter or Goliath more than a member of the family."

"You're an excellent judge, Cleo. I trust your opinion. May I suggest you go now, before Cobbit leaves for the day?"

Cobbit's shift wouldn't end for some time yet, but Mr. Hobart seemed keen to get it over with, and I had nothing better to do.

I exited via the front door, greeting Frank as I passed. "Good afternoon. Pleasant day, today."

Without a member of my family or any guests within earshot, he was once more his usual testy self. "What's pleasant about it? It's too hot."

"The clouds are starting to come in. Perhaps tomorrow will bring rain to cool everything down."

"Then I'll get wet standing out here. It's not just the rain falling from the sky, you know. It comes from the guests shaking out their coats and umbrellas all over me, and the passing carriages driving through puddles. I'll be drenched in an hour, just you wait and see."

"As much as I'd like to hear more, Frank, I have a task to perform for Mr. Hobart. Must dash."

I hurried to the mews where the Mayfair stabled its horses and kept two carriages for the use of family and guests. Lord Dunmere's Peugeot occupied one of the coach houses and the other was empty, neither carriage in sight. A young groom peered into the vehicle as his lordship's mechanic, seated in the driver's seat, explained how to make the contraption work. The lad listened intently. A third man stood behind the vehicle, the doors to the compartment that housed the engine open. He didn't see me. His attention was entirely focused on the inner workings.

I should have turned and fled before he looked up, but I did not. Uncertainty pinned me to the spot.

When Harry did look up, he grinned that lopsided, devilish grin of his, the one that made my heart flutter even while I felt trapped.

CHAPTER 3

"What are you doing here?" I blurted out.

Harry approached, wiping his hands on a rag. He wore dirty overalls over his clothes, and oil smudged his cheek, but I didn't point it out. Knowing him, he'd ask me to wipe it off and I did not want to touch him. That might lead to kissing him, and I'd vowed not to let that happen again. I'd decided to set aside my feelings for the sake of my independence. It wasn't fair to let Harry, or any man, think we had a future together when I had no intention to marry.

Harry sometimes made it difficult to stay on track, however, especially after an absence and when he looked at me with chocolate-colored eyes that danced merrily upon seeing me.

"Last time Lord Dunmere was here, I asked his mechanic to show me how the engine worked." Harry jerked his thumb at the mechanic giving the groom a lesson. "I've spent an hour or two here every day since his return."

Harry had an affinity for all things engineering, so it wasn't surprising the workings of the Peugeot intrigued him. I suspected his intelligent mind meant he already knew all there was to know about it.

"How was your holiday?" he asked.

"Lovely, but I'm glad to be home."

His crooked smile flashed again. "Miss me, did you?"

"You would think that."

"What other reason could you have to come to the mews on the same day as you arrived back? You rarely come here."

"Mr. Hobart sent me to check that Cobbit wasn't too put out by that." I indicated the automobile.

"Cobbit's not here. He drove some guests to the Tower, something Uncle Alfred would have known. He sees the travel schedules in advance."

I bristled. "He did send me!"

Harry smirked. "I believe you."

"The last place I want to be is in a smelly, airless mews with a man who has nothing better to do than be annoying. I have a new case, as it happens, and it requires my attention."

"I have to leave, too. I have an appointment in the tearoom on Piccadilly. I'll walk you to the end of the mews and you can tell me all about your case." He began to remove his overalls.

I didn't wait.

"Cleo!" he said, catching up to me as he put his jacket on. "Why wouldn't you wait for me? Are you afraid I'll try to steal your case?"

"No. There's no client."

He adjusted his necktie. "So, tell me about it."

"No."

"Why not? We work well together."

"Because there may not be a case. If there is, I have plenty of other people to discuss it with, including Monty."

"Monty?"

"D.S. Forrester."

"I know who Monty is, I just…" He sighed. "Never mind. Are you cross with me because I teased you about missing me?"

"Not at all." We reached Piccadilly, where we had to part ways. I gave him no opportunity to press me further about my abruptness. I didn't want to be forced to answer. I didn't know *how* to answer. "Goodbye, Harry."

"Cleo, wait." He caught my elbow but quickly released it. His gaze softened, leaving me in little doubt of his feelings toward me. The intimate moment was somewhat ruined by the smudge of oil on his cheek. "I want you to know that I missed you, too."

I crossed my arms, shot him a defiant look, and said, "I will ask Mr. Hobart to tell you that he *did* send me to the mews to speak to Cobbit. Then you'll feel even more of a fool than you look."

"How do I look?"

I smiled, turned around, and strode away without telling him about the smudge. I resisted the urge to glance over my shoulder the entire way back to the hotel entrance.

Inside, Mr. Hobart smiled guiltily at me. So, he *had* sent me to the mews knowing Cobbit wouldn't be there, and Harry would. I ought to tell him to stay out of my affairs, but I didn't have the heart. He was sweet and kind, and I knew he was fond of me in a fatherly way.

Besides, I didn't want to explain why I was avoiding his nephew. I suspected he'd try to talk me out of my conviction, and I wasn't ready for that conversation.

* * *

I PLANNED to spend the following morning catching up on my correspondence. I'd sent postcards to my friends in my former hometown of Cambridge while I was away, but wanted to go into further detail about my Brighton holiday. Writing letters also provided a distraction as I waited for Monty to call me back about any luggage that may have been left behind at Victoria Station. The more I thought about it, the more concerned I became for R.P. I was positive she hadn't changed carriages during the journey. That left only one explanation for her disappearance.

The arrival of Miss Hessing was another welcome distraction. The bride-to-be couldn't stop talking about her fiancé, and their future plans. Her bubbly chatter was a far cry from the shy woman I'd met when she and her mother first arrived at the hotel some months ago. It was clear from the way she cheerfully discussed the upcoming wedding that she didn't know her mother was pressuring Floyd and Harmony to reduce the cost. I wouldn't be the one to tell her. No one should. Her wedding day ought to leave her with wonderful memories.

Miss Hessing left an hour later, only to be replaced by

Flossy, carrying some magazines in her arms. "I thought I might find Harmony here," she said, taking a seat on the sofa.

"I haven't seen her since breakfast. She's very busy with the wedding."

"That's what I wanted to talk to her about. I wanted to give her these." Flossy fanned out the magazines on the table. "Before we left for Brighton, she borrowed a few to give her inspiration for the reception. I thought she might like to view the ones that came while we were away."

"That's kind of you to think of her. I'll pass them along."

There was a knock at the door and Floyd let himself in before I reached it. He thrust his wrist out to me. "Can you do up my cuff links?"

"Nice to see you, too, Floyd."

"Sorry, yes, nice to see you, Cleo. You look well. Did you enjoy the holiday?"

"I did, thank you, particularly the sea bathing."

"Flossy said you went every day. Did you miss me?"

"Of course."

"Truly?" He sounded surprised yet pleased.

I finished attaching one cuff link and he handed me the other. "Hopefully you can join us next year."

He made a face. "No thanks. My favorite time of the year is when everyone leaves London and I'm left to fend for myself."

I laughed, thinking he was joking, but he looked quite serious. "Floyd, you haven't fended for yourself a day in your life."

Flossy called out from the sitting room. "He just likes the freedom that comes with our parents not peering over his shoulder."

"It must have put a dent in your plans when your father returned after only a week," I said.

He *humphed*. "Unannounced, too."

I finished with his cuff and fixed his tie for him. "Don't you have a valet to do this?"

"I do, but he's hopeless. I think he must have slept in today."

"Why do you keep him on?"

"Because he's discreet."

"Ah. You mean he doesn't spy on you for your father."

He winked at me. "I'd better run. Harmony wants to see me about something, and she's a stickler for punctuality. If I arrive late to a meeting, she gives me the meanest look."

Flossy joined us from the sitting room, carrying the magazines. "Pass these on to her for me. She might like to browse them for ideas."

Floyd wouldn't take them. "It's too late to change anything now. Anyway, those are English."

"So?"

"Harmony felt an American style of wedding would be more to Mrs. Hessing's taste."

"What is an American style of wedding and how is it different to an English one?"

Floyd shrugged. "Harmony spoke to some of our American guests, and they gave her the society pages of their magazines and newspapers. She claims the articles and photographs of the weddings of wealthy American families gave her a lot of inspiration, but I'm not privy to the details. I'm more of a higher-level manager. She takes care of the minutiae." He thanked me for my assistance with the cuff links and let himself out.

Flossy caught the door before it closed and watched him stride off along the corridor to the lift. "My brother is finally maturing."

"Why do you think that? Because he's up before midday?"

"Because he hasn't teased me about the last time I went for a paddle in Brighton."

"What happened the last time?"

Flossy hugged the magazines to her chest and hurried from my suite.

* * *

WITH LITTLE TO DO FOR the rest of the day, I planned to join my friends in the staff parlor that afternoon for a chat. I wanted to gauge their thoughts on the missing R.P., and whether I was overreacting. Harmony might not be there, but I hoped to see Goliath, Frank, Peter and Victor, one of the cooks. They sometimes helped me in my investigations. They were also good company.

I didn't reach the parlor, however. I'd barely set foot in the foyer when Peter drew my attention to a guest sitting on one of the burgundy leather armchairs, reading a newspaper. The long-legged man held the paper up so that it obscured his face, but it was oddly angled, as if he were peering past it in the direction of the check-in desk.

"It's Harry Armitage," Peter told me. "He came in thirty minutes ago and hasn't moved."

I quickly scanned the area, looking for my uncle. Thankfully he wasn't there. "What's he doing here?"

"When I asked, he said he was waiting for someone, but he wouldn't say who. I'm worried what will happen if Sir Ronald sees him."

While Peter and the other staff knew my uncle had dismissed Harry from his position as assistant manager several months ago, they didn't know that it was because he'd discovered Harry had been arrested for theft as a thirteen-year-old. Uncle Ronald's fury was clear to everyone, however, and whenever Harry set foot in the hotel, the staff grew anxious that Uncle Ronald would have him thrown out. Last time, he'd been civil to Harry. It remained to be seen if that was a fleeting moment that would never be repeated.

"Have you informed Mr. Hobart?" I asked. If anyone could discover the real reason for Harry's presence, it would be his uncle.

"He's in a meeting with Sir Ronald. I'll tell him when I see him. Unless he's in the company of Sir Ronald, that is."

The lift door opened, and we both stared at it. I released a breath when two guests emerged.

I thanked Peter for informing me, then walked up to Harry. I pulled down the corner of his newspaper so we could make eye contact. "You're making Peter nervous. He doesn't know whether to ask you to leave or distract Sir Ronald if he comes downstairs."

Harry folded the paper. "Don't be nervous."

"I said Peter is nervous, not me."

"I'm working."

"That doesn't make his decision easier. If anything, it

makes it harder." I glanced toward the counter where a new guest was checking in. "What does your investigation have to do with the guests? Or are you observing the front-of-house staff?"

"I can't tell you."

"I tell you about my cases."

"Only when you need my help."

"I never *need* your help, Harry." It wasn't true, but I wasn't going to give him the satisfaction of admitting it.

His dimples appeared with the flash of his smile. "That means you involve me because you like my company. I knew it."

I'd walked right into that one. "Seriously, Harry, you shouldn't stay. If my uncle sees you, it could be awkward. Tell me who you're watching, and I'll take over for you. I have nothing better to do anyway."

"Your case has ended already?"

"I'm still waiting on some news from Monty." I sat on the armchair beside Harry and nodded at the check-in counter. "Are you spying on the staff or guests?"

He hesitated a moment before unfolding the newspaper. "My investigation is confidential, Cleo."

"I'd never break a confidence, especially yours." I laid a hand on his arm. His gaze lowered to it. "You know you can't stay."

"Sir Ronald won't throw me out."

"I admire your confidence, but that's not what I meant. The newspaper provides only so much cover. Sooner or later, some of the guests will recognize you, particularly the ladies arriving for afternoon tea. You were a great favorite of many when you worked here, and they'll want a brief chat before they enter the sitting room."

He didn't like his popularity being pointed out to him, but he knew I was right. "Very well. I'll tell you in case you have to take over. After I left the mews yesterday, I met with Mrs. Hessing. She believes a gossip columnist has checked into the hotel in an attempt to find out more about the wedding preparations."

"Find out from the staff?"

"Apparently."

"Staying in one of our rooms is a rather expensive way to gather gossip." Even the Mayfair's cheapest rooms on the fifth floor cost a considerable sum for one night. "Doesn't Mrs. Hessing want the attention anyway? I would have thought she'd enjoy seeing her daughter's wedding in the society pages."

"She does want it, but on her terms. She's worried the columnist will reveal too much too soon and spoil the surprise of the spectacle. She's also aware that events like this often don't have smooth lead-ups and she's worried that will overshadow the reception itself."

I couldn't blame Mrs. Hessing for wanting to control the story rather than leave it to chance. The press could focus on one small negative and ruin everything. Even so, hiring Harry to flush out the columnist was an extreme method to ensure privacy.

"What does the columnist look like?" I asked as a man wearing a purple silk waistcoat and cravat made a beeline for Mr. Chapman, who was reading the reservations book near the entrance to the sitting room. "Is it him?"

"*She's* aged in her thirties with blonde hair, a long nose and sunken chin." Harry raised the newspaper as a lady walked by. "That's Mrs. Hessing's description, not mine. Mrs. Hessing doesn't know which newspaper this columnist works for, but she has already approached Liddicoat, trying to goad him into admitting he's marrying Miss Hessing for her fortune."

"What a ghastly woman."

"She also approached both Mrs. and Miss Hessing, but Mrs. Hessing realized she was insinuating the same thing and sent her away before Miss Hessing caught on."

It wouldn't matter if she had. Miss Hessing wouldn't believe it. She was sure of Mr. Liddicoat's love for her now. Even so, the gossip columnist was wretched for stooping to such a tactic. "Why does Mrs. Hessing believe she's staying at the hotel?"

"She saw the same woman at the reservation desk the day before yesterday. When Mrs. Hessing demanded Uncle Alfred find out what she wanted, he discovered she'd made a reservation for tonight and tomorrow night. She hired me to thwart the woman's attempts to gather information after my uncle and yours refused to cancel the reservation without knowing for certain she was the gossip columnist."

"What name is the reservation under?"

"Mrs. Blaine. She hasn't checked in yet."

We both looked toward the check-in counter. The clerk passed a gentleman the key to his room, and the guest went on his way. There was no one waiting to be served.

"I'll watch for her," I said to Harry. "You should go before Uncle Ronald sees you."

"It'll be fine."

"Because you're working for Mrs. Hessing? Harry, she won't be staying here forever. Once she's gone, my uncle will remember that you sat here for hours after he expressly told you not to come back. I wouldn't put it past him to…" I waved my hand in the air, not quite sure what my uncle would do to Harry.

He took my hand as I lowered it to my lap. "Cleo, I like that you're worried about me, but you don't have to be."

I slipped my hand free and rose. "I'll keep an eye out for your suspect, but if you don't want me to replace you, I should go so as not to draw attention." I turned away before he noticed my face heating.

Peter approached after having a brief discussion with the check-in clerk. He had a message for me. "A Detective Sergeant Forrester called and has asked you to telephone him as soon as possible."

I turned to Harry. "I'll do what I can to help, but if my uncle throws you out, don't blame me. I did try to warn you."

I walked off to ask the check-in clerk if I could use his telephone. I'd just lifted the earpiece off the hook when the lift door opened, and Uncle Ronald and Mr. Hobart stepped out. Mr. Hobart tucked a clipboard under his arm and headed to his office. Uncle Ronald, however, stopped. As if he sensed an intruder in his domain, he suddenly turned toward the armchair where Harry sat.

Their gazes met.

My uncle's back stiffened.

Harry nodded at him.

To my surprise, Uncle Ronald nodded back. Then he went on his way without a word to anyone.

Harry smirked at me, wiggled his fingers in a wave, then raised the newspaper to obscure his face again. He must have already had a word with my uncle. Or Mrs. Hessing had. Either way, Uncle Ronald wasn't surprised or cross to see him there. Harry would probably have admitted it if I hadn't cut him off when I became flustered that he'd held my hand, so I only had myself to blame.

When Monty came on the line, I turned my back to the foyer to avoid distractions. I wanted to give him my undivided attention. I was glad I did.

"I need your help, Cleo," he began. "You could be right about the woman you saw—or didn't see—leaving the train. A man reported his sister missing late yesterday. He was told to call back if she still hadn't appeared this morning, which he did. He claims his sister was supposed to be on the ten-thirty express from Brighton. At Victoria Station, she should have caught a taxicab home, but she never arrived. As the day wore on, he checked with her employer and she hadn't gone there, either. The case was assigned to one of the other detectives, but he's disinclined to investigate because he thinks she's run off with a fellow and will turn up. It sounded like your missing woman, so I thought you might want to look into it while my colleague drags his feet. Time is of the essence with missing person cases, but my hands are tied."

"Thank you, Monty. I'll begin an investigation immediately. Did you look into the uncollected luggage at the station?"

"I did, but there was none. According to the brother, she only took a carry bag with her anyway, not a trunk."

"What was her name?"

"Ruth Price." He then gave me the description given by the brother. It matched the woman I'd met in Brighton and seen get on the train but not get off.

I pressed a hand to my stomach. I had a terrible feeling that Ruth Price had met her end on the express to London.

CHAPTER 4

$\mathcal{M}$onty's voice crackled down the line. "The missing woman is an assistant to a journalist."

"Does the journalist work for *The Evening Bulletin*?" I asked.

"How do you know?"

Aware that our conversation could be overheard by a telephone operator, I gave him the barest details. "She mentioned that newspaper when I met her in Brighton." It explained why she'd mentioned only *that* newspaper in her threatening message to me. "Monty, she wanted me to help her with something, and she planned to speak to me about it once we were back in London."

"I'll pass that on to the detective. Hopefully he'll want to question you." From his tone, he didn't sound convinced.

I hung up, then asked Peter if he had a few moments to join me in the staff parlor. I signaled for Goliath to come, too. He fetched Frank then went to the kitchen to see if Victor was free.

Harry watched us from behind his newspaper. As I drew closer, he arched his brows in question. He wanted to know what was going on.

I smiled and wiggled my fingers in a cheery wave identical to the one he'd given me earlier.

A few minutes later, the four men sat in the staff parlor, cups of tea in hand, and listened as I explained the case of the missing Ruth Price, and my connection to her. I finished by telling them Scotland Yard were not yet treating her disappearance as suspicious.

"The lead detective thinks she ran off with a man," I said. "Mind you, he has no evidence to support his theory. Monty isn't impressed and wants me to look into it."

"Monty, eh?" Goliath snickered. "You and him courting, Miss Fox?"

"No."

"You soon will be, I reckon." He winked.

Frank made a sound of disgust in the back of his throat. "That doesn't mean anything, idiot. She calls us by our first names, too."

"That's not the same thing. We're staff. He's her equal. When folk who are social equals start calling each other by their first name, it means something."

Frank looked aghast at him. "Her equal? You really are an idiot. *She's* a Bainbridge. That fellow is just a local plod."

"I'm a Fox, not a Bainbridge," I cut in before the conversation got heated.

"And that fellow is a detective sergeant," Peter said with a glower for Frank. "He deserves some respect."

Victor rolled his eyes. "Being a sergeant or detective doesn't mean he should be respected. It's character that matters."

Before he worked for the hotel, the baby-faced cook had led a colorful life conning wealthy people out of their money. While he'd reformed his ways before the law caught up to him, he was not inclined to think favorably of policemen. He'd seen too many bad ones to blindly respect them all.

Frank and Peter looked like they'd disagree with Victor, so I quickly moved the conversation on before I lost control completely. If Harmony were here, she wouldn't have let them stray off course as quickly as they had. Victor, for one, would listen to her.

"I need your ideas," I told the men. "There may be something I've missed, something obvious. Ruth Price got on the train ahead of me. I passed her in her compartment before taking my seat. She was alone. To reach the next carriage, she would have had to pass our compartment, but I didn't see her."

"Your door had a window?" Frank asked.

"Yes. We could see anyone who passed."

"You didn't close your eyes?" Goliath asked.

"No. I was reading, but I would have seen someone pass."

"Doesn't the express make some stops before it reaches Victoria Station?" Peter asked.

"There are two. I wanted some air, so I opened the window and looked out while we stopped. No one got on or off our carriage. The conductor confirmed that, when I asked him once we reached our final destination and I realized she was missing. I asked Flossy if anyone passed our compartment on their way to the next carriage while I had my head out of the window, but she saw no one. So, what do you all think?"

"Perhaps she fell out of her compartment window," Goliath said.

"She would have screamed. She didn't, so that also rules out the possibility that she was pushed out while conscious."

Peter had a theory that could explain that. "What if she did scream, but the train whistle masked it?"

Frank scoffed. "It would be impossible to get the timing right not knowing when the whistle was going to blow."

"Improbable, not impossible."

Victor got up and set his teacup on the table. "I need paper, a pencil and a map of the area between Brighton and London with the train line marked."

Peter went to fetch the items.

"You think she was murdered first, don't you, Miss Fox?" Goliath asked. "Someone stabbed her and pushed her dead body out of the window. That's why she didn't scream."

"I'm afraid so. I can't think of another explanation. There was nowhere to hide in that compartment, and she didn't leave the car at any point en route."

"Was there blood in her compartment?" Victor asked.

"I didn't check, but I assume not, or the police would have been notified." That ruled out his stabbing theory.

"You said she had a bag with her. You didn't see it when you passed the empty compartment at Victoria Station?"

"I'm quite sure it wasn't there."

Peter returned with the items and laid the map out on one of the tables. He traced his finger over the black railway line between Brighton and London. It branched off at one point only to rejoin it again, to allow for the faster express train to overtake the train that stops all stations.

Goliath, standing behind us since he was taller, raised a good question. "Is there a slow section? Somewhere she could jump out without getting too hurt?"

Frank scoffed. "A woman jump out of a moving train?"

"Don't you call me an idiot again."

"Then don't say idiotic things. Women don't jump out of trains."

I leaned closer to the map to study it. "While I generally agree with your sentiment that women tend not to do stupid things, Frank, I can think of one reason why she might jump out of a slow-moving train—she was trying to escape. However, the express doesn't slow down except when it pulls into a station." I pointed to the two stations on the line before Victoria, both in built-up areas. "They're too public and it was broad daylight. We would have heard about witnesses seeing a woman jump from her compartment window by now. It had to have happened in the countryside, where no one was about. The train sped along without slowing, so I doubt anyone would survive the landing."

Victor pointed to the Ouse Valley Viaduct. "My guess is here. There are a few scattered farmhouses, but none close to the viaduct."

Peter offered the paper and pencil to Victor. "Did you want these to make a copy of the map?"

Victor took them, then passed them along to me. "Draw the layout of the carriage, taking note of who was in each compartment and where the exits are."

I sat down and the men crowded around as I sketched the first-class carriage's layout. "At the front end is the door that exits onto the platform. It's the only direct access for passengers getting on or off. The compartments are on the left side of the narrow corridor. In the first compartment, starting at that end, was Ruth Price. She was alone. In the second compartment was the lady with the large hat who bumped into me on the platform in Brighton before I got on. I didn't notice until we got off that there was another woman in there with her. She also wore a large hat. In compartment number three was Clement Beecroft."

"The actor?" Goliath asked.

"Actor and impresario. There was a second man in his compartment. He was…odd."

"In what way?" Peter asked.

"He looked like a laborer. Or a pugilist. His nose was somewhat squashed in."

"In a first-class carriage?" Frank tutted. "What's the world coming to?"

"Maybe *he* killed her," Goliath agreed.

"I don't think we should jump to conclusions based on a man's clothes or nose," I said wryly. "But I admit that he seemed out of place. In compartment number four were Lord and Lady Pridhurst and their grown daughter, Odette. I met them in Brighton. They stayed at the same hotel as us. Then it was we three, in the final compartment. No one passed our door to reach Ruth's, so we can discount passengers from other carriages. Nor did Ruth go in the opposite direction to the next carriage. If she was murdered then bundled out of her window, the murderer must be someone occupying the compartments between hers and ours." I counted up the dots I'd placed in each square that signified compartments. "Seven suspects. But something has just occurred to me."

The men looked at me, but it was Victor whose mind worked most like mine. "You never saw their faces?" he asked.

"I did not."

"Whose faces?" Peter asked.

I pointed to the second compartment, the one next to Ruth's. "There were two women in here wearing large hats that obscured their faces. The one with the wine-red flowers on the brim had bumped into me just before I saw Ruth get on the train, but I didn't see the other woman get on. I only saw her when I got off. What if *she* was Ruth? She may have carried the hat and clothes in her bag and changed into them before changing compartments at some point during the journey."

"Why would she do that?" Goliath asked.

"To escape someone," Frank told him.

I rather liked my theory, mostly because it meant Ruth was still alive. Even so, it would be unwise to dismiss the awful notion that she'd met her end on the express train from Brighton and her body had been discarded out of the window like a piece of rubbish.

The viaduct seemed the most likely place to find her, given its isolation, but tunnels were also a possibility. Somehow that method of disposal seemed more gruesome.

I folded up the map and handed it back to Peter. "I'll catch the train to Balcombe tomorrow and search the area near the viaduct." I'd probably be gone all day, so I needed to think of an innocent excuse to satisfy my family. I doubted my aunt and uncle would accept me going off in search of a dead body. It wasn't the genteel sort of investigation they preferred me to conduct.

"I can come with you," Victor said. "I have the day off tomorrow."

We arranged to meet at Balcombe station so as not to raise suspicions if anyone saw us together. Victor said he'd inform Harmony when his shift ended that evening, and I set about laying the foundations of my excuse. In the end, the only thing I could think of that would deter Flossy from asking to join me on my day out was to tell her I was visiting the museum.

As expected, she wrinkled her nose and declared she had more interesting plans.

* * *

VICTOR and I traveled together in an omnibus out of the village of Balcombe. It was rare for us to spend time together without the presence of either Harmony or Harry, and the journey began awkwardly. I attempted to strike up a conversation by asking him about his work as a cook in the hotel kitchen, but his brief answers cut that short. The reason for his disinterest soon became clear. His mind was elsewhere.

"Miss Fox, may I ask you a question about Harmony?"

"You may, although I may not answer it, depending on its nature."

"Fair enough." He removed his cap and stroked the brim between his finger and thumb. He was uncertain, a trait that Victor rarely displayed. Now I was even more intrigued. "Do you think I have a future with her?"

"Aren't you two already together?"

"Aye, but beyond now."

"I'm sure she wouldn't be with you if she didn't see a future with you. Victor, has something been said?"

"I haven't asked her to marry me, but I wanted to gauge her interest, so I mentioned moving out of the residence hall one day. She said she's happy as things are and doesn't want to think too far ahead. Why would she say that if she's sure about me?"

"Perhaps because you didn't ask her to marry you. Sometimes you have to ask a clear question to get a clear answer."

"Do *you* think I should ask her?"

While I wanted to encourage him, I would feel awful if the result was heartbreak. The truth was, I didn't know Harmony's wishes for the future any more than Victor did. "Harmony's career is going swimmingly at the moment," I told him. "Although her appointment as assistant to my cousin is temporary, it could lead to other promotions later. Marriage could put an end to that chance."

"I wouldn't stop her working if she didn't want to."

I smiled, but did not nod in agreement. Some men might say that, and mean it, but when they realized how much work went into keeping house and raising children, they changed their minds. Indeed, some married women gave up work they enjoyed out of sheer exhaustion. Juggling several demanding roles was difficult without the help of servants.

Harmony knew how the world worked. She also knew more opportunities would come her way if the wedding reception was a success. I wasn't sure what she would choose to do if she had a choice or was forced to make one. Even if I had an inkling, it wasn't my place to tell Victor.

"You have to have a proper conversation with her," I urged him.

"And if I do and she rejects me, it will all come to an end."

He slapped his cap back on his head. "I don't want that. Not yet." Decision made, he turned to look out of the window at the verdant pastures until we reached our destination.

We alighted from the omnibus when the viaduct came into view. It was an impressive structure with multiple arches spanning the wide valley carved out by the River Ouse. If Harry were here, he'd tell me about the design and construction. Victor and I merely sighed as we realized how large our task was.

We began our grim search at the northern end, on the western side of the viaduct since that was the Brighton to London side. Although it cut through paddocks, the immediate vicinity was rather bushy. There'd not been much rain of late, but even so, I was glad I'd worn sturdy boots that I didn't mind getting muddy.

A train sped along the line some hundred feet above, but once it disappeared into the distance, the only sounds came from birds. We took our time, checking near the base of the hollowed-out brick supports as well as further afield, until we reached the river itself. It was smaller than I expected. It would be almost impossible to time it so that an object dropped from the fast-moving train landed in the river. It was also highly doubtful anyone would survive such a big fall.

"Miss Fox! Over here." Victor held up a tortoiseshell hair comb.

We exchanged glances before continuing the search. It wasn't long before we found the brown leather bag belonging to Ruth. It had burst open, and its contents were scattered about. A chemise and a pair of bloomers were stuck to bushes and glass bottles with jewel-colored enamel lids had smashed on impact. They would have been a lovely travel set used at her toilette. Her opera glasses had suffered a similar fate.

I looked around for documents or a journal, but found none. There wasn't even a book or newspaper that she could read on the journey. I did find two pencils, however.

"Don't come any closer." Victor accompanied his warning with a hand extended to ward me away. "I've found her."

All I could see were a pair of lace-up boots attached to a woman's legs. One of the ankles was twisted at an unnatural angle. The rest of the body was hidden by the bushes.

I heeded Victor's warning at first, but after some thought, I decided I had to see the body. There might be clues on it and two sets of eyes were better than one.

Although I'd solved a few murders, I'd rarely seen a dead body. Falling from a great height would cause considerable injury. Despite steeling myself, I wasn't prepared for the sight of poor Ruth Price. She was bloodied and broken, her skin discolored with bruising, her limbs askew.

I turned away and drew in a few deep breaths before looking again. This time, I was more clinical, taking in as many details as I thought might be necessary.

"There's a lot of blood," I said. "That indicates that the impact with the ground killed her. No one heard her scream, so we can rule out an accidental fall from her compartment window. That leaves suicide or she was pushed out by someone. I don't believe she planned to kill herself and if she didn't scream, she must have been rendered unconscious in her compartment first."

Victor crouched near her head. "It's impossible to tell if she was struck first. I doubt even an autopsy could determine that. But I do agree with you. Given all the blood, she must have died here. Are you sure suicide can be ruled out?"

"I suppose not entirely without speaking to someone who knew her state of mind, but she made plans to meet me upon our return to London. People who are about to kill themselves don't make arrangements for rendezvous."

I asked Victor to look away while I lifted her skirts. Her petticoat and bloomers were still in place and showed no rips, so I was reasonably sure she hadn't been sexually forced. I lowered her skirts then checked her pockets. Empty.

I was about to stand when I noticed something. "Does that mark on her neck look out of place to you? I don't think a fall would have caused such a straight injury." It looked to me like she'd been strangled. If her airway had been cut off by strangulation, that would render her unconscious.

Victor looked closer. "It is very straight but there's so much bruising, I'm not sure. A medical professional should know."

We walked back to Balcombe, where we alerted the local sergeant to the body. I advised him to contact Scotland Yard and ask for Detective Sergeant Forrester. Even though it wasn't Monty's case, I hoped requesting him would change that.

It did not. The team that arrived at the site where we waited was led by Detective Sergeant Fanning. I'd met him when investigating the murder of a polo player in June. While not outwardly hostile toward me during that case, he'd been disinclined to listen to me. He was also rather incompetent. He agreed with the Balcombe police who'd already forbidden me from getting close to Ruth Price's body, even though I explained that I'd already seen it. Apparently my 'delicate female sensibilities' would find it too overwhelming and they didn't want a fainting woman on their hands in addition to a dead one.

"Very well, I won't come any closer, but may I draw your attention to the straight mark on her neck. It seems out of place compared to the rest of her injuries."

While most of the men dealt with the body, I searched the area again with Victor and some of the constables. By the time Ruth's body was ready for transportation, we'd found her purse with coins strewn about, several hairpins, and a second tortoiseshell comb. There were no letters, books or papers.

I traveled back to Balcombe with D.S. Fanning and two of his men, while Victor preferred to ride separately with the Balcombe police. I took the opportunity to tell Fanning I'd caught the same train as Ruth Price and been the one to alert D.S. Forrester when I didn't see her get off at Victoria Station.

"Forrester says you were alarmed," he said. "Based on what evidence?"

"She didn't leave the carriage at either of the other stops and she didn't get off before me at Victoria Station. Her compartment was empty."

D.S. Fanning reached into his jacket pocket and removed a pencil and small notebook. He flipped to a blank page and wrote my name followed by my statement. "Did you hear a scream?"

"No."

He lowered the pencil. "How well did you know her?"

"I met her in Brighton. She asked me to help her with something."

"What?"

"I don't know. She said she'd tell me when we returned to London."

"Why you?"

"I don't know."

"She must have needed a lady detective."

"There's no need to add the word lady before detective."

He looked confused. "But you *are* a lady, Miss Fox."

I sighed, then told him everything I thought he ought to know, from the moment I first noticed her on West Pier watching the Pridhursts, to *not* seeing her when I passed her compartment as the train rolled into Victoria Station.

He wrote down some of it, but not all. "Are you sure you didn't hear a scream coming from her compartment during the journey?"

"As I already told you, no, I didn't."

"Well, if you're sure." He put away his pencil and notebook. "Shame. I saw the photograph the brother left with us yesterday and she was pretty."

"I fail to see what that has to do with anything," I said hotly.

"Now don't get upset, Miss Fox, it was just an observation that it's a shame a pretty young thing would end her own life."

I bit my tongue, but it was no good. On rare occasions, my anger took on a life of its own and would not be contained. This was one of those times. "Is it not a shame when *anyone* takes their own life, Detective, pretty and young or otherwise?"

"I was just—"

"And what makes you so sure she killed herself?"

His nostrils flared. "I don't have to justify my professional opinion to you."

"Is it because she didn't scream? That's your only reason? As I just told you, she made plans to meet me in London. A woman wanting to kill herself on the way doesn't make plans for the near future. You need to wait for the results of an autopsy to determine the cause of death, and you should speak to someone close to her to know more about her state of mind before accepting or rejecting any theory. The brother who reported her missing would be a good place to start."

D.S. Fanning stiffened. "It was evident that she died from the fall."

"I didn't say she was killed in her compartment, just that she may have been rendered unconscious first then bundled out of the window by her assailant. The mark on her neck requires closer inspection by a medical professional. Hopefully an autopsy—"

"I'm not going to bother the coroner with this one, Miss Fox. The Balcombe police say the viaduct is a common place for suicides."

"And Scotland Yard is a common place to find intelligent people, but idiots do happen to work there, too." Perhaps I shouldn't have said that. I instantly regretted it and was about to apologize when D.S. Fanning said something that changed my mind.

"This is what happens when women are exposed to sights like the one you saw back there. You are overwrought, Miss Fox. I advise rest and a cup of tea."

It was so ridiculous that I could only laugh. It held no humor, but it did have the effect of confusing Fanning. He watched me warily the rest of the way back to Balcombe, as if he expected me to turn into a wild creature and attack.

He didn't offer to drive us back to London. I wouldn't have accepted anyway. As I stepped out of the carriage at the railway station, I held the door open and leaned back in. I may not like him, and I may think him incompetent, but he was a necessary evil at this point. "Please, Detective, ask the coroner to perform an autopsy, and suggest he pay particular attention to the mark on Ruth's neck."

D.S. Fanning grabbed the door and wrenched it out of my grip then slammed it closed.

Victor and I caught the train back to London. We didn't sit together, which was just as well. I wasn't good company. My blood was still boiling after my discussion with Fanning.

I telephoned Monty when I returned to the hotel, but he said he didn't have the authority to force Fanning to keep an open mind. He also pointed out the case might be a joint operation between the Sussex police and Scotland Yard, since

Ruth Price's body was found in West Sussex, yet she lived in London.

"I'm afraid Fanning is somewhat lazy," he went on. "If he can find a reasonable explanation for her death without too much effort on his part, he'll take it. There's a chance the Sussex division will keep him on his toes, so all is not lost." He did not sound hopeful, however.

In light of that, I asked him to give me the address for Ruth's brother. If Fanning was going to rule her death suicide, I was going to see if her family agreed. If the brother claimed she was melancholy, I'd let Fanning have his way. But if he didn't think his sister was likely to take her own life, then I'd go with my instinct and treat her death as murder.

CHAPTER 5

Over breakfast the following morning, Harmony agreed with my decision after I told her about our gruesome discovery and my frustrating encounter with Detective Sergeant Fanning.

"I'm afraid I lost my temper with him," I told her. "I called him an idiot."

She peered over her coffee cup at me. "Is he an idiot?"

"Evidence and witness accounts suggest he is."

"Then I don't see the problem."

"I might need his help in the future."

"You have Monty for that." Her sly tone and smirk implied what she thought about me being on a first-name basis with D.S. Forrester.

Time to change the subject. To make it appear that I was making casual conversation and not fishing for her opinion on her future with Victor, I picked up a piece of cold toast and pretended to give it a thorough inspection. "What do you think about women continuing to work after marriage, by choice, not necessity? Is it possible to do both or would the effort of keeping house while working be too much?" I nibbled a corner of the toast.

She lowered her cup so quickly a little liquid spilled over the rim. "Are you considering marrying him?"

I choked on a crumb. "I hardly know Monty!"

"Not him, Harry. Did he ask you? When? How? Did he get down on one knee?"

I put the toast back on the plate and dusted off my fingers. "Harry hasn't asked me, nor will he. He knows my views on marriage. I was specifically asking about *your* views." I waited, but she sat back with a disappointed look on her face.

"Speaking of Harry—"

"We weren't," I said.

"Are you going to ask him to help you with this case?"

I sighed. It seemed we both had topics we wished to avoid. "I have no reason to involve him. Besides, he's busy with his own case."

"Ah, yes, the reason he's camped out in the foyer." She lifted her cup again and peered at me through eyes sparkling with mischief. "The maids were all aflutter with the news that he was back. They hope he's on the verge of returning to work here. He has been missed."

If she was trying to make me jealous, it wasn't going to work. I already knew some of the maids placed Harry on a pedestal.

"Mrs. Hessing told Mr. Bainbridge she hired Harry to keep an eye out for a gossip columnist," Harmony went on. "He informed Sir Ronald."

That explained why my uncle hadn't thrown Harry out when he saw him in the foyer yesterday. "He's watching for anyone matching her description arriving at the check-in counter. Apparently, she should have checked in yesterday."

"You could find out if he's still in the foyer when you leave the hotel."

"I don't want to talk to him."

"Yes, you do."

I sniffed. "His case is none of my business. I have no reason to speak to him. If I do, he'll get the wrong idea."

"We wouldn't want that," she muttered into her coffee cup.

* * *

HARRY WAS in the foyer again. I did not approach him. I barely even looked at him. Not properly, anyway, merely out of the corner of my eye as he approached.

He cut me off before I reached the door. "Are you hurrying in order to avoid me?"

"I'm hurrying because I have things to do."

He lowered his voice. "I heard you found a body yesterday. Nasty business." I liked that he didn't comment on my feminine sensibilities being overwhelmed by the sight. He knew I could cope with it more than most.

"News travels fast," I said.

"One of my father's former colleagues told him last night when they met for a drink. They meet regularly to discuss cases, both old and new. My father enjoys it, and my mother likes getting him out of the house."

"Most retired men take up fishing or bird-watching."

"He tried fishing once. His line got tangled and he came home grumpier than when he left."

I tried picturing D.I. Hobart relaxing, but couldn't. It didn't suit the hearty man whose life had revolved around his work. If he hadn't been forced out by the commissioner, he'd still be there. His departure was a loss for Scotland Yard. He would have been an ally for me now, too, although it seemed I'd made a name for myself if he'd been informed that I discovered Ruth's body.

"Was it Monty who mentioned my involvement?" I asked.

Harry shook his head. "Another sergeant. He doesn't know you, but he told my father that an annoying female private investigator suggested the woman was murdered, when it was clearly suicide. Based on a description like that, my father knew it was you."

I shot him a withering glare. "Very droll. Your father doesn't find me annoying at all. He likes me."

I'd been trying to make him laugh, but instead, his gaze softened. "He is an excellent judge of character. He wanted me to tell you to trust your instincts over Fanning's. If you think the woman was murdered, you should investigate."

"I already planned to. But tell him thank you when you see him. Speaking of the case, I should begin." I made to leave but stopped when he spoke.

"I can help you, if you need it. You only have to ask."

"You already have a case of your own."

He glanced toward the desk where guests were checking out. Even though London was quiet at this time of year, the Mayfair Hotel was always busy mid-morning. "Your investigation is more interesting than mine."

"Mine has no client and therefore no fee. Yours does. But thank you, I'll keep it in mind if I need another mind to mull over clues."

"I hope you do."

The sound of his warm, rich voice stayed with me all the way to Enoch Price's house in Chelsea. The area wasn't as exclusive as Mayfair, but it was still appealing with handsome houses, clean porches, and respectable shops. A pinch-lipped housekeeper answered my knock and wouldn't let me inside until I told her I was there about Ruth.

She clutched the cross hanging around her neck and left me waiting in the sunny front parlor. Either the room was rarely used, or the housekeeper was very good at her job. There wasn't a speck of dust on any surface and the grate gleamed. Photographs on one of the occasional tables were positioned for best viewing from the doorway and the wooden cross on the wall was perfectly straight. Even the fringing on the carpet was aligned.

A few minutes later, a man entered. The resemblance to Ruth was obvious, from the spectacles and freckled nose to the serious set of his mouth. Although I suspected his balding head made him appear older than he was, I still guessed him to be at least ten years older than his sister.

I introduced myself. "May I begin by saying I'm sorry for your loss, Mr. Price. Losing a loved one is difficult, but when she was so young..."

He invited me to sit then hitched up his trouser legs and sat too. "Thank you, Miss Fox. I'm still in shock. My little sister...gone. It's quite awful."

"The police informed you yesterday?"

"Early evening, yes." He blinked dry eyes back at me through his spectacles. "Forgive me, how did you say you knew Ruth?"

"I met her in Brighton. She asked for my help, but never

told me why. She said she'd contact me when we returned to London."

He stiffened at the mention of Brighton. "I don't understand. What sort of help could she have needed from you?"

"I was hoping you might shed some light on that. I'm a private detective, so I think she wanted to employ me."

The curl of his top lip was ever so slight, but I noticed it. I suspected I was meant to. "I can't think of a reason."

"Ruth worked for a journalist at *The Evening Bulletin*, didn't she? Is that why she was in Brighton?"

The top lip rose higher. It would seem he wasn't just appalled by my profession, but by his sister's, too. "I don't know. We didn't discuss it."

"What was the name of the journalist she worked for?"

His gaze lifted to the wall behind my head where the cross hung. "I don't recall. Miss Fox, I don't mean to be rude, but I have no need of a lady detective. The police are looking into Ruth's death. I'm sure they'll be thorough." He stood, a prompt to get me to leave.

I stayed seated. "Are you aware that Detective Sergeant Fanning thinks Ruth killed herself?"

"She didn't! She wouldn't!" The explosive denial held more emotion than anything he'd said since my arrival.

"I agree. Someone making plans, such as a meeting, has no intention of committing suicide. But why do *you* say Ruth wouldn't? Was she happy? Did she have something to look forward to?"

"Marriage, children, a settled life." Enoch sat down and glanced at the cross on the wall again.

"She was engaged to be married? Can you tell me her fiancé's name?" I reached into my bag for my notebook.

He shook his head. "You misunderstand. I meant she would one day have those things to fulfill her. A girl such as her looks forward to having her own home and family."

"A girl such as her?" I echoed.

"She was a good girl. Naturally, she wanted those things. Her interest in journalism was merely a passing phase that she would grow out of when the novelty wore off. It's not uncommon these days for females to perform a little task here and there to earn some pin money before settling down. As long as it's respectable, no harm is done, and there's nothing wrong with being an assistant to a journalist." It sounded like a speech he'd practiced. Or one he'd heard.

I had so many thoughts about his comments, but I held them all back. Allowances had to be made for his grief. "Is there a more specific reason why she wouldn't take her own life? She was happy?"

He indicated the cross. "She was deeply devout. Taking one's own life is a sin. She simply wouldn't do it, and I'll explain as much to that detective."

"I'm afraid it won't do any good. D.S. Fanning believes Ruth threw herself off the train and he is disinclined to look for another cause of death."

He shot to his feet again. One arm crossed his middle, and he lifted a hand to nibble on the thumbnail before turning away so I couldn't see his face. Perhaps I shouldn't have been so blunt, but I needed him to realize that an incorrect cause of death would likely be recorded, and it would be there forever.

"I'm not asking for money, Mr. Price. I want to take on this case for Ruth's sake, as well as for my own satisfaction. All I want from you is to answer a few questions. And to let me see her room."

He turned back to face me, calmer and more composed. He nodded.

"You reported her missing when she didn't come home after her visit to Brighton, is that right?" I asked.

"Yes."

"Do you know why she was there?"

"No. I didn't even know she'd gone until I read the note she'd left for me in her room."

"Why wouldn't she confide in you?"

He hesitated before answering. "Because I wouldn't have approved of her going to a place full of licentiousness."

"It's not like that at all. Most of the holidaymakers in Brighton are families."

His jaw firmed. "The note said she'd return on the ten-thirty express three days later. I telephoned the police when I got home from the office that day, and she wasn't here. They said she'd probably missed her train and to call back the next day if she still hadn't returned, which I did."

"Can you think of a reason why she would go to Brighton?"

"No."

"Was it to do with her work for the journalist?"

"I don't know. We never discussed the particulars of her employment."

It was hardly surprising Ruth kept the details to herself. Mentioning it would probably start an argument with her brother, given his views.

"How was her demeanor when she left London?"

He shrugged. "Fine."

"What was on her mind in the days leading up to her departure?"

He looked at me askance. "I am not a mind reader, Miss Fox."

"What did you talk about?"

He shrugged again. "Nothing out of the ordinary. She asked me what I'd like for dinner. We discussed the Sunday sermon." He swallowed heavily. "I scolded her for not listening. She has—had—a habit of not paying attention, but I'd catch her out by asking certain questions about the service."

"Did she have any friends she might confide in?"

"Ruth confided in God. She needed no other confidante."

I closed my notebook and returned it to my bag. "May I look through her belongings?"

He led the way upstairs to her bedroom and stayed while I searched. The bed was made with a precision I was used to at the hotel, but never bothered to achieve when I made my own bed. A Bible sat on her nightstand; a set of rosary beads draped over it. The pages of the Bible were well thumbed. A plain wooden cross hung above the bed. Enoch was right. Ruth was devout. Her faith wasn't just for appearances to satisfy her brother.

I searched through drawers and cupboards, checked inside coat pockets and under the mattress. I found no papers or journals, nothing out of the ordinary for a young woman.

In the corridor, the housekeeper watched me, her pinched lips even thinner than when I'd first introduced myself. "May I ask you some questions about Ruth, Mrs...?"

Her nostrils flared. "I have nothing to say. Mr. Price, Father Dominic is here to give his condolences."

"Take him through to the parlor. Close the door so he doesn't see Miss Fox leave." Mr. Price watched the housekeeper head down the stairs. When she was out of earshot, he turned to me. "When you make your inquiries, please respect my sister's stature in the community and do not mention her work at the newspaper. It wasn't an important part of her life, so not worth making a song and dance over. Also don't tell anyone that she was in Brighton alone. We'll put it about that she visited a friend there."

I made no promise, since I couldn't keep it. It was likely I'd need to mention both those points as I made my inquiries. I merely thanked him for his time.

His final request was that I leave silently. That was a request I could accommodate. I tiptoed down the stairs and exited without another word.

* * *

THE EVENING BULLETIN had a reputation for a sensational style of journalism. Facts were only printed if they were scandalous, speculation was rife, and provocative headlines were the norm. It was a formula that sold a lot of copies.

While I waited my turn to speak to the harried clerk at the front desk, I peered through a large window behind him to the inner sanctum. Like Fleet Street outside, the newsroom was a scene of hectic activity, despite it being Sunday. Newspapermen with pencils tucked behind their ears wrote furiously at their desks or dictated to a stenographer. Sometimes they clicked their fingers above their heads and a youth standing off to the side would come running to accept the handwritten papers. The papers were then either added to a pile on a typist's desk or taken into an adjoining office. I was surprised by the number of women. All of the stenographers and typists were young females.

A member of the public in front of me had a lot of complaints about the latest edition's inaccuracies. The poor clerk dutifully wrote them down, although I doubted the editor would see them. I picked up a copy of the latest edition from a pile and skimmed the articles while I waited. There was no report of Ruth's death. I didn't even know if the journalist she worked for knew she'd died. I'd forgotten to ask Enoch Price if he'd informed her employer.

The man in front of me finally finished his diatribe and left the building. The clerk set his notes aside and looked at me as if he expected me to spout a long list of grievances against the newspaper, too.

"How may I help you?" he asked blandly.

"My name is Cleopatra Fox. I'm a private detective investigating the death of Ruth Price."

He straightened, his gaze sharpening. "I...uh... Who?"

"I already know she worked here, and I can see that you recognize her name. What I don't understand is why you're denying knowing her."

"Let me find someone for you to talk to."

He pushed open the door to the newsroom and strode past the journalists and typists to the far side where he opened another door. Moments later he returned with a white-bearded, pink-faced, red-nosed man in tow.

I put out my hand. "Cleopatra Fox. Private detective."

"Finlayson. Editor." He shook my hand.

"I'm looking into the death of Ruth Price. She worked here, I believe."

The editor's pursed lips emerged like two slugs from his snowy beard before disappearing again. "She did."

"You know about her passing?"

"We were informed early this morning."

"May I speak with the journalist she worked for?"

"Journalist?" His burst of laughter sent spittle flying out of his mouth and onto his beard. The laugh evolved into a chesty cough that turned his face even pinker and his nose redder.

The clerk rose, as if to fetch help, but sat again once Mr. Finlayson's cough subsided.

"She isn't a journalist," the editor went on. "She writes our gossip column."

Puzzle pieces I didn't know I needed slotted into place, but I wouldn't jump to conclusions yet.

"Who told you she was a journalist?" Mr. Finlayson went on.

"It's not important. May I speak to her?"

"I'm afraid that's out of the question."

"Why?"

"You may speak to me instead."

"Do you know what stories Ruth was working on at the time of her death? Do you know why she went to Brighton?"

His lips pursed again as he considered his answer.

I saved him the effort of coming up with something. "It seems you can't help me, Mr. Finlayson. What is the gossip columnist's name?"

He picked up the newspaper I'd put down a few minutes earlier and flipped the pages until he reached the relevant section. He pointed to the byline. "We call her Mrs. Scoop."

"Is that her real name?"

"Of course not. She stipulated anonymity in her contract." He folded up the newspaper and slapped it back onto the pile. "The passing of Ruth Price is very sad. That's all *The Evening Bulletin* has to say on the matter at this point." He indicated the door to the street. "If that's all, Miss Fox…"

Something wasn't right. The clerk had fetched someone to speak to me about Ruth, and Mr. Finlayson had immediately put aside whatever he was doing to meet me. The newspaper's editor would be very busy. So why bother with me at all?

"Why won't you talk to me about Ruth?"

"There's nothing to tell," Mr. Finlayson said.

"Her work here may be related to her cause of death. You see, I don't believe she threw herself off that train."

"Why not?"

"I met her brother this morning. He claims she believed suicide to be a terrible sin."

"What led you to speak to the brother? You must have already had a reason to think she wouldn't kill herself. What was it?"

I could have told him I'd met Ruth in Brighton, but I held that information back. His questions were unsettling, particularly when I was supposed to be the one questioning him. "I don't understand why you're obstructing me, Mr. Finlayson.

Don't you want me to get to the bottom of the mystery? Don't you think Ruth Price deserves justice?"

"You seem to be suggesting she was murdered, Miss Fox. If you are a private detective, someone must have hired you. Was it her brother?"

His habit of answering my question with his own was becoming frustrating. My patience was thinning. Was this how it felt to be on the other end of one of my interrogations?

I employed a tactic some of my suspects used on me and stayed silent.

Mr. Finlayson was undeterred. "Are you a private detective, or are you an assistant to a journalist at another newspaper?"

I blinked at him. "Why would I lie?"

"The death of a young woman on a train from Brighton to London is a good story, particularly if there's more to it than suicide. If anyone prints the story, it will be *The Evening Bulletin*, not one of our rivals. She was *our* employee, and we should be the ones to print it first. But thank you for confirming a common opinion around the office. Now we know to pursue the story."

I stared at him, open-mouthed.

He indicated the door again but did not wait for me to leave. He turned and marched back into the newsroom.

The clerk at the desk cleared his throat and glanced pointedly at the exit. At that moment, the door opened and two people entered. The first was an elderly gentleman brandishing a copy of the latest edition of the newspaper. He slapped it down on the front desk and began to list his complaints about the contents.

The person who entered behind him was a thin, blonde woman around forty years of age with hawkish features. She brushed past me, her head down as she read a piece of paper. An unkind person would describe her as having a long nose and sunken chin.

Seeing her confirmed the earlier thought that had taken root when Mr. Finlayson told me Ruth worked for a gossip columnist. The blonde woman must be the same one Harry was looking for, the one who wanted to gather information about the Hessing-Liddicoat wedding. Her features were too distinctive for there to be another. Ruth Price worked for her. When she saw us in Brighton, or overheard the Bainbridge name, she linked us to the hotel venue for the wedding reception. I doubted we were the reason she was in Brighton, but she saw an opportunity to gather information while we were there.

I was that opportunity. Somehow, she knew I solved murders, and she was counting on the fact I wouldn't want my sleuthing becoming public knowledge. When she returned to London, she planned to blackmail me into revealing some wedding details to pass on to her employer, Mrs. Scoop.

While the clerk's head was bent over his notes to write down yet another complaint from a member of the public, I slipped into the newsroom. Despite the open windows, it was warm and smelled faintly of ink. The chorus of chatter and mechanical rhythm of typewriter keys was surprisingly comforting. Perhaps that was because it meant everyone was too busy to notice an intruder in their midst.

Before I reached the room where Mrs. Scoop had gone, the door opened, and she re-emerged. She passed me with a long-legged strut, her attention once again focused on the paper in her hand. She exited the newsroom altogether.

Sometimes, situations change, and a good detective must pivot accordingly. Mrs. Scoop's departure could benefit me. Like Mr. Finlayson, she probably wouldn't divulge anything to me willingly. I needed to employ more devious methods and her absence was perfectly timed.

I reached the door with the name Mrs. Scoop painted on the glass pane. Not a single person in the newsroom had stopped me and asked why I was there. For a profession that prided itself on being inquisitive, the journalists were surprisingly unobservant within their own environs.

I slipped into the office and closed the door. The information Mrs. Scoop dealt with was sensitive, so I wasn't surprised to find one of the three desk drawers locked. I quickly set to work with my picking tools and unlocked it. Inside were two large envelopes. I removed two photographs from one of the envelopes, along with some handwritten notes. In one of the photographs, Lord Pridhurst was seated at a table playing cards. In the second, he stood on the street with another man, exchanging something. It wasn't clear who was handing what to whom, but they seemed to be attempting to hide behind a tree.

I returned the photographs to the envelope then quickly scanned the page of notes. Someone had written sample headlines in a spidery scrawl: 'Lord Pridhurst's Shame', 'Does his Family Know?', and the most provocative, 'Duped! Lord Desperate to Marry Off Daughter Before Truth Exposed.'

The rest of the notes appeared to be a list of times and dates with a single name attached: Keats. I doubted it referred to the poet. It was probably the other man in the photograph.

I returned the paper and photographs to the envelope and opened the second one. It contained a single piece of paper. My breath caught in my chest. The heading stated 'Hessing-Liddicoat Wedding at the Mayfair.' Below that was a list of names. All were staff at the hotel, except for the last one.

Me.

It confirmed what I'd realized when I saw the woman who fit the description Mrs. Hessing gave Harry for the gossip columnist. His quarry was Mrs. Scoop, the woman who employed Ruth Price. Among other tasks, Ruth was trying to find out details about the Hessing-Liddicoat wedding, and she planned to blackmail me into being her source. Her death had put an end to that plan before it had begun. What I'd merely speculated until now was here in black and white for anyone to see.

It was evidence of a motive for murder. If Detective Sergeant Fanning suspected Ruth's death was the result of foul play, he would place me on the list of suspects if he saw these notes.

I no longer felt compelled to push him in that direction.

The door suddenly opened and Mrs. Scoop stood there, one clawlike hand gripping the door handle. "Who are you?" Her voice was as needle-sharp as her glare. "What are you doing in here?"

CHAPTER 6

"I'll explain," I said. "Once you close the door." I did not want Mr. Finlayson to throw me out before I had a chance to get answers from the woman who employed Ruth.

The gossip columnist closed the door and held out her hand for the envelopes. I passed them to her, and she slotted them back into the desk drawer with a vigorous shove. She remained standing and crossed her arms, her needle-thin eyebrows raised. Now that I was closer, I could see she'd drawn them on.

"Well? Answer me. Who are you?"

"My name appears on the bottom of your list of potential sources at the Mayfair Hotel."

Her gaze lowered to the drawer.

"Miss Cleopatra Fox," I clarified. "I won't be a source, by the way."

"You were always an unlikely option, but we weren't sure how loyal you were to the family that you were once estranged from." She knew far more about me than a stranger ought.

"Now that I know which staff are on your list, they won't be a source of information, either."

She pulled out the chair and sat. "As you wish. The wedding reception is only a sidepiece anyway. It doesn't interest me overmuch."

She hadn't invited me to sit, but I sat anyway. "Then why did you make a reservation to stay at the hotel?"

She stilled. Then she waved her hand in dismissal. The movement was jerky, abrupt, as if she barely had the time to do it. "I could have you arrested for trespass, Miss Fox."

"And I could warn Lord Pridhurst that you plan to print something about him. I met him in Brighton. He would believe me." I looked around her office, but it was quite bare. There was nothing of a personal nature on display, no photographs or even newspaper clippings that she might be proud of writing. "Do I call you Mrs. Scoop?"

She opened the top drawer of her desk and removed a slender silver tin. She opened it and pulled out a cigarette. She offered me one. I tried not to reveal my surprise—few women smoked—as I declined. "Anonymity keeps my work and private life separate. A woman in your position would understand the necessity for separation from time to time."

I gave her a tight smile. "You've heard that Ruth Price is dead."

She used a match to light the cigarette, then leaned back in the chair, cigarette held near her lips. "Ruth was supposed to come into the office after returning from Brighton on Thursday. She didn't. Nor did she come in the next day. Yesterday, I called at her home. Her brother told me he'd reported her missing, then early this morning he sent a message to say her body had been found at the Ouse Valley Viaduct. I didn't want to trouble him at such a time, so I went to Scotland Yard to find out more. I was informed by a rather stupid officer that Ruth threw herself off the train." She rolled her eyes as she took a drag on her cigarette.

"I agree with your opinion of D.S. Fanning and Ruth's cause of death. I've decided to look into it. The first time I saw her, she was watching the Pridhursts. Then, later, I received a note asking me to meet her. I did, and she told me that if I didn't help her, she would expose me in this very newspaper."

Mrs. Scoop watched me as she drew on her cigarette then blew the smoke across the desk between us. "And you think she wanted your help to gather information about the wedding reception?"

Her question surprised me. "Is there another reason?"

"No," she said before slotting the cigarette between her lips.

"What scandal was she investigating in Brighton?"

Mrs. Scoop tapped the closed drawer. "Lord Pridhurst."

"Yes, but what was he involved in?"

"I can't tell you that. It's confidential until it appears in my column."

"Mrs. Scoop, you don't understand. If Ruth was killed because she was watching Lord Pridhurst and reporting to you, then your life could also be in danger."

She gave a brittle laugh. "Don't be absurd. Lord Pridhurst isn't a killer."

"Then what is he? What has he done? I can be discreet. No other newspaper will discover the scandal from me."

She watched me closely as she sucked on her cigarette. "All right." She blew out smoke through her nose. "He's in enormous debt. He's about to lose everything, including part ownership in a shipping company. That isn't unusual and, while devastating for him personally, it's not a scandal. However, he has plans to marry his daughter to the son of a very wealthy man by the name of Holland. The union will solve Pridhurst's immediate financial problems."

"And Mr. Holland doesn't know?"

"Precisely. Again, not so much of a problem if he finds out, as long as he cares for the girl. The thing is, I doubt he's marrying her for love. You see, Mr. Holland's canned goods business wants to expand into America, and he can't do that without a shipping company to ship his cans. I have it on good authority that part of Odette's dowry was an exceptionally good rate."

"No shipping company, no incentive to marry," I said.

She pointed the cigarette at me. "Precisely."

"You don't think that's enough of a motive for Pridhurst to kill Ruth? Or you? Kill the journalist, kill the story."

"He doesn't seem like the type, but..." She lifted one shoulder. "I concede that it's a possibility. Don't worry, I will be careful."

"What other stories was Ruth working on?"

"Just the Pridhurst file and the Hessing-Liddicoat

wedding." She watched me as she drew on her cigarette. "Perhaps we're reading too much into this, Miss Fox. Neither you nor I know much about Ruth. We don't know her state of mind when she caught that train."

"You didn't discuss personal matters with her?"

She scoffed. "She was my assistant, not my friend. Perhaps there were events or people in her life that drove her to end it all. That brother of hers, for example." She sniffed. "Controlling misogynist."

I heard the booming voice of Mr. Finlayson in the newsroom outside, shouting at the hapless journalists for their tardiness and ineptitude. I ought to go before he came in to speak to Mrs. Scoop about printing a story on Ruth's death before their competitors got wind of it. "If you think of anything relevant, please contact me at the Mayfair Hotel."

"Am I welcome there?"

I simply smiled. Before I exited, I peered through the glass pane in the door but couldn't see Mr. Finlayson. I opened the door, then something occurred to me. "Ruth was the one who was supposed to check into the Mayfair Hotel under the name Blaine, wasn't she? Not you. But she never arrived, because she died."

Mrs. Scoop huffed, sending smoke from her cigarette billowing from her mouth and nose. "Very clever, Miss Fox. Yes, I made the reservation intending for Ruth to check in, although I hadn't told her yet. I planned to, when she got back. She was better at that sort of thing than me. She was extraordinarily observant. Wallflowers often are. People underestimated Ruth all the time." She placed the cigarette between her lips, but removed it again without taking a puff. "My style is more direct, which is why I approached Mrs. Hessing first. I thought she'd be the sort who would appreciate it and allow me to exclusively cover the wedding." She huffed again. This time it was self-deprecating. "I was wrong."

* * *

BACK AT THE MAYFAIR, I found Harry seated on the same armchair with a current edition of *The Times* opened to obscure his face as he watched the comings and goings of the hotel foyer. As I'd done the first time I saw him there, I hooked a finger over the top of the newspaper to draw it down.

"I hope you plan to stay awhile," he said, folding it up. "I could do with the company."

I sat in the other armchair. "Is your investigation dull?"

"Immeasurably. Yours sounds far more interesting. Tell me about your suspects, the clues you've found and theories you've formed. They don't even have to be fully formed, just talk to me to keep me awake."

"I can do better than that. I can tell you who your gossip columnist is, as well as which hotel staff she was hoping to blackmail or bribe into being a source of information about the wedding."

He blinked slowly at me. "Are you muscling in on my investigation on purpose?"

I knew he was joking, but even so, I felt compelled to deny it. "I would never do that, Harry."

"Not even to get your name on my office door?"

I laughed softly. "In the process of conducting my own investigation into Ruth Price's death, I happened to stumble upon your target. Ruth worked for her."

"I thought she was assistant to a journalist."

"I think it's what she wanted everyone to believe, even her brother. The gossip columnist works for *The Evening Bulletin* and goes by the pseudonym Mrs. Scoop. I've just come from her office."

"What's her real name?"

"She wouldn't tell me. I recognized her from the description Mrs. Hessing gave you."

"And she simply gave you the names of staff she planned to interrogate about the wedding?"

"I wouldn't say she *freely* gave the list to me. I found it in her office before she arrived."

"She didn't have that sort of information securely locked away?"

"Um..."

"You broke into a locked cabinet, didn't you?"

I put up my hands in surrender. "She caught me red-handed, but I managed to convince her not to throw me out. You're not the only one who can charm people, Harry."

He smirked. "Give me the list of names and I'll warn them not to talk."

"I can't remember them all, and anyway, you may not need to. Ruth Price did most of Mrs. Scoop's dirty work. She was the one who was going to check in here and speak to the staff, but her death put an end to that. I don't think Mrs. Scoop has plans to come in her stead. She doesn't seem all that interested in the wedding, actually. She seems to have bigger fish to fry."

"Such as?"

"Lord Pridhurst." In a low voice, I told Harry what I'd learned about Lord Pridhurst's debts and how he didn't want Mr. Holland to find out. "If Holland learns the shipping company will be lost to Pridhurst, Mrs. Scoop thinks he won't make an offer for Odette's hand, and Pridhurst needs him to. That's a motive for murder. If he found out what Ruth knew, he could have killed her to silence her. He was also seated only three compartments away from her on the train. That's opportunity."

"But clearly Mrs. Scoop also knows about Pridhurst, so killing Ruth won't stop the story."

"*He* may not know that. I've warned Mrs. Scoop to be careful, but she doesn't seem too concerned."

"Are you going to talk to Pridhurst?"

I'd been thinking about my next move on the way home and decided that Pridhurst would most likely deny it if confronted. I needed more evidence before I accused him of anything. "I want to talk to him without letting him know that I know about his financial troubles. I plan to speak to as many passengers as possible who were seated in the compartments between ours and Ruth's and ask them if they saw anyone moving about the carriage. If his name is mentioned, then I'll confront him."

"Mapping out their movements is a good plan," Harry said, nodding. "Although the killer will lie."

"Hopefully I can catch them out in the lie. I already know where everyone was seated. I just need to speak to them. There are three passengers I can't yet identify, unfortunately.

Without their statements, I'll be leaving a rather large gap in my knowledge."

"Draw me a seating plan of the carriage," he said.

"I already have one, but I have no intention of showing it to you. I'm working this case alone."

"Don't be petulant."

"Petulant! I simply want to solve this one on my own, thank you."

"I know you, Cleo," he purred. "You're afraid if you spend too much time with me, you'll succumb to your feelings and kiss me again."

"Again? Ha! *You* kissed *me*, Harry."

"Last time, yes, but you kissed me first in St James's Park. I know you remember it."

He was so sure of himself, so arrogant. It was even more irritating because he was right. I remembered that kiss very well. "I am not involving you in my case, Harry."

"Then why did you sit down and tell me about it?"

I liked to pride myself on being good at thinking on my feet, but Harry had a way of making me trip over them instead. Going by his satisfied smirk, he knew he'd caught me out.

The appearance of Mrs. Hessing stepping out of the lift was a welcome distraction. The arrival of Uncle Ronald via the front entrance was even more welcome. Both he and Mrs. Hessing looked directly at us.

Harry rose and did up his jacket button. "I need to speak to my client about these latest developments."

Uncle Ronald stopped in the middle of the foyer. His gaze tracked Harry as he intercepted Mrs. Hessing. He frowned, something he did a lot, but this time I worried it was the precursor to a lecture about being seen with Harry. I would set him straight before he had the opportunity to open his mouth.

"Good morning, Uncle," I said.

He checked his watch. "It's the afternoon." As he tucked it back into his waistcoat pocket, his narrowed gaze sought out Harry again.

"We were just chatting," I said quickly. "It would be rude of me not to greet him."

"You don't have to pretend with me, Cleopatra."

"Pretend?" I asked weakly.

"I'm pleased that you and Armitage are working together for Mrs. Hessing. I like that you're taking an interest in hotel affairs." His gaze softened. "You're an asset when you put your mind to it." He stroked his moustache, seemingly embarrassed at speaking so affectionately. "Make sure his paramour doesn't find out. You don't want to upset her."

He hailed Mr. Hobart before I had the opportunity to reply. Not that I would have spoken up. I wasn't going to be the one to tell him Harry and Miss Morris were no longer together. It would only make him worry that I was in Harry's sights, then he'd forbid me from seeing him, and perhaps even forbid me from investigating. Uncle Ronald still didn't believe I had no interest in marriage, and therefore no interest in Harry. If he wasn't going to listen to my continual denials, I wasn't going to set him straight now.

Harry rejoined me as Mrs. Hessing headed to the post desk, her walking stick clicking on the floor tiles with firm precision. "You waited for me. Is everything all right with Sir Ronald?"

"He thinks we're working together for Mrs. Hessing. He likes that I'm taking an interest in hotel affairs."

His smile was rueful. "So that's why he doesn't mind us talking."

"That, and he believes you are still with Miss Morris."

He arched his brows at me. "Cleo, you should tell him I'm not."

I cleared my throat. "You get your wish. You may help me with my case so that it appears we're working together to appease my uncle. Shall we discuss it over lunch at Luigi's?"

He indicated I should leave the hotel ahead of him. "I knew you'd give in."

"You did not. Anyway, I'm not giving in because I want to be near you. I'm giving in because if I don't, Uncle Ronald will grow suspicious. If he finds out I'm not helping you with Mrs. Hessing's situation, but am trying to solve a murder, he might forbid me from sleuthing. I am merely protecting my freedom."

We both greeted Frank as we passed him, then headed up Piccadilly.

"Of course," Harry finally said. "Have it your way."

"What does that mean?"

"It means you can tell yourself whatever you like, but you gave in without much of a protest, from what I could see."

"Then you weren't looking properly. I'm hungry. Are you hungry? It's been an age since I've had a bowl of Luigi's pasta. I think I'll have the spaghetti today. What about you?"

I walked off before he could tease me about my tendency to chatter when I was nervous.

* * *

FIFTEEN MINUTES LATER, I placed the sketch I'd made of the first-class carriage on the table between us. Harry and I sat in our usual spot in the window of Roma Café below his office on Broadwick Street, Soho. One of the other tables was occupied by two women speaking in rapid Italian to each other. They looked a little familiar, but it wasn't until one of the dark-eyed beauties gave Luigi a simpering smile as he approached us that I recalled seeing her in the café before.

Harry and I placed our orders for spaghetti Bolognese, and I also ordered a pot of tea. Luigi shook his head in disappointment as he walked off, then repeated my order in Italian for the benefit of the women and the two leathery-skinned men seated on the stools at the counter. I didn't speak much Italian but understood enough to know that Luigi told them I was still drinking dirty water.

I took out my notebook and pencil from my bag and placed them beside the diagram. "Starting from the front of the carriage is Ruth Price's compartment. She sat alone. In compartment number two were two women, both wearing large hats. The one with the wine-red flowers decorating her hat bumped into me on the platform in Brighton. I don't know their names and didn't see their faces."

I flipped open my notebook. At the top of a blank page, I wrote 'Compartment Two' and 'Woman in Red Hat' beside it. On the next page, I repeated the compartment number and wrote 'Other Woman in Big Hat.'

"In the third compartment was the actor and impresario, Clement Beecroft." I wrote that down on the next page of my notebook as I told Harry how my maid had seen Beecroft swimming up to a bathing machine. "I overheard the woman in the hut giggle, so I presume they were enjoying themselves." I wrote that detail down, then suddenly looked up. "Jane thinks he's married, so the woman could have been his wife, but he has a reputation as a philanderer."

"It won't be difficult to find out if he's married."

"Mrs. Scoop didn't mention Beecroft to me when I asked if Ruth was investigating other scandals, but that doesn't mean Ruth didn't stumble across him having a romantic liaison while she was in Brighton watching Pridhurst." I wrote down the word 'Affair' on Beecroft's page. "He wasn't alone in the carriage compartment. There was a man with him." I described the flat-nosed fellow's clothing. Harry agreed that he sounded out of place in the first-class carriage. I assigned the fellow a page of his own in my notebook then moved on to the final compartment. "Lord and Lady Pridhurst sat in there with their daughter, Odette."

Harry traced his finger along the corridor from compartment four to one. "If Pridhurst is the killer, he had to pass these two compartments without being seen. Did all the doors have windowpanes in them so the occupants could see into the corridor?"

"Yes, but if someone bobbed down as they passed the door, they wouldn't be seen." It wouldn't be comfortable for a woman to bend over, thanks to her corset, but it wasn't impossible. I gave each of the Pridhursts their own page in my notebook. "As far as we know, Lord Pridhurst is the only passenger with a motive for murdering Ruth."

He tapped his finger on compartment number four. "Lady Pridhurst and Odette must also be considered suspects. Neither would want Mr. Holland to learn about Lord Pridhurst's financial troubles."

"That's if they're aware of it. Not all men confide in their wives and daughters." Even as I said it, I thought of something. "When Flossy and I met them on the pier, Odette was happy. But when I saw her later, just before I got off the train at Victoria Station, I saw her teary reflection in the window. I think her father took the opportunity to tell her about his predicament."

"She might have been upset enough to confront Ruth then and there, and perhaps kill her."

"That would be a shame. Odette seemed sweet."

"Even sweet women can turn nasty when they're worried about losing the man they love."

"Speaking from experience?" I couldn't help asking.

"So far, no woman has murdered for me." He indicated the compartment with the two ladies in hats. "Do you think they knew one another?"

"I didn't see them talking, so it's impossible to say. The same with Mr. Beecroft and the man in his compartment. Speaking of Beecroft, we'll begin with him. Someone in one of the theaters around here should know where we can find him."

"We can start with the theater near my flat. I know several of the regular actors and dancers now."

Luigi set bowls of pasta in front of us, stopping me from teasing Harry about how well he knew the dancers. It was probably best that I didn't know anyway.

While we ate, I told him about my visit to Ruth Price's home, and why I'd come to the conclusion that she wouldn't have taken her own life. "Ruth was too devout to do something she saw as a terrible sin. Her brother, Enoch, made a point of telling me how devout. He doesn't want her death recorded as suicide."

"Perhaps he'll pay you a fee when you prove it was murder," Harry said. "What was he like, Enoch? Could he be a suspect?"

"He wasn't on the train."

"He could have hired the unknown man seated in compartment three with Beecroft."

I stopped eating, my fork halfway to my mouth. "You think that man is a hired assassin?"

"You did say he looked like a thug with his battered nose. We certainly can't discount the possibility."

If he was, then anyone could have hired him, including Enoch Price. "Enoch was condescending about Ruth's occupation. He also told me she wanted to settle down one day."

"So?"

"What if she wasn't interested in settling down? What if she told him just before she left for Brighton that she never wanted to marry and would rather work? What if that angered Enoch?" A lump formed in my throat. I couldn't imagine being killed because my family didn't like my choice for my future. I wasn't convinced Enoch would do such a thing either. "I think he was ashamed, rather than angry," I went on. "He didn't want anyone knowing she'd gone to Brighton alone. It wasn't respectable, so he said. He ushered me out of the door while the priest wasn't looking, too. Even after her death, he wanted Ruth's career to remain a secret."

"It will probably come out at some point."

"Particularly if the editor at *The Evening Bulletin* thinks there's enough of a story surrounding her death to sell more newspapers." I made a face. "Horrible man. Ruth was nothing to him, just another nameless employee he passed in the office." Mrs. Scoop hadn't shown any emotion either, and even Enoch was more worried about how Ruth's death would be recorded than the loss of his sister's life. The dispassionate reactions made her death seem all the more tragic.

With our bowls of pasta finished and our stomachs full, we walked to the street where Harry lived. He greeted the tobacconist smoking a slim cigar on the pavement outside his shop and pushed open the backstage door of the theater opposite.

The air in the dimly lit corridor was cooler than outside. It smelled faintly of sweat, but that scent gave way to a mixture of florals further along. Voices and laughter drifted down from the far end. The closer we drew to them, the busier the corridor became. A man wearing a red cape and waistcoat rehearsed the words for his act as he passed, not even pausing when he nodded at Harry. Going by the way he announced the disappearance of his assistant, he must be a magician.

We stepped to the side to allow two stagehands carrying a crate between them to pass, then again as a woman holding a crimson gown over her arms bustled along the corridor. Three giggling dancers clad in white feathers and very little else emerged from a room up ahead and stopped upon seeing us. Or, rather, upon seeing Harry. They smiled.

The tall one with legs almost as long as Harry's thrust a hand onto her hip. "Back again? Leave something behind last time?" The lick of her lips was as bold as her outfit of white beaded bodice and feathered skirt that reached only to mid-thigh. Long white ostrich plumes shimmered high above her head, making her seem even taller.

"You're wasting your time trying to make her jealous, Claudine." Harry jerked his head in my direction. "Miss Fox and I are merely colleagues."

The dancer named Claudine smiled silkily. "So, there's hope for me yet?"

"I think Sir Garfield would have something to say about that."

Claudine shrugged her bare shoulders and pouted. "You do know how to deflate a girl."

"Can we ask you some quick questions for an investigation we're working on?"

She looked at the other two girls who both nodded. "We have a few minutes before rehearsal starts."

The three dancers headed back into the room, but Harry held back.

Assuming he was being gentlemanly, I peered inside where a further nine scantily clad women filled the space. "They're all dressed," I told him.

He bent to whisper in my ear. "In case you weren't aware, Claudine was teasing. Sometimes I stop to chat to them if they're outside getting air between their performances, but I haven't been back here in months."

"You don't have to explain to me, Harry. What you do in your spare time is your business. You said it yourself, we're merely colleagues."

The room smelled better than the corridor, thanks to the bottles of perfume on each of the four dressing tables. There were at least two girls sharing each of the dressing table mirrors as they applied color to their lips and cheeks, and kohl around their eyes. A seamstress knelt behind one of the girls, fixing her tail feathers. They paid us little attention until Harry closed the door.

Once they noticed him, they greeted him with smiles. Even the seamstress knew his name. Some cast curious glances at me, and I recognized a few from a previous visit. Harry introduced me.

"Miss Fox and I are investigating the death of a woman on the express train from Brighton. Clement Beecroft was on that train. Do any of you know him?"

"His productions appear at the Laneway Theater," Claudine said. "I've never met him."

"I have," one of the others said. "I used to dance there last year."

"What's he like?" Harry asked.

"Like all the leading actors. He thinks we should worship him." She rolled her eyes.

"Is he married?" I asked.

"Yes, but it didn't stop him from looking."

"Just looking?"

"Depends whether you believe the rumors or not. Apparently, he always installs his current mistress in the lead female role of his plays."

In my experience, rumors usually held at least a kernel of truth, and sometimes much more. "Have you met Mrs. Beecroft?"

"No. He used to joke that she didn't like the theater, and that's why their marriage worked." The dancer shrugged. "I don't know what he meant by that."

It meant that Mrs. Beecroft's absence from his workplace allowed her husband to get away with having affairs with his leading actresses.

We thanked the dancers and headed to St. Martin's Lane, not far away. The posters outside the Laneway Theater announced the upcoming production of a musical comedy starring Clement Beecroft and Geraldine Lacroix. The illustrator had drawn an excellent likeness of Beecroft smiling down at a pretty woman who stared simperingly back at him. According to the posters, the opening night was a week away.

We found the backstage entrance and asked a stagehand carrying a toolbox where we could find Mr. Beecroft. He instructed us to follow him to the stage where more staff were constructing a house without walls over two levels. The only way I knew it would be a house was because the upstairs area had a fireplace painted on the backdrop and the downstairs one had a stove. There was obviously still a lot to be done in the next week.

Clement Beecroft clearly thought so, too, going by the way he shouted at the set designers from where he stood in front of the first row of seating. "I'm not paying you to stand there and stare at me! Get back to work!"

The orchestra in the pit started tuning their instruments. The whine of violin strings set my teeth on edge. It sent Beecroft over the edge, figuratively and almost literally. He clutched his clipboard in both hands and leaned over the barrier to shout at the musicians in the pit.

"Stop that infernal noise! I can't hear myself think." He slammed the clipboard down on the barrier.

The men constructing the set stopped and glanced anxiously at one another. The musicians dutifully kept quiet, and a stagehand who'd been hovering nearby, turned and left.

Harry and I brazened it out. Using the theory that he wouldn't shout at a woman he'd just met, I indicated to Harry that I would do all the talking. Harry hung back.

"Excuse me, Mr. Beecroft." I put out my hand. "My name is Cleopatra Fox. I'm a private detective. May I ask you—"

He flung the clipboard at me.

I ducked and it clattered to the floor. By the time I'd recovered my balance, Clement Beecroft had run off. Harry had been a few feet behind me and stopped to see if I was all right. If he hadn't, he might have caught Beecroft. Nevertheless, Harry was quick and should be able to stop Beecroft leaving the building.

But how far would the angry actor—who clearly had something to hide—go to avoid answering questions?

CHAPTER 7

*H*arry dodged stagehands and props that had been left in the corridor as he chased Beecroft. Someone in one of the rooms he passed screamed, but I wasn't sure why until I reached it and saw her hastily throwing on a dressing gown. She wore bloomers and a tightly laced corset, which was more than the dancers we'd seen earlier wore.

Harry disappeared around a corner. I picked up my skirts and raced after him as best as I could. I was surprised to catch up to him at a closed door. He tried the handle. Locked.

"I know you're in there, Beecroft," he called out.

The sound of a door or drawer slamming shut came from inside, but Beecroft didn't answer.

"If I have to break this door down, it won't go well for you when I get my hands on you."

"Leave me alone," Beecroft shouted back. "I don't have the money."

"What money?" Harry asked through the door.

There was a moment's silence, before Beecroft answered. "You, er, said you were private debt collectors."

"Private detectives," Harry corrected him.

The lock tumbled and the door opened. Harry charged in and I followed. Beecroft stepped back and stared at us. The small room must be his office and dressing room. It smelled faintly of cigarette smoke. Aside from the desk there was a narrow storage cupboard with a full-length mirror attached to the door. A yellow armchair with gold braid detail was tucked into the corner. The walls were covered with framed posters of the shows he'd starred in and photographs of the actor in various poses that accentuated his handsome features. He had the classic good looks that made women swoon, much like Harry. But unlike Harry, there was a showiness in the gold cravat, the needle-thin moustache and heavily oiled hair.

He smoothed the palm of his hand over his hair before checking his appearance in the mirror. Satisfied, he sat at his desk and removed a cigarette from a battered old tin. "I misheard you. I thought you were here to collect a payment." He offered a cigarette before lighting his with a match.

"You owe money?" Harry asked.

Mr. Beecroft suddenly smiled as if lighting his cigarette had flicked on an electrical switch within him. "Doesn't everyone?" He pointed the two fingers holding the cigarette at the guest chairs. "Please, take a seat. I do apologize for the mess," he added as he gathered up pages that appeared to be a script with notations in the margin. "The week before opening is always hectic, but I can spare a few moments."

He might be a good entertainer, but his acting skills were clumsy. I didn't believe for a moment that he'd misheard me when I said I was a private detective. So, what was he hiding?

Whatever it was, he wouldn't tell the truth if I simply asked. I decided to play along and make him believe he was assisting me, even though his odd behavior made him a suspect.

"A young woman died on the ten-thirty express from Brighton on Thursday. I happened to be on the same train, hence my interest. You were also on that train."

"Good lord, I had no idea. Was she ill?"

"I believe she was pushed out of her compartment window after being rendered unconscious first."

He gasped. "Murder! Surely, I would have read about it in the newspapers."

"The police are treating it as suicide, but I have grave doubts."

He sat back heavily, blowing out a breath that puffed out his cheeks. "The poor woman. And to think there was a killer on the train." He shook his head only to suddenly stop and focus on me. "Am I a suspect? Is that why you're here?"

"I haven't found anything linking you to her." It was true. I hadn't. It was simply a guess that Ruth had unearthed his liaison with his mistress while in Brighton.

His chest rose and fell with his deep breath before he switched on a smile again. "I can assure you, I haven't killed anyone." He pointed the cigarette at the door. "Despite what you saw out there, I'm actually quite a good-natured fellow. That was a performance. I've found the only way to keep them on track is to turn into a ghastly beast and shout. I wish I didn't have to, but with only a few days to go until opening…well, you saw the state of that set." The more he spoke, the more of a cockney accent seeped through his cultured one.

"I will be speaking to everyone who occupied the compartments between mine and the victim's." I removed my notebook and pencil from my bag and drew the layout of the carriage again, this time only noting Ruth's location, my position, and Mr. Beecroft's. "She was in the first compartment, and you were in the third with another fellow. Did you see anyone pass by your compartment during the journey?"

He stroked his thumb across his lower lip until the smoke from the cigarette got in his eye. He lowered his hand to the desk. "Nobody passed, but the fellow in my compartment left for a few minutes." He straightened and leaned forward, frowning in thought. "I was reading my script for a while, which made me drowsy. I closed my eyes but didn't fall asleep. I heard the man get up. When I heard the door to our compartment close, I opened my eyes, and he was gone. He returned a few minutes later. Good lord," he muttered. "Could *he* have killed her? Was I sharing a compartment with a murderer?"

"It's possible."

"Oh, God. What if he knows I'm a witness? He could easily find me. I'm very well-known. My face is everywhere." He indicated the photographs and posters.

"Don't worry," I assured him. "The police aren't treating

her death as suspicious. They're not even looking for the fellow. He has no reason to panic unless they do."

"But it might be a good idea to keep your doors locked," Harry added. "Just to be safe."

Mr. Beecroft placed the cigarette to his lips with a shaking hand. "He looked like a killer. Mean eyes. Ugly face, as though he's taken a few beatings in his life."

"Had you ever seen him before? Perhaps in Brighton?" I asked.

"No."

"Did you speak to one another?"

"I said good morning when he entered, and he responded in kind. He only just made it before the train departed. I knew there was something wrong about him. He wasn't dressed like your typical first-class passenger. The conductor checked his ticket and clipped it without question, so I assume he paid the correct fare like the rest of us."

"What about the two women in the compartment next to yours?" I asked. "Did you recognize them?"

He thought about it a moment then shook his head. "They both wore very large hats. I couldn't see their faces. I doubt they could see me, either. What was the victim's name?"

"Ruth Price."

He showed no indication the name meant anything. "Poor girl. Her family must be distraught."

"Her brother is, as are her colleagues at *The Evening Bulletin*."

His gaze held mine several moments too long. "She was a typist?"

"Assistant to the gossip columnist who goes by the name Mrs. Scoop."

He picked up the script and shuffled the pages. "I've read her column."

"I'm sure you've even appeared in it a number of times."

He gave me a flat smile.

I thanked him and rose. As he walked Harry and me to the door, I engaged him in what I hoped he mistook for idle conversation. "I enjoyed my holiday in Brighton. Did you find it relaxing?"

"Not entirely." He indicated the script on the desk. "I went there to learn my lines in peace and quiet. I find a few days of uninterrupted rehearsal is the only way to remember them all."

Harry laughed good-naturedly. "You have an understanding wife to let you go to Brighton alone."

"Mrs. Beecroft gives me the space my creative process needs. Anyway, I was ensconced in my hotel room for much of the time. It was hardly the glamorous holiday that yours would have been, Miss Fox."

"I stayed at the Grand Brighton Hotel," I said. "Were you there, too?"

He pointed the cigarette at me, sending a clump of ash onto the carpet. He smiled at me. "I can't tell you that. I hope to stay there again, in peace, and the gossip columnists would have a field day if they found out."

"I wouldn't pass it on."

"Even so." He reached past me to open the door. "I hope you'll attend a performance one evening. It will be spectacular. The script is terribly funny, and the music will have you tapping your feet all night. You can purchase tickets from the box office when you leave."

Neither Harry nor I spoke as we strode along the corridor. We passed a door labeled Geraldine Lacroix but didn't stop. Clement Beecroft stood in the doorway to his office, watching us.

Once we were safely out of earshot, I pointed out that Beecroft had made sure we left the premises without speaking to the woman who was most likely his mistress.

"We can't say for certain that she is," Harry said. "We are merely assuming, considering his well-known fondness for his leading ladies."

"You're right, I won't jump to conclusions. I am reasonably sure Ruth Price's name meant nothing to him, though. Do you agree?"

"I do, but he was lying about other things, including the fact he misheard you when you said you were a private detective."

"For someone who makes his living on the stage, he's not a great actor."

Harry huffed a humorless laugh. "One thing I can't decide

is whether he was lying about the other man in his compartment leaving it for a few minutes."

That part had seemed convincing, but like Harry, I
wouldn't believe it unless others verified it. The compartment
between Beecroft's and Ruth's had been occupied by the two
women, but unless I identified them, I couldn't question
them.

We crossed over St. Martin's Lane, heading in the direction of Harry's office, even though we'd not discussed a destination. "I think Beecroft needed to hide something in his
office from us, that's why he rushed there," Harry said. "The
question is, what?"

"The other question is, when do we break in to find out?"

Harry's steps slowed and his gaze slid to me. He didn't
try to talk me out of it, however. That was most unlike him.

"No dire warning about what could go wrong?" I asked.
"No attempt to forbid me?"

"That tactic has never worked with you. Besides, we'll be
breaking into a theater, not someone's home. It'll be empty. I'll
allow you to join me this time."

"How magnanimous," I muttered.

We made plans to meet later, then parted ways when we
reached Piccadilly. As I entered the hotel, Frank stopped me
with an ominous warning.

"Miss Bainbridge is looking for you. She asked me to tell
you to join her and her friends for afternoon tea if you're back
in time." He removed his watch from his pocket and checked
the time. "You only have fifteen minutes to get ready."

Ordinarily I wouldn't mind partaking in afternoon tea if I
had nothing else to do, but I wanted to nap for a while
knowing my sleep would be interrupted later to conduct the
search of the theater. If I were to join Flossy and her friends, I
needed to change into something more appropriate first, then
sit through an hour or two of gossip.

Gossip. Perhaps I would make the effort, after all.

Jane was in my room when I arrived, having anticipated
that I might need her assistance if I was going to afternoon
tea. She'd already chosen an outfit for me to wear and set out
matching jewelry. "If you don't mind, Miss Fox, I've also
chosen your outfit for dinner."

"Dinner?" I asked her reflection in my dressing table mirror. "I wasn't aware of any plans."

"Sir Ronald has requested the family dine together in the restaurant, since it has been some time since you were all home."

I sighed. "Thank you, Jane. Prepare whatever outfit you think will look nice."

"You look nice in everything, Miss Fox, but the blue gown does go well with your eyes."

Fifteen minutes later, I joined Flossy and two of her friends for afternoon tea. Although much of society's elite had left London, the sitting room was still full. The Mayfair's legendary afternoon teas were so popular that reservations were a must. If left too late, patrons missed out. It was a little easier to get a table in August, however.

A full room meant a hot room. Almost every lady flapped a fan at her face, some more vigorously than others. From the entrance, they looked like butterflies amongst the potted palm trees that were placed strategically between tables to allow for privacy. Mr. Chapman was very particular about the positions of the tables, ensuring gossip could be safely exchanged without being overheard, if one kept one's voice low.

Once the waiter delivered the finger sandwiches and pastries, I steered the conversation to someone I assumed the other girls knew. "Did Flossy tell you we met Odette Pridhurst in Brighton?"

The two sisters, Cora and Mary Druitt-Poore, gave me blank looks.

"They don't know her," Flossy told me.

"Mr. Holland was with them. His family is in canned goods."

More blank looks.

Flossy changed the subject. "Speaking of Brighton, we saw Clement Beecroft, the actor, on our train home. He's so dashing in real life. I wanted to talk to him, but was too shy."

"What was he doing in Brighton?" Mary asked.

"Having a holiday," Flossy said as if Mary was silly. Which, to be fair, Mary often was.

Cora, who at nineteen was the elder of the sisters, leaned

forward conspiratorially. "I wouldn't be so sure about that," she whispered. "Earlier this week, I read that the actress in his next play was in Brighton, too. Coincidence?" She picked up her teacup and arched her eyebrows. "I think not."

"Where did you read that?" I asked.

"Either *The Evening Bulletin* or *The London Tattler*. They have the best scoops."

Mary scolded her sister. "You're wicked to spread such rumors, Cora. Mr. Beecroft is far too gentlemanly to do what you're suggesting."

"How do you know he's gentlemanly?" Cora asked.

"I can tell by looking at him. He has such a nice smile on his posters."

Cora rolled her eyes.

I excused myself from the sitting room as soon as I'd finished my tea. Instead of heading upstairs to my suite, I made my way to the staff parlor. Goliath was chatting to one of the footmen over cups of tea and cake. Neither was surprised to see me there, but the footman greeted me with more formality and awkwardness than Goliath.

I reached for the stack of newspapers on the table in the corner. "Don't mind me."

I sorted through the stack, separating the newspapers according to the paper's title then sub-sorted them by date. There were several papers represented in the pile, including *The Evening Bulletin* and *The London Tattler*. Some of the editions dated to a week prior, but most had been printed in the last four days, although none in the past twenty-four hours

I began with the editions of *The Evening Bulletin*, even though I doubted I'd find what I was looking for. As suspected, there was no mention of Geraldine Lacroix in Mrs. Scoop's column.

The footman left and Goliath joined me, cup of tea cradled in the palm of his big hand. "What are you looking for, Miss Fox?"

"An article about Geraldine Lacroix in Brighton. Have you read it?"

"Can't say I have, but I don't read the gossips much." He

sat and picked up a copy of *The London Tattler*. "If it appeared in today's edition, it won't be here. The maids rescue the papers the guests throw out, but no one throws them out on the day they come."

"It was printed earlier this week, so it might not be in any of these. It's certainly not in *The Evening Bulletin*."

"Did you expect it to be?"

"No, but I wanted to rule it out." So far, there was still nothing connecting Beecroft to Ruth Price. I continued to search with Goliath's help.

He found the article about Geraldine Lacroix in *The London Tattler*. The anonymous reporter claimed she'd been seen in Brighton enjoying the 'numerous entertainments on offer.' It didn't mention sea bathing, or who she was with, nor was there any mention of Clement Beecroft.

"Not very scandalous," Goliath said, folding the newspaper. An article on the back page about cheating rumors at an automobile event caught his attention and he stretched out his long legs as he read it.

The door opened and Peter popped his head inside. "Goliath! There you are! I've been looking for you."

Goliath continued to read without looking up. "It's not Miss Fox's fault."

"I didn't say it was." Peter strode in and snatched the newspaper out of the porter's hands. "You're needed."

Goliath hauled himself to his feet. "This place would fall apart without me."

Peter clapped him on the back. "It's true. You're indispensable. No one moves luggage like you."

Goliath rounded on him. "I was being sarcastic."

Peter pushed him toward the exit. "I don't have time for your sarcasm, but I can assure you, you are a valuable member of the front-of-house team. Nobody carries heavy luggage with as much ease as you do."

Goliath scrubbed a big paw across his jaw. "Thanks, Peter. Don't mind me. I've been spending too much time with Frank lately. His sullenness is contagious."

I followed the two men out of the parlor. "Peter, have the hotel's copies of the evening newspapers arrived yet?"

"Some. They're in the smoking room."

I crossed the foyer, keeping my eyes peeled for my uncle. He didn't like me entering the domain of the male guests. The billiard and smoking rooms were spaces for the gentlemen to be themselves, so he'd told me. If ladies insisted on joining them, where could men go to discuss topics unsuitable for female ears? He hadn't liked it when I listed a number of other places, from gentlemen's clubs to parliament.

I'd not snuck into either room on the hotel's ground floor for months. I'd had no reason to do so. Uncle Ronald wouldn't be pleased, particularly if the two guests enjoying cigars and whiskey complained. Hopefully they didn't know I was the niece of the owner and wouldn't take their complaints to him.

"Don't mind me," I said. "I'm looking for the latest edition of *The Evening Bulletin*. I'll be but a moment."

One of the gentlemen picked up the newspaper from the table beside him and handed it to me.

I turned the pages, skimming each article. Once again, there was no mention of Ruth Price's murder. Mrs. Scoop's column was about the secret guest list for an upcoming royal event that she'd managed to see. I wondered if Ruth had been the one to ferret out that information before her death.

I handed the newspaper back. "Enjoy your cigars, gentlemen."

I lingered in the foyer for a while, chatting to Miss Hessing. Or, rather, she did all the chatting while I listened. Her enthusiasm for the wedding spilled out of her. It was infectious, and I encouraged her with smiles and nods until it was time to change for dinner.

In my suite, Jane had been replaced by Harmony. "I sent her to Miss Bainbridge's," she said as she laid out a sage green and silver dress on the bed.

"Why?"

"I expected you'd want to tell me about your progress on the investigation."

I sat at the dressing table and removed the pins from my hair. "We could talk over breakfast tomorrow. You don't need to assist me in the evenings while you're working with Floyd, you know that."

She helped me with the pins. "I don't mind."

I turned my attention back to the mirror's reflection. Behind Harmony, the beads on the dress shimmered in the light. "I thought I was wearing the blue gown tonight."

"You wore the blue last time you had dinner with your family in the hotel restaurant."

"Did I?" I frowned, thinking back.

"Be still so I can do your hair. It's a mess."

"It's not that bad."

To prove her point, Harmony ran the brush firmly through it. When I protested, she simply shrugged. "It's knotty."

"If it is, it's not Jane's fault. It's because I've been outside most of the day and wind attacked it."

When she didn't answer, I laid a hand on her arm. "Harmony, what's wrong?"

She lowered the brush to the dressing table. "All right, I admit it. I miss your company. Mr. Bainbridge is testing my nerves. He's kind and not too demanding, but he's not my friend. Not like you. When we have spare time, he doesn't want to talk about interesting things like books or mysteries. He talks about cricket or automobiles."

I pressed my lips together to stop myself laughing. "I miss you too, Harmony. But you don't have to pretend to want to help me get ready in order to talk to me."

"All right." She sat on the bed. "Tell me how your investigation progresses."

"Well, now you have to help me get ready for dinner, since you got rid of Jane." I turned to face the mirror. "Although I think I can manage my own hair tonight. You'll just have to help me with the buttons on my dress."

She picked up the brush again. "Don't be ridiculous. You're dreadful at doing your own hair." She passed the brush through my hair with gentler strokes. "What did Ruth Price's brother say about the police verdict?"

I told her that Enoch Price didn't think his sister would take her own life, and how speaking to him led me to call at the office of *The Evening Bulletin* on Fleet Street. "According to Mrs. Scoop, Ruth went to Brighton to find out more about Lord Pridhurst. Apparently, he's about to lose his share of a shipping company, which will cause Mr. Holland to lose interest in Odette. Isn't that dreadful? Imagine never knowing if a man was interested in you for yourself or for your money and connections."

Flossy faced the same problem. It was a good thing I'd vowed not to marry. I wasn't a wealthy heiress, but not many people knew that, and with my close connection to the Bainbridges, most assumed I was worth a fortune, too.

Harmony wasn't listening, however. "Mrs. Scoop, the gossip columnist?" She dug a pin a little too firmly into my hair, scraping my scalp. "I've had it up to my neck with the gutter press. Victor told me about a fellow Mrs. Poole threw out of the kitchen this morning. Apparently, he was trying to find out what would be served at the wedding reception." She slid another pin into the arrangement, this time gentler. "You should inform Harry. He's looking for a gossip columnist who wants to check in and spy on us."

"I did. It's her, Mrs. Scoop."

Harmony's jaw dropped. She stared at me in the mirror's reflection for a moment before pressing her lips together and once again poking my scalp with a pin. "I have a mind to march into her office and demand she stop. Not that it will do any good, but it will make me feel better."

"She told me she's not that interested, after all."

"And you believed her?" Her *humph* implied I was naive.

"I think she's a little deflated after the death of Ruth. I think Ruth was the one who did all the real work, gathering evidence, following leads. Rather like me. Mrs. Scoop merely writes up the article when she has all the information."

"At least Harry knows, I suppose," she said as she admired her handiwork in the mirror. "He can give her name to Mrs. Hessing, and Mrs. Hessing can confront Mrs. Scoop if she wants to."

"He plans to, but hasn't yet. We were busy the rest of the day."

She frowned. "He helped you?"

"We questioned Clement Beecroft together. Before you say anything, working with Harry is for my benefit, not his. My uncle thinks I'm helping Harry investigate for Mrs. Hessing. If he knew I was investigating a murder, he'd demand I stop and take only genteel cases, like finding missing puppies."

"Missing puppies are a tragedy, Cleo." Harmony sifted through the hair combs in the box on my dressing table and found the silver one with the aquamarines that went well with the gown she'd chosen. "What did Beecroft say when you asked him why he was in Brighton?"

I told her how our interview had started, and how it ended, and that Harry and I planned to break into the theater to find out what Beecroft was hiding. "We both think he was behaving oddly."

"Just be careful. I don't want you getting arrested this close to the wedding."

"As opposed to any other time?"

"You know what I mean. A scandal could overshadow the event. Speaking of the wedding, I've told Jane which dress you should wear and to sweep all of your hair up with a few little delicate curls hanging loose at the sides. That style always looks fetching on you, and it's simple to do. Tell her to attach a string of pearls at the back of the arrangement. Miss Bainbridge will make her own decisions, so at least Jane doesn't have to worry about that."

I took her hands in mine and leveled my gaze with hers. "I appreciate you thinking of me, but you don't have to. You have enough on your plate. Besides, Jane is perfectly capable. Now. Deep breath." She obliged. "And another. Better?"

"Not really."

I kissed her forehead. "The reception will be marvelous. Don't worry. You're the most organized, efficient person I know. You won't let Miss Hessing and Mr. Liddicoat down."

"It's not me I'm worried about. I can control what I do and don't do. It's everyone else that I can't control, particularly the mother-of-the-bride and the suppliers. If she gets her way, someone will have to pay. In practical terms, that could be your uncle. Figuratively, it could be me."

* * *

FLOSSY AND I went downstairs together. We were early, but her brother was even earlier. He stood at the steward's desk at the entrance to the restaurant, studying the reservations book. Mr. Chapman was nowhere in sight.

"Are you filling in as steward tonight?" Flossy asked.

"Don't be absurd," Floyd said without looking up. "Chapman's probably replacing the flower in his buttonhole. In fact, this would go faster if he was here because I could just ask him."

"Ask him what?"

"Whether Mrs. Hessing is dining here tonight." His finger skimmed over the last few names before reaching the end. "Good. She isn't." He suddenly smiled. "I can enjoy myself." His gaze slid past us and tightened. "Chapman's back. Let's find our table. I don't want to have to explain myself."

We took our seats at the family table but did not stay seated long. As diners began to arrive, we got up to welcome them. It was something my uncle insisted upon doing whenever possible. He claimed the personal touch was what set the Mayfair apart from other luxury London hotels. After experiencing the Grand Brighton Hotel's service, I tended to agree with him. The Mayfair had a warmth about it that hotel lacked.

Conversations were not so varied tonight. Indeed, they were generally limited to two and divided according to gender. The men exchanged gossip about a motor vehicle cheating scandal and the women wanted to know about the arrangements for the Hessing-Liddicoat wedding. Considering Flossy and I couldn't divulge anything, and indeed knew nothing, those conversations were rather short.

I extricated myself once my aunt and uncle arrived, but my heart sank upon seeing her. Her pupils were huge, her gaze darting about, and her movements were jerky as if she had too much energy coursing through her. They were all signs she'd just taken a dose of tonic. What worried me more, however, was seeing the way Uncle Ronald fussed over her. He quickly pulled out her chair before she asked, signaled for the menu to be brought over immediately, and asked my aunt several times if she needed anything. He didn't get up and converse with guests as he usually would, but stayed with my aunt. He settled for watching Floyd play host instead. He must be worried about Aunt Lilian, too.

"What do you think, Cleopatra?" Uncle Ronald asked. "Will the wedding be good enough for Mrs. Hessing?"

"Floyd is doing a fine job with the arrangements," I assured him. "And Harmony is an excellent assistant. She'll make sure everything is perfect."

Uncle Ronald's lips flattened as he once again watched Floyd.

Aunt Lilian sniffed. "Stop undermining him, Ronald." Never had I heard her snap at him. She'd been brusque with Flossy, Floyd and me, but never her husband.

He seemed just as taken aback. "I, er…"

"It's typical of you to doubt his ability. It's no wonder he struggles, with you being so critical all the time."

Uncle Ronald glanced at me, but I wasn't sure what he expected me to do. I didn't dare say a word in case Aunt Lilian turned her wrath on me.

"Don't defer to Cleopatra," she whispered loudly. "She isn't her mother, no matter how much she looks and behaves like her. My sister may have been gone all these years, yet you still value her opinion above mine, and above Floyd's. Cleopatra may be cleverer than he is, but this hotel is in his bones. He was born here. It's the only home he's ever known, and he deserves a say in its future, since it will be his one day." She paused as the sommelier poured wine into our glasses, and resumed once he was out of earshot. "It's time you stop favoring your niece over your own son."

I wanted to list all the times my uncle had argued with me, or forbidden me from going somewhere or doing something, to prove that he *didn't* favor me. But my aunt was in no mood to listen, and the restaurant wasn't the right place for such a conversation. Besides, a part of me knew there was some truth to her claims. Uncle Ronald did value my opinions, and he could be cruel to Floyd. But that was changing. I hoped.

Dinner was a tense affair. Aunt Lilian turned sullen, barely managing smiles for the friends who greeted her. Uncle Ronald sat stiffly throughout the first course. Sensing something was amiss, Flossy and Floyd exchanged worried glances.

I excused myself early and retired to my room. I had to get some rest if I was going to wake up in a few hours to meet Harry. The trouble was, I couldn't fall asleep. I went over

Aunt Lilian's words in my head, wondering if I could have said something to reassure her. That led to the realization that her addiction was getting worse. If she didn't stop taking the tonic soon, she was going to destroy her relationship with her family or destroy herself.

CHAPTER 8

The starless night shrouded the backstage door of the Laneway Theater in darkness. It was the perfect evening for breaking and entering. Any roaming constables wouldn't spot us in the recessed doorway of the lane.

Once Harry inserted the lock picks, he was able to do the rest by sound. The satisfying *click* of the lock signaled his success. He rose, catching me yawning. "Long day?"

"Yes, and even longer evening."

I could just make out his chiseled cheekbones and jawline as he studied me in the darkness. "What happened?"

"Not now, Harry." I gave his arm a little shove. "We have work to do."

Once inside, I struck a match and lit the lantern I'd brought with me. It hissed to life and cast enough light so that I could lead the way along the corridor without knocking over props.

Clement Beecroft's office door wasn't locked. The desk surface was tidy, with no sign of the script there or in the drawers. There were bills and receipts, contracts to be signed and correspondence about future projects. Nothing out of the ordinary. In the closet with the long mirror on the door, we found two woolen coats, a cape, three hats and a spare pair of shoes. A selection of ties hung from a rack on the inside of the door. Like the desk, it was neat and tidy.

My hopes of finding a journal belonging to Ruth were dashed. If she had made notes on Beecroft's movements while in Brighton, and he'd taken them before pushing her out of the window, they weren't in his office. There was no evidence that he'd gone anywhere near her at any time.

We left and headed back along the corridor. I paused at Geraldine Lacroix's door. I had a hunch and hoped it might be confirmed if I searched her dressing room. I tried the handle. Unlocked, just like Beecroft's office door. Either they both had trusting natures, or they had nothing to hide.

Harry followed me inside. With the lantern held high, we took in our surroundings. Unlike Beecroft's office, Geraldine's dressing room was untidy. A petticoat and skirt hung over the privacy screen, and an annotated script was strewn across the dressing table, the pages out of order. There seemed to be no organization to her pots of stage makeup and the odd hairpin appeared here and there on the floor where she'd dropped them.

But what struck me was the fashionably large hat decorated with wine-red flowers and feathers.

I plucked if off the corner of the privacy screen. "This is the same hat the woman in compartment two wore. I think we can safely assume that was Geraldine, considering *The London Tattler* reported she was in Brighton."

"And she and Beecroft are most likely having an affair."

Harry rifled through the dressing table drawers while I checked the closet. Neither of us discovered a journal or any other incriminating evidence.

We left the dressing room and exited the theater. Outside, we clung to the shadows near the shops along St. Martin's Lane as we hurried back to the hotel. Most of the city was asleep, but London was never completely silent, even at three AM. A hansom cab sped past, and somewhere in the distance, the motor of an automobile spluttered to life. Two drunken youths stumbled arm in arm down the other side of the road, talking loudly about their female conquests. They didn't see us.

While their crude discussion of a particular woman's attributes made me giggle, Harry must have been embarrassed. He tried talking over the top of them. "Why didn't

Geraldine remove the hat? She must know it made her easily identifiable, not just by us, but by gossip columnists who might be out to learn more about her affair with Beecroft in Brighton."

"I don't think she particularly cares who knows," I said. "I don't think he does, either. It seems to be common knowledge that he takes his current leading lady as his lover. The secret is well and truly out, and there's no point attempting to hide it now, either from the public or his wife. Either Mrs. Beecroft doesn't mind or suffers in silence."

Harry agreed with me, but pointed out one thing I'd overlooked. "If Beecroft isn't overly concerned about keeping his affair with Geraldine Lacroix a secret, why did he hurry to his office when you introduced yourself as a private detective? What did he have to hide, if it wasn't evidence of his extra-marital relations?"

That was a very good question. "Evidence of Ruth's murder?" But that didn't make sense either. "Why would he murder her, though, if he's not concerned about his relationship with Geraldine being discovered?"

"It seems he doesn't have much of a motive for murder, after all."

"He rushed back to his office for a reason, Harry. Unless we believe his excuse that he thought I worked for a private debt collector, he *is* hiding something."

Harry escorted me down the lane beside the Mayfair to the servants' entrance. He caught me yawning. "Get some rest, Cleo. Meet me at my office mid-morning and we'll question Geraldine together. With opening night so close, she should be at the theater by then for rehearsal."

He seemed to assume I'd involve him in the investigation from here on. I didn't refuse, since his assumption was correct. The ruse had to be convincing to make Uncle Ronald think I was helping him with Mrs. Hessing's gossip problem.

That was absolutely, positively, the only reason I was involving him.

* * *

THE HOTEL WASN'T a place I wanted to linger the following morning. Everyone from my uncle down to the maids were busy as a stream of deliveries arrived. With the wedding only days away, there were many things still to be done, some of them small, others large. Yet not a single guest would have realized. The foyer was calm. The front-of-house staff smiled as they carried out their duties with professional pleasantness. The engine of the hotel, however, hummed with activity.

I bought two coffees from Luigi and took them up to Harry's office. I entered without knocking, a common enough occurrence that he no longer commented on it.

We discussed the plan for our interrogation over coffee, then set off. As planned, we asked the box office attendant selling tickets whether Geraldine had arrived for rehearsal yet. It took Harry slipping him a few coins for the youth to confirm.

"We can ill afford bribes," I told Harry. "There's no client for this case."

"My business is doing fine, Cleo. Don't worry."

I knew he was getting more work thanks to his agency's name appearing in the newspaper a number of times in relation to cases we'd solved together, but I didn't know whether that translated into a trickle of income or a flood. "How well *is* it doing?"

His lips tilted with his smirk. "Sorry, I can't tell you that. Only staff can know my financial situation."

I gave him a withering glare. "Need I remind you that you refused to take me on as an associate when I suggested it months ago."

His smirk became a devilish grin. "Is this another attempt to get your name on my door?"

Before I could answer, the theater door opened, and Clement Beecroft exited. Harry and I both turned our faces away. Thankfully he didn't see us, and continued on, striding up St. Martin's Lane. At least we could question Geraldine without worrying he would catch us.

We found her rehearsing a jaunty song in her dressing room. She hesitated upon seeing us, then said we should come back later if we wanted her to sign something.

Harry set her straight. "We're investigating the death of a

woman named Ruth Price. She was a passenger on the ten-thirty express from Brighton, the same train you caught back to London after your holiday."

She glanced past us to the door.

I closed it. "You're not a suspect," I lied. "Indeed, the police think Ruth killed herself. Mr. Armitage and I are simply trying to tie up loose ends for her family."

Geraldine visibly relaxed. She was quite the beauty, with fair hair and wide blue eyes. Her languid movements as she invited us to sit on the sofa held a dancer's grace and the self-awareness of someone used to being noticed. She didn't seem to recognize me, so I didn't tell her I was also on the train, and that she'd bumped into me on the platform in her hurry to catch it.

"Witnesses mentioned seeing you in the second compartment of the first-class carriage." It was another lie, but I had to explain how we knew she was the woman beneath the red hat without telling her we'd seen it in her dressing room the night before. The hat was in the same place, perched on the corner of the privacy screen. "Ruth Price was in the first compartment. Do you recall seeing her?"

"No, sorry." Her voice was as smooth and assured as everything else about her. "Who did you say saw me on the train?"

"I'm not at liberty to say." I gave her a description of Ruth, but she simply looked blankly back at me. "She was an assistant to a gossip columnist."

Geraldine's nostrils flared. "Was she following me?"

"Perhaps. Or perhaps she was following Mr. Beecroft."

Her gaze held mine before shifting to Harry. "I thought you said I wasn't a suspect."

"We're just trying to establish the movements of everyone in that carriage," he said, his voice friendly, encouraging. "You occupied the compartment next to Ruth's, but our sources say you weren't alone. Who sat with you?"

The concern that had tightened her face disappeared, replaced with the eagerness to impart some shocking knowledge. "I don't know. *He* was a stranger." She waited for us to take in what she'd said with a look of triumph. "That's right, I said *he*. 'E was most definitely a man dressed as a woman, which I can see from yer faces that yer didn't know."

I tried to digest her revelation and think of a follow-up question. Indeed, it wasn't just what she'd said, but how she'd said it. The twang of a cockney accent was unmistakable.

Harry beat me to it. "Are you sure she wasn't simply a woman with masculine features?"

She laughed. "Mr. Armitage, I work in theatrical comedy. I've seen my fair share of men dressed as women." The cultured accent had returned. If she was aware she'd slipped into a cockney one, she gave no indication. "A man can't hide his Adam's apple without a high collar, and hers—his— wasn't high enough."

"Can you give us a more thorough description? Was he tall?"

"Not really. He was quite slim, too. But he was awfully ugly, either as a woman or man." She touched the left side of her face. "The skin here was all wrinkled and puckered. I'd say it was an old burn scar."

"Did you speak to him at any point?"

"No."

"Did he get up and leave?"

"No. But someone did pass our compartment, as it happens. Another man, also rather ugly but in his case, it was because of his flat nose. There was a mean look about him, too. I didn't like him." She made a face. "I'm not sure which compartment he came from."

"Did anyone else pass yours?" I asked.

"Just him."

That matched with what Beecroft had claimed. Of course, if someone had ducked low, Geraldine wouldn't have seen them.

"Thank you for your time," I said, rising. "As for the gossip columnists, if they print that you were in Brighton, it's not because of us. We don't share our findings with journalists."

She lifted one shoulder, unconcerned. "Be sure to purchase a ticket for the production. It'll be spectacular."

We saw ourselves out and waited until we were away from the theater before discussing the interview.

"We need to find that thug with the flat nose," Harry said.

"He does seem guilty. Did you also notice her accent change? Beecroft's did, too. I think they both had humble origins. The question is, is there something from their pasts they want to hide?"

"You think Ruth found out something scandalous and they killed her to keep her quiet?"

"It's possible. I don't want to rule anything out yet." I glanced at the clock above the theatrical wigmaker's shop. It was five minutes past eleven.

"Where to now?" Harry asked.

"Victoria Station. The express from Brighton will arrive soon. Hopefully the same conductor as last Thursday is working."

* * *

ACCORDING TO THE STATIONMASTER, the same conductor was indeed working on the morning express from Brighton. We'd arrived a few minutes before it was due, and I would have liked to ask the stationmaster some questions, but he was too busy to chat. The platform was thick with passengers waiting to catch the next train, many making last-minute purchases of newspapers or sweets. Porters and other staff dressed in smart uniforms sporting the London, Brighton and South Coast Railway company's badge on their caps were just as busy, so we could do nothing but wait.

The train's arrival was announced by the staff moments before the locomotive appeared. It chugged to a stop in a cloud of steam. Harry and I rushed to the first-class carriage, determined to have the maximum time to speak to the conductor before the train departed.

The bearded fellow was indeed the same conductor working on that fateful journey. I introduced myself as one of the passengers that day and introduced Harry as a fellow private investigator.

"We're making inquiries into the death of another

passenger whose body was found at the Ouse Valley Viaduct. Do you know about it?"

"'Course I do! It was the talk of the railways when they found her. Sad business."

"Her connections would like us to tie up some loose ends. Can we ask you some questions, Mr...?"

"West. Jack West. Aye, you can ask. I remember you, Miss Fox." He removed a battered cigarette tin and matchbox from his pocket. "You asked me about the woman from the first compartment when we arrived here at Victoria. I should have been more concerned then, when she didn't get off, but I just thought she'd moved to the next carriage when I wasn't looking. If I'd listened to you..." He shook his head. "I feel real bad about it."

"You couldn't have done anything by then. It was much too late. Tell us what you recall of Ruth Price."

He lit his cigarette then shook out the match to extinguish it. After drawing in his first puff, he blew the smoke out of the side of his mouth. "Only that she sat in the closest compartment to the door here."

"Did you hear any noises or voices coming from that compartment?" Harry asked.

"Nothing.

"Do you recall any other passengers from that journey aside from Miss Fox?"

"Aye. Let's see now." He scratched his beard with the hand that held the cigarette. "I definitely remember that actor, Beecroft, and the actress. I can't recall her name."

"You recognized them from their posters?" I asked.

He shook his head. "I'm not interested in the theater. The stationmaster at Brighton pointed them out. He and his wife like to go to Beecroft's shows whenever they get up to London. He was real excited to see them." He shrugged. "But they stayed in their compartments the entire journey. I s'pose they could've moved about when I wasn't looking."

I glanced past him to the conductor's seat at the front of the carriage. Unless he closed his eyes, it would be impossible to miss a passenger in the corridor. "What about anyone coming and going? Do you remember seeing passengers moving between compartments?"

"Aye." He tapped the side of his head. "I've got a good memory for faces. There were three passengers that I saw, and they all went into that poor woman's compartment. A young girl who didn't want to be seen by the folk in the compartments between the one she occupied with her parents and the first compartment."

He must be referring to Odette Pridhurst. "Do you mean she bobbed down so they couldn't see her pass?"

He nodded. "When she stepped out of the dead woman's compartment again, she was crying. Another woman also entered the first compartment. She wore a big hat."

"Was it red?"

He shook his head. "That actress wore the red hat. It was another woman."

I removed my notebook and pencil from my bag. "Can you describe her?"

He hesitated. "I don't like saying this, but if it helps…she wasn't very nice to look at it. Her face was disfigured here." He scratched the side of his beard. "And she looked mannish, if you get my meaning."

Geraldine Lacroix had described her compartment companion in a similar fashion. "And the third person you saw moving around?"

"Another ugly person, this time a man. Flat nose, a laborer's clothes. If I hadn't seen his first-class ticket with my own two eyes, I'd have thought he snuck on without one. But I swear to you, I gave it a good look before I clipped a hole in it."

"He also entered Ruth's compartment?" I clarified.

"Aye."

"At which point of the journey did the passengers enter her compartment?"

"And in what order?" Harry added.

Mr. West leaned one shoulder against the carriage as he blew out a puff of smoke. "This is where my memory fails me. I think the cove with the squashed nose was last, but as to the other two, I'm not sure. I reckon they all paid their visits to compartment one in the first half of the journey."

"Before the viaduct?" I asked.

He nodded.

"Is there anything else you can tell us about the flat-nosed man? Did you see him meet anyone here when he arrived?"

"Sorry, Miss, I didn't. I get busy, seeing off passengers, communicating with the guards, that sort of thing."

The stationmaster approached and cleared his throat to get Mr. West's attention. The conductor hurriedly extinguished his cigarette and apologized to us. "I have to get back to work, but can I ask why you want to know everyone's movements? I was told that girl threw herself off the train, but your questions make it sound like you suspect someone pushed her."

I wasn't sure whether to tell the truth or not. I didn't want to worry him that there might be a murderer on the loose, but he could prove useful if he remembered something important. If he did, he'd be more inclined to inform us if he knew why it was important.

While I dithered, Harry stepped in with a ready explanation. "The police think she killed herself, but her brother doesn't believe it. We hope our investigation will confirm one way or another for his peace of mind." He handed the conductor a business card. "You can contact Miss Fox or me at my office. Thank you for your time, Mr. West."

The conductor tucked the card into his pocket and gave us a nod before joining the stationmaster.

Harry suggested we stop and ask the other railway staff if they recalled the flat-nosed man getting off the first-class carriage last Thursday. Considering they saw hundreds of passengers pass them by every day, we weren't surprised when none could remember him.

"He's the key to this," Harry said as we crossed the concourse to the exit. "Three witnesses have now claimed to have seen him moving about the carriage—Beecroft, who shared his compartment, Geraldine who saw him pass hers, and now the conductor says he saw him enter Ruth's compartment."

"How do we find the identity of one man in this city? His appearance is distinctive, but that's all we have to go on."

"Don't get discouraged, Cleo. We'll keep digging."

"We will, but I don't want to discount the other suspects yet. West says he saw the man dressed as a woman moving about, but Geraldine didn't mention him leaving the compartment they shared."

"She probably fell asleep," Harry said.

"She didn't mention it when we questioned her, and she *did* notice the flat-nosed thug. So she must have been awake when he passed. West also mentioned Odette, but no one else did, likely because she ducked under their windows. I think it's time we question Lord Pridhurst. I want to hear his explanation for why his daughter was seen entering Ruth's compartment."

"Do you know where to find him?"

"Hopefully he still has business here in London. If he does, he'll be staying at the Coburg Hotel."

"Are you sure you want to be seen entering enemy territory?"

We stepped out of the station and into the sunshine. I raised my parasol and lowered it enough so that it hid part of my face. "No one will recognize me. You, however, are distinctive, Harry. Perhaps I should go alone."

"You have it the wrong way around. *I'll* go alone. Nobody cares if I come and go from rival hotels, and I have the business cards to prove I'm a private detective. Pridhurst knows who your family are, Cleo. If he doesn't like your questions, he'll have no qualms informing Sir Ronald."

He didn't need to explain what would happen if my uncle learned what investigation I was really working on. "All right, you can question him. But I want to hear what he has to say."

* * *

BEING the middle of a warm August day, the Coburg Hotel was relatively quiet. Lord Pridhurst wasn't there. The manager told Harry that he hadn't checked out, but was merely conducting business elsewhere in the city. Harry left a written message for his lordship at the post desk requesting he meet him at Speakers' Corner at Hyde Park since the closer garden of Grosvenor Square was for the use of residents only.

In Hyde Park, I sat on a bench seat, pretending to read a newspaper, while Harry stood near the temperance reformer decrying the evils of alcoholic consumption from her platform of an upturned milk crate. She didn't attract much of a crowd, so I easily spotted Lord Pridhurst when he arrived. Harry approached him and, after introductions, led him toward me. They sat on the bench seat next to mine. Even though Harry made sure Lord Pridhurst had his back to me, I kept my newspaper raised so that only my eyes and hat would be visible if he looked.

"What is the meaning of this?" Pridhurst snarled. "Your message mentioned my daughter is in some sort of trouble. How can she be when she is safely at home?"

"The trouble relates to the journey from Brighton to London last Thursday," Harry said. "I'm investigating the death of a passenger. She was thrown out of the moving train as it traveled over the Ouse Valley Viaduct. A witness saw your daughter enter the woman's compartment."

I expected Lord Pridhurst to spray Harry with a blistering denial, but he went very quiet. When the denial finally came, it was ice-cold. "Your so-called witness is lying. I don't know why he or she is trying to besmirch my name, but leave my daughter out of it. She is innocent. She never left our compartment."

"There's a second witness who saw Odette looking upset at the end of the journey."

"Another lie. You, Armitage, have a responsibility not to smear the names of the innocent. Tell the dead woman's family that the police verdict is correct. Whether they like it or not, that is the truth." He stood.

"Sit down, Pridhurst," Harry said, calmly. "I haven't finished."

Lord Pridhurst pointed a finger at Harry. "Now hear this. If you continue to harass my family, I will not hesitate to inform the police. I have friends in high places who will destroy your pathetic little agency." He slapped his hands together behind his back and marched off.

"Will you tell them Ruth Price knew about your meeting with Keats?" Harry said. He did not rise from the bench. He didn't even raise his voice.

But Lord Pridhurst stopped dead.

Harry continued. "Will you also tell the police that to

repay the debt you owe Keats you'll have to sell your share of the shipping company, and that if Mr. Holland discovers you no longer have ownership, he no longer has a reason to court Odette?"

"How dare you." Lord Pridhurst's low voice was barely audible. It seemed it finally worried him that I could overhear.

I raised the newspaper higher, completely obscuring my view. I heard Harry get up and join him. Now out of earshot of their whispers, I could only guess what transpired between them. I lowered my newspaper to my lap.

Lord Pridhurst's finger did a great deal of aggressive pointing. Harry let him rant, perhaps hoping he would drop an important detail in the verbal stream. It ended when his lordship stormed off. The problem was, he stormed off in my direction. He looked at me, frowned harder, then walked on by.

I didn't dare glance over my shoulder to see if he turned back around.

Harry joined me. "I'm not sure if you caught any of that, but if not, you didn't miss anything. There were a lot of vague threats that usually began with him saying 'Do you know who I am?' or 'I know people in high places.' He finished with the accusation that I was 'no better than the gutter press', which I thought was ironic."

"I'm sorry to put you through that, Harry."

"I've experienced worse from angry hotel guests who didn't get things they wanted when they wanted them. At least now I don't have to be concerned I'll be reported to my superior. I rather like being my own governor." It seemed to be a new personal revelation for him, one that pleased him.

We walked past the new orator, a wizened old man with a flowing white beard. Although the crate on which he stood appeared to be the same, his topic was quite different to the temperance reformer's. He'd attracted a larger crowd, too, who listened intently as he told them the end of the world was mere weeks away.

Neither of us was in a hurry as we made our way to the Apsley House end of Hyde Park. The weather was warm without being hot, and Hyde Park was in full summer glory.

Picnickers lazed beneath shady trees after enjoying their midday feast, and children played games on the lawn while their governesses or mothers sat nearby, reading or chatting. A lady and gentleman on horseback passed us, heading to Rotten Row to show off their high-stepping mounts. Somewhere in the distance, a band played. The bright, brassy tune reminded me of the ones preferred by the bands in Brighton, and instantly conjured memories of the joys of holidaying at the seaside.

"We should go to Brighton," I blurted out.

"That's a bold suggestion, but all right. I'll pack my bathing costume."

I knew he was joking and didn't really think I was proposing a seaside tryst, but I felt compelled to set him straight anyway. "Just for the day. If we catch the first express there and the last one back to London, we can spend several hours investigating. We'll begin with speaking to the staff at the hotel where Ruth stayed."

"Do you know which hotel?"

"No, but Mrs. Scoop does. We'll head to her office now and ask her."

I quickened my steps, and Harry's long strides effortlessly kept pace. "What will you tell your family?" he asked.

"I'm not sure yet, but it will either involve the library or museum."

He laughed softly. "We'll also make sure we don't get on the train together, just in case someone on the station recognizes you."

"Actually, I've changed my mind, and I don't think you should come, Harry. There's no need, and as you say, we don't want anyone seeing us together."

"I'm coming, Cleo."

"I don't need you there."

"I'm not going to help you. I'm going because I haven't been to the seaside in a long time, and I have a desire to go. Honestly, you think everything is about you."

I was about to defend myself when a quick glance at him revealed he was grinning at me.

"Besides," he went on, "I'm rather enjoying seeing you

panic about spending an entire day with me at a seaside holiday town. I want to see how it plays out."

"I am not panicking. Honestly, Harry, you're the one who thinks everything is about you. Fine. I will allow you to come, but do not pack a bathing costume. There'll be no time for anything other than investigating."

I hoped he didn't see my face heat as the panic he'd noticed set in further. He was right. I'd realized after suggesting it that spending time at the popular destination for newlyweds and holidaying couples was a dreadful idea.

CHAPTER 9

The clerk at the front desk at *The Evening Bulletin* recognized me from my last visit. Somewhat reluctantly, he went to fetch Mrs. Scoop only to return without her. "She says to go through, Miss Fox."

I hesitated. Through the window behind him, I could see Mr. Finlayson railing at a hapless journalist. The ridged veins on the editor's forehead were visible from where we stood, his words also clearly audible. The journalist had missed a deadline.

"We'll wait a moment," I told Harry.

After shooting a final round of blistering words at his target, Mr. Finlayson stormed into his office and slammed the door. The young journalist looked like he wanted to crawl under his desk, but he stayed to accept the sympathetic pats on the back from colleagues.

"Now we can go in," I said, leading the way.

As with my last visit, few of the journalists paid us any attention. The typists and stenographers, however, looked twice—at Harry, not me.

Mrs. Scoop was the only woman to give me more attention than Harry. Her gaze narrowed upon seeing him, but she otherwise paid him no mind. "The police still think Ruth died by her own hand, Miss Fox. I spoke to them myself. So why is your investigation ongoing?"

I took my cue from her and didn't bother with pleasantries. I didn't even introduce Harry. "Is that why your newspaper hasn't printed anything about her death?"

"It's hardly newsworthy. People throw themselves off trains all the time."

Considering the person in question was her assistant, her response seemed heartless. "What hotel did she check into in Brighton?"

Mrs. Scoop reached for her cigarette tin and removed one. Was she delaying? Why would she, if she had nothing to hide? "Rutherford House."

It wasn't familiar to me, but Brighton had many accommodation options catering to a variety of visitors. I thanked her and was about to leave, but Mr. Finlayson emerged from his office at that moment to shout at another journalist.

I dawdled in the relative safety of Mrs. Scoop's office. To make conversation, I asked her again what investigations Ruth was working on.

"I told you last time," she said. "Pridhurst and the Hessing wedding. A short memory will do you no good in your profession, Miss Fox. Is that why he's here? To take notes for you?" She jabbed her lit cigarette in Harry's direction. "Or is it for his looks?"

I bristled. "Mr. Armitage is an excellent private investigator. We're working on this case together." Considering I teased Harry about his looks and the way women responded to him all the time, my defensive reaction surprised me.

Mrs. Scoop blew smoke through her nose along with her huff.

My annoyance drove me to press her harder. "Don't you find it surprising that Ruth didn't see Clement Beecroft or Geraldine Lacroix in Brighton?"

She rounded the desk and reached for the door handle. "Not at all. Ruth had enough on her plate."

"*The London Tattler* knew about Geraldine. Did it upset you to miss out on the scoop?" At the sound of Mr. Finlayson's office door slamming shut again, I added, "Did it upset your editor?"

She gave a brittle laugh as she opened the door. "I'll see you out."

Harry waited for us to exit ahead of him, but Mrs. Scoop

insisted he go first. I suspected that was so I could see the effect he had on the typists. Their heads turned to follow him as he passed their desks.

My assumption was proved correct when Mrs. Scoop caught my elbow. She bent to whisper in my ear. "Be careful, Miss Fox. Handsome men can ruin an intelligent girl's life."

I pulled free and hurried after Harry. Once in the reception area, I peered through the window behind the front desk, catching Mrs. Scoop watching us.

"I'm sorry," I said to Harry as we exited onto Fleet Street.

"For what?"

"For teasing you about your looks."

"I don't mind it coming from you, because I know you value me for all my other attributes."

My irritation with Mrs. Scoop suddenly vanished. Harry had a way of dragging me out of bad moods like no one else. "*All* your other attributes?"

"I could list them for you, but it would take too long, and you already know them anyway."

I laughed. "Careful, Harry. Your arrogance might have me changing my mind."

"Would you like me to balance it by listing all the wonderful things about you, too?"

My cheeks flamed. For the second time in as many hours, I quickened my pace to outstrip him. Once again, it was no use. His long strides easily kept up. A sideways glance proved he realized his compliment unsettled me, and he was enjoying himself.

Drat him.

* * *

THE MAYFAIR'S OLD RESTAURANT, now the ballroom, was off-limits to everyone, including me. Mr. Chapman had instructed a footman to stand guard and turn away curious guests and staff alike. The steward smirked at me after my attempt to peek inside failed. I wondered if he would also refuse my uncle entry or whether it was just me. I was probably the only family member banned from entering. Mr. Chapman didn't like me much.

I took the stairs to the fourth floor, but didn't enter my suite. I'd not spoken to my aunt for more than a few minutes since returning from Brighton. I couldn't avoid her forever. Nor should I. She needed to know we all cared about her. If she was irritable, I wouldn't take it to heart. Indeed, I'd see it as a good sign because it meant she hadn't taken her tonic and the withdrawal was affecting her mood.

My uncle and aunt's suite was larger than mine, with the best view over Green Park of all the hotel's rooms. While my suite had been furnished in fine style, it had few personal touches aside from my photographs and books. Theirs housed paintings and decorations chosen by my aunt, as well as dozens of framed photographs on the occasional tables. There was even a photograph of my mother and father on their wedding day. Considering Aunt Lilian had been forbidden from attending her sister's wedding by their parents, the photograph must have been sent directly to her by my mother. It was a testament to her love for my mother that she'd kept it, and most likely even hidden it from her parents while they were still alive.

Aunt Lilian reclined on the sofa in a loose-fitting gown that made her thin frame seem skeletal. A whirring electric fan ruffled her hair, which was hanging past her shoulders. The silvery-gray strands were a similar color to her skin. There were no books or magazines within reach, just a dry cloth and a basin of water.

She didn't smile at me. She didn't even attempt one. Nor did she greet me with her usual kindness. In the past, even when Aunt Lilian was at her worst, she always gave me a warm welcome. Now, she could no longer manage even that.

"What is it, Cleo?" she asked on a heavy sigh.

I didn't want to tell her I was worried about her, or that I felt guilty for not seeing much of her these last few days. In her current mood, she'd accuse me of pitying her. Instead, I asked for help.

"You always know so much about members of society, Aunt. I hoped you could tell me about Lord and Lady Pridhurst of Wellingborough."

She raised herself up from the cushions and swung her bare feet to the floor. Her lips pinched. I thought it was because the movement caused her pain, but it may have been because my question, or my presence, irritated her. "What do the Pridhursts have to do with anything, Cleopatra? Are you investigating again?"

"I… Uh…"

"Can you not leave good people alone? Everyone has secrets, but it doesn't mean they should be exposed for all and sundry to gossip over. Why must you open old wounds?"

My last investigation had indeed opened old wounds for a family my aunt would consider 'good people' and this investigation threatened to expose fresh ones the Pridhursts were trying to hide. She'd only just met them in Brighton, but that encounter was enough for her to identify with their need for privacy.

"I'm sorry, Aunt." I took the cloth and dipped it into the basin. The water was no longer cool, but a damp cloth should give her a little relief. "Place this on your forehead then I'll leave you be."

She pushed my hand away. "Fetch my tonic. It's beside the bed."

I chewed the inside of my lip.

"Cleopatra! I asked you to fetch my tonic."

"I don't think you should have any more. It's not good for you."

She clicked her tongue in irritation and pushed herself to her feet. "You're not a doctor," she snapped as she carefully made her way to the adjoining bedroom.

I slipped out of her suite and almost bumped into Uncle Ronald about to enter. He must have realized from the look on my face that I'd had an uncomfortable encounter with Aunt Lilian.

He reached past me and closed the door. "Perhaps I'll come back later."

He went to walk off, but I stopped him. "She's still taking the tonic."

"We have a dinner party to attend tonight. She needs to get through it in lively spirits."

"She *needs* to stop taking the tonic altogether. It's doing more harm than good."

He patted my shoulder. "It's kind of you to worry, but her doctor has prescribed it. He knows what he's doing, Cleopatra. He has a great deal of experience with treating female melancholia."

I watched him walk to his office, wondering if I should continue to press my point.

Floyd didn't give me a chance to make a decision. He raced out of the stairwell, glanced at the lift door beside it, and grabbed my arm. "Your rooms, Cleo. Now."

He ushered me inside before closing the door behind us. He leaned back against it, his breathing coming in ragged bursts.

"Did you run up the stairs?" I asked.

He nodded.

"Who are you avoiding?"

"The Hessing witch."

"That's not nice, Floyd."

"Trust me when I say it's the nicest word I can think of. I was waiting for the lift in the foyer when she saw me. She called out to me, so I pretended not to hear and took the stairs instead. I'd wager good money she caught the lift and followed me up here."

"She may not be following you. Her room is on this floor."

He pressed his ear to the door, listening. "I should've taken the service stairs down to the kitchen instead of coming upstairs. She wouldn't chase me there. She abhors seeing how hard the staff work almost as much as she abhors subtlety."

I was about to tell Floyd that she may have merely wanted to say hello, when a sharp rap on my door startled him. It sounded like it was made with the end of a walking stick.

Floyd jumped. "Get rid of her, Cleo." He hurried away down the short corridor to my sitting room.

"Floyd," I hissed.

"I know you're in there, Miss Fox," came the brusque American voice of one of our most important guests.

I wasn't sure how Mrs. Hessing knew I was in my suite. She could have been guessing, but I opened the door anyway. I smiled. "Mrs. Hessing, what a lovely—"

"Is he in here?" She tried to peer past me, but I stood my ground. She couldn't enter unless I got out of the way.

"Who?"

"Don't act the fool. Your cousin, Mr. Bainbridge. I saw him run up the stairs."

"He's probably in his own suite."

"I doubt that. If he's avoiding me, he'd come here. He knows you'd protect him."

"My dear Mrs. Hessing, why would I want to protect him? I think my cousin is a ridiculous fellow, not to mention a coward, and I'd find it amusing to see him squirm." I folded my arms over my chest and smiled.

She narrowed her gaze at me. She wasn't sure if I was joking or not. "When you see him, tell him I do not like to be taken advantage of by anyone."

"Is Floyd taking advantage of you?"

"Not him. The florist and the suppliers of the decorations. Tell Mr. Bainbridge that he *must* negotiate prices down. I will not be the laughingstock of London's tradesmen. I have a reputation to uphold."

"Mrs. Hessing, no one would dare laugh. I think they're all very aware that there is nothing amusing about you."

Her eyes narrowed further. "Good day, Miss Fox."

"Good day, Mrs. Hessing." I closed the door and marched into the sitting room.

Floyd sat on the edge of my writing desk, his arms and ankles crossed. "Ridiculous? A coward? Good lord, Cleo, it's lucky I know you adore me or my feelings might be hurt."

"Very amusing. We both know you don't have feelings, Floyd."

He pushed off from the desk and pecked the top of my head. "Thank you, Cousin." Genuine warmth softened his voice. "You saved me."

"I ought to charge you a fee for every time I rescue you."

He grinned. "But that would take all the fun out of it for you."

* * *

EARLY THE FOLLOWING morning I passed Mr. Hobart entering the hotel, a newspaper tucked under his arm. I told him that if anyone should ask for me to tell them I was spending the day at the museum. I could see from his smile that he didn't believe me, but he asked me which one.

"All of them," I said before strolling past Frank as he held the door open for me.

I met Harry on board one of the second-class cars of the express train to Brighton. Neither of us wanted to pay the first-class fee. The carriage was full. Harry and I sat opposite a couple who were clearly newlyweds going by the way they stared into one another's eyes. Harry and I didn't speak.

A chill ran down my spine as we passed over the Ouse Valley Viaduct. I glanced at Harry, only to see him watching me. We exchanged grim looks.

A taxicab took us from Brighton Station to Rutherford House. Situated a few streets back from the beach, it was quieter than the Grand Brighton Hotel, and a great deal smaller. The hotel occupied two elegant cream-colored Georgian terraces with black wrought iron balconies outside every window on the lower floors. The terraces would have been originally owned by wealthy gentlemen, but now guests paid by the night. I suspected the cost was high enough to ensure the tradition of wealthy occupants continued.

Understated elegance continued inside. The cool marble columns and counter were welcome on such a warm day, while the soft greens, blues and sandy colors of the furnishings oozed seaside luxury rather than city opulence. Like the Mayfair, floral arrangements and potted palm trees were popular. Thanks to its small size, however, the greenery made the Rutherford House foyer feel a little too much like a jungle. The detective in me couldn't help thinking that it offered numerous places to hide, for both clandestine meetings and to eavesdrop.

Not only was the foyer small, but the entire hotel couldn't have had more than twenty rooms. With so few guests at one time, it would be easier for the staff to remember Ruth Price. Her name didn't ring any bells at the check-in desk, however. When I told the clerk that I was investigating her death, he even searched through his register. Her name didn't appear.

Harry and I left without any clue where to try next. We stood on the pavement near the portico entrance, both of us lost in thought. There were so many hotels in Brighton. It would be impossible to find where Ruth had stayed.

"Why did Mrs. Scoop lie?" I looked up at the black lettering of the hotel's name above the entrance. "She must know we'll return to London and accuse her of being deceitful. It only makes her look suspicious."

Harry shrugged. "Perhaps she simply forgot, and this is a hotel she once stayed in herself."

I wasn't convinced. Mrs. Scoop was too sharp to forget the name of the hotel that she must have booked and paid for. I gasped as a thought occurred to me. "Mrs. Scoop organized Ruth's accommodation, just like she planned for Ruth to stay at the Mayfair Hotel to spy for her. She made that reservation under a false name: Mrs. Blaine."

Harry indicated I should walk back inside ahead of him. The doorman, who'd been standing there watching us with a curious expression, opened the door again.

"Do you recall a guest named Mrs. Blaine staying here about a week ago?" I asked him.

"The name is familiar. What did she look like?"

"Young woman, spectacles, brown hair, freckles. Oh, and she carried a brown leather bag with her."

"I remember her! She wouldn't let the porter carry her bag."

"What else do you remember about her?"

"She was very interested in some other guests staying here. I saw her watching them from behind a palm tree. Sometimes she'd write notes in her notebook, too."

So, she did have a notebook. It hadn't been found with her other belongings at the Ouse Valley Viaduct.

"Who were they?" I asked.

The doorman shook his head. "I'm afraid I can't tell you."

Harry held out his hand. The doorman shook it then slipped his hand and the bribe into his pocket. He closed the door he'd been holding open the entire time. "An actor and actress from London. Beecroft was his name, but I don't recall hers. It sounded foreign. They weren't staying together, but they were together, if you understand my meaning." He winked, to make sure that we did.

Not only did we now know for certain that Geraldine and

Beecroft had conducted an affair, we also knew that Ruth knew about it. According to Mrs. Scoop, Ruth hadn't been sent to Brighton to watch them, so she must have simply stumbled upon them while staying in the same hotel.

"Do you think either Beecroft or his lady friend noticed Ruth watching them?" I asked.

The doorman scrubbed his jaw. "Hard to say. Beecroft did seem anxious from the very start of his stay. When he got out of the cab on his arrival, he looked around, as if he was worried he'd been followed from the station. Then for the duration of his stay, he kept asking me if I'd seen anyone lurking nearby who shouldn't be here."

"Did he describe the person he thought might be watching him?" I asked.

"No."

"*Was* anyone lurking?"

"Not that I noticed. His anxiety got worse after the first telephone call."

"First?" Harry prompted.

"Beecroft received two while he was here. The only telephone device is at the front desk, but it's not for the use of guests to make outgoing calls. It shouldn't really be for the guests' use at all, but he's famous and the front desk clerk told me both callers wanted to speak to Beecroft in person, not leave a message." The doorman leaned closer to us. "The first call was on the Tuesday, the day after Beecroft arrived. The second was on the Wednesday, the day before he checked out. Both conversations got heated."

"Did you overhear anything specific?"

"Not from here, but the clerk at the front desk told me the first call was from a man, and it sounded like Beecroft was agreeing to meet him, but reluctantly. He refused at first, but the man on the end must have been insistent, because Beecroft eventually gave in."

"Do you know where the meeting took place?" Harry asked.

"The clerk didn't catch that part."

"And the second call, on the Wednesday?"

"That was from a woman, and the call came from London. Beecroft argued with her, telling her to stop pestering him. He called her a name which I can't repeat in front of a lady, Miss Fox, but if you want to hear it, sir, I can whisper in your ear."

Harry declined the offer. "Is there anything else you can tell us? Anything that struck you as odd?"

"There was one thing. Beecroft's accent changed to a cockney one when he spoke on the telephone." The doorman looked pleased with himself for discovering that piece of information. "I bet the London gossips would like to speculate about his past if they knew that."

He was right, but reporters would want more details first. Perhaps Ruth had uncovered those details, even learning the identity of the man and woman on the other end of the telephone line. Perhaps she planned to give her notes to Mrs. Scoop upon her return to London, but Beecroft stole the notebook then killed her.

I asked the doorman if there'd been any guests at the hotel matching the description of the man with the burn mark or the man with the flat nose.

He shook his head. "Do you reckon one of them made the first telephone call to Beecroft?"

Neither Harry nor I commented.

"You should speak to my friend," the doorman went on. "He works at his father's pharmacy." He pointed down the street in the direction of the beach. "Their silence cabinet is the closest one to this hotel, and my friend reckons he's always listening in to people's telephone calls."

"Isn't the point of a silence cabinet that calls can't be overheard?" Harry asked.

"My friend is nosy. He found a way. He might remember one of your suspects making a telephone call to the hotel, on account of their faces being distinctive."

It was a good theory. If I was watching Beecroft and wanted to arrange a meeting with him but do so without showing my face at the hotel, I'd do it over the telephone, and I'd choose the closest one.

Harry and I headed in the direction of the pharmacy. "Do you think the woman who telephoned Beecroft was his wife?" I asked.

"It would be my first guess, particularly as the call came from London."

I glanced back toward the Rutherford Hotel's doorman. "Hotel staff make good witnesses. They can go almost anywhere, and no one pays them any attention."

"Their low wages also make them susceptible to bribery," Harry added with a wry grin.

"I think we should go to the Grand Brighton Hotel next and speak to the staff who were on duty when Ruth left me a message to meet her. Their shift had ended by the time I received it, and the change of staff meant no one remembered her, but hopefully we'll find one of them today."

"Good idea. We'll go after we speak to the pharmacist's assistant."

The pharmacy's silence cabinet was located beside a display of Dr. Gunston's Hair Oil stacked on a table off to the side. A sign on the shop window advertised the booth's availability for members of the public to use to make telephone calls in private, for a modest cost. We found the hotel doorman's friend reading a detective novel in the staff room.

Harry described the two suspects to him, but the youth shook his head. He seemed disappointed that he couldn't help. On a whim, I asked him about Beecroft, but again, he shook his head.

"He's the actor who stayed at Rutherford House, isn't he?" the youth asked.

"He is."

"Someone did make a call from our booth, and they mentioned him—Clement Beecroft—to the person on the other end."

"Was it a woman with spectacles, freckles, and carrying a brown bag?"

The youth nodded eagerly, and offered up as much information as he could recall. We didn't even have to bribe him. I suspected the well-thumbed Sherlock Holmes mystery had something to do with his enthusiasm. "I heard the woman say she'd stumbled on a big story, and that the person on the other end had to print it. She said that more than once: 'You *have* to print it.' The woman became frustrated, and I reckon the person on the other end didn't like her tone. The call was ended mid-sentence."

"When was this?" I asked.

The assistant thought back. "It was around midday last Wednesday. I remember because my mother makes eel pies on Tuesdays and always packs leftovers for Dad and me to have on Wednesdays for lunch. They're delicious cold."

Wednesday was the same day Beecroft received his second call, and the day I first saw Ruth watching the Pridhursts, then met her later.

It was the day before she died.

"Is there anything else you can tell us about the woman who made that call here?" Harry asked.

The youth shrugged. "She tucked a notebook back into her bag after she came out of the silence cabinet. Is that important?"

Neither of us answered him.

Outside, I led the way to the Grand Brighton Hotel on Kings Road. A cool breeze drifted off the sea, ruffling my skirts, and making the midday sun more bearable. My thoughts were fixed on what we'd learned about our victim and main suspect, but Harry's were not.

"Perfect day for it," he declared.

"For sleuthing?"

"For swimming."

I followed his gaze to the sea. Sunlight glinted off the water as it gently lapped against the sand. Several women's bathing machines were out, and children paddled in the shallows or made sandcastles. Men swam out from the beach but were too far from the women and children to be seen clearly. The segregation of the sexes protected the modesty of everyone. It was a peaceful summer scene compared to the busy piers with their colorful and noisy entertainments.

"A shame you didn't bring your bathing costume," I said. "The hotel is this way."

"Let's have something to eat first."

We purchased fish and chips from a small wooden hut on the beachfront promenade and sat on the beach to eat it. I removed my lace gloves to keep them clean, while Harry opened up the paper wrapping to make it easier to share. It wasn't long before we had to fend off hungry seagulls. One even dared come between us and snatch a chip off the paper.

"I'm naming that one Cleopatra," Harry said.

"Why?"

"Because it's clever and brave. It waited until the end when we're both full and feeling lazy, then made its move."

"I was ready to be insulted. You rather took the wind out of my sails by paying me a compliment."

"If I'd known comparing you to a seagull was the way to give you compliments without causing you to run away, I would have done it earlier."

We were venturing into dangerous territory again, so I made no comment. To ensure I stayed silent, I decided to fill my mouth with more food, even though I was quite full. Harry must have had the same idea. We both reached for a chip at the same time. Our hands touched. I should have quickly withdrawn but did not. Something compelled me to linger and lift my gaze to see his face.

Harry's little finger stroked mine. While I watched him, he studied our hands, as if fascinated by my bare skin, usually hidden within my glove.

I didn't want to move away. I was frozen there, my skin tingling where he'd touched me. My heart clanged like a bell in my chest. Was it warning me? Or announcing something?

Either way, I knew in my bones that this moment would be one I remembered forever.

CHAPTER 10

A child's ball suddenly plopped onto our fish and chip wrapper, breaking the spell.

I quickly whipped my hand back. Harry stared at the ball for several beats before picking it up and tossing it to the boy who'd thrown it.

I felt his gaze on me as I gathered up the leftovers in the paper. "We should go."

He silently followed me up the beach. Perhaps, like me, he couldn't think of anything to say.

But Harry was a charmer, a smooth conversationalist who always knew the right thing to say. Had the moment we shared rendered him speechless? Or did he simply know that silence was the wisest option now?

* * *

The doorman at the Grand Brighton Hotel remembered me and greeted me by name. It was a good indication that he had an excellent memory for names and faces, so we began with him.

"On the day before I checked out of the hotel, a woman named Ruth Price came here and left me a note at the post desk while the clerk wasn't in attendance. Does that name mean anything to you?"

"Sorry, Miss Fox, it doesn't. What did she look like?"

I described Ruth's appearance, but it was the brown bag that he remembered. "One of the porters offered to carry it for her, thinking she was checking in, but she refused. She got a little stroppy, which we thought was odd. She kept trying to look past us toward your party. Do you know, I reckon she'd followed you here."

She must have followed us all the way from the West Pier where we'd seen her watching the Pridhursts. The only reason she would do that was because she hoped to find out how we knew Lord Pridhurst. Perhaps she thought we were connected to his scandal in some way. I didn't think she knew I was a private detective at that point. How could she?

"*Then* did she go to the post desk?" I asked.

"No. She waited a while before heading upstairs. I reckon if you ask the lift operator, you'll find she went to your floor, Miss Fox. All very mysterious, she was. Her interest in your party was very strange."

"Do you recall if she went upstairs before or after I'd left with my maid to go for a swim?"

"I reckon it was after, but I can't be sure. It wasn't until she came downstairs again a few minutes later that she went to the post desk."

I tried to link all of Ruth's movements together, from the moment she spotted Beecroft at the Rutherford Hotel, to her death on the train home. I needed to write down what I knew to get it all straight in my head.

Harry asked our final questions to the doorman, describing the two unidentified men we also sought, but the doorman shook his head. Not only did he not recognize them, but he vowed he never forgot a face, particularly a distinctive one.

I followed Harry across Kings Road and back to the promenade, my mind occupied with sifting through what we'd learned rather than my surroundings. "I can't believe Ruth followed us to the hotel from West Pier and I never noticed. And I'm supposed to be a detective!"

"To be fair, you weren't working on a case, nor did you think it would matter."

"Still, I should be more aware of my surroundings."

"What flavor?"

"Pardon?"

"What flavor ice cream do you want?"

I'd been so distracted by my thoughts, I'd once again failed to notice my surroundings. It really would not do. "Strawberry, please, although I don't deserve it. Honestly, I could kick myself for not seeing Ruth."

"Everyone deserves ice cream, Cleo."

Harry ordered strawberry for me, and nothing for himself. Once he'd paid and handed the cup and spoon to me, he indicated we should walk down the ramp to the beach.

"I once stole an ice cream cart," he said as we sat on the sand.

"A whole cart?"

"It wasn't just me. I was part of a gang of boys that stole it. We made ourselves sick after sharing the spoils." At thirteen, Harry was living on the street after running away from the factory where he worked for a cruel employer. He rarely spoke of it, although I suspected it had left its mark. "At the time, I thought it was righteous punishment for my crime."

"And now?"

"And now I believe every boy deserves ice cream." He whisked the spoon out of my hand and scooped out a dollop of my ice cream from the cup. "Even big boys."

I held the cup out to him. "You should finish it. I'm still full from the fish and chips."

"No thanks." He stood. "I'm going for a swim."

"But you didn't bring a costume."

"I'll hire one. I won't be gone long."

There were a number of establishments providing bathing costumes for those visitors who didn't own one, particularly near the men's swimming area. Although tempted to sneak closer to the section of the beach where I was forbidden to go, I decided not to. I didn't want to cause a scene. Nor did I want Harry to think I wanted to see him in nothing but a damp, tight-fitting costume.

I finished the ice cream and removed my notebook from my bag. I turned to a blank page and jotted down what I knew about Ruth's movements in Brighton. She'd stayed only a few nights, the same as Beecroft. Perhaps they'd even caught the same train from London, and she'd seen the person Beecroft believed followed him from the station. The next day, Beecroft received a telephone call from a man who demanded to meet him.

The day after that, Wednesday, Beecroft received another call, this time from a woman in London. Ruth also made a telephone call *to* London, but it wasn't clear whether that was before or after Beecroft received his call. According to the pharmacy assistant, Ruth used the silence cabinet around midday, which was a few hours before I first saw her on West Pier watching the Pridhursts. At about four PM, she followed us back to our hotel, waited until I left again to go sea bathing, then went upstairs and presumably spoke to Aunt Lilian and Flossy. She returned downstairs and left a message for me at the post desk, blackmailing me into meeting her. When I met her at six she was going to ask for my help, but was put off when she saw a man watching us from behind his newspaper.

I also wrote down some other facts—such as seeing Beecroft swimming away from a bathing machine—as well as theories I'd formed about that day. Even though neither Jane nor I had seen Geraldine Lacroix, it was very likely she was the woman giggling inside the hut. It was also extremely likely Ruth overheard the telephone call Beecroft received from the man, then followed to see who he met. I noted, too, that she must have been speaking to Mrs. Scoop over the telephone, strongly advising her to print a story she'd uncovered.

Was the story about the affair of Beecroft and Geraldine? Or something more scandalous? Something to do with the man Beecroft had spoken to over the telephone, then met?

I tapped the pencil against the notebook as I considered the possibilities, unaware that I was staring in the direction of the male swimming area. It wasn't until Harry was only a few feet away that I realized. He strolled toward me, his shirt sleeves rolled to his elbows, his jacket slung over his shoulder. It wasn't the first time I admired his strong forearms, or the way his biceps filled out his shirt. At least I could blame my pink cheeks on the heat.

He sat beside me with a satisfied sigh. "That was invigorating."

I returned my notebook and pencil to my bag. "We should go."

He asked me to hold his jacket while he rolled his sleeves down. I found myself drawn to his warm skin as it disappeared inch by inch beneath his shirtsleeves. For the first time, I noticed a small birthmark near his elbow.

He cleared his throat loudly. "Would you like me to go slower?"

"No! We don't want to be late." I looked out to sea, ignoring his light chuckle.

With his sleeves down, he stood and offered me his hand. I passed him his jacket and graciously accepted his assistance. It would be petty not to.

* * *

HARRY MADE a telephone call to his parents from the public booth at Brighton Station while we waited for our train. He was due to have dinner with them, but was unlikely to make it on time. He also informed his father of our progress. Perhaps D.I. Hobart could contact his former colleagues at Scotland Yard and have them put pressure on D.S. Fanning to re-examine the case. If he could tell them to exhume Ruth Price's body and have an autopsy performed to determine cause of death, that would be even better. I was still convinced the mark around her neck wasn't caused by a fall. I doubted D.I. Hobart had that much sway anymore, however.

Harry and I didn't discuss the investigation on the way home. There were too many other passengers nearby for such a gruesome conversation. Instead, he asked me about my previous visits to the seaside as a child. That led to me talking about my parents, something I didn't do often. Their deaths had been traumatic. Although extremely fortunate to be raised by loving grandparents from that point, as opposed to Harry who had no one after his mother died, I'd nevertheless found their loss profoundly difficult. Even more so because I'd been in the cart when it overturned. I'd been thrown clear and wasn't badly injured, but I'd witnessed the entire thing, including their arguing beforehand.

That argument had distracted my father. He'd not seen the deep ditch on the side of the road or noticed the horse move wide. It wasn't until the wheels plunged into the ditch that he'd tried to correct our course. But it was too late.

It wasn't until the train slowed down as we approached London that I realized I'd done most of the talking. "Sorry," I said, turning to look out of the window. "That was rather a lot."

Harry's hand folded over mine, resting on my lap. His fingers curled underneath my hand, and his thumb caressed the back of my glove. "It helps."

I looked at him, frowning. "Helps with what?"

The locomotive's whistle blew as we approached the station. It wasn't our stop, but people moved about to get off. Harry removed his hand and gave me a gentle smile.

He offered no answer to my question, and I didn't ask again.

* * *

FLOSSY DENIED MEETING Ruth Price at the Grand Brighton Hotel on the day before we left. She claimed she spent a few minutes settling her mother in her suite then went in search of a copy of the latest edition of *The Queen* in the hotel's library.

Aunt Lilian must have been the one to tell Ruth I was a private detective. I didn't want to have another encounter like the last one with my aunt, but my desire for confirmation overrode my trepidation.

I found her dressing for a theater outing with the aid of her lady's maid. Uncle Ronald was nowhere in sight, although he was due to go with her. She must have taken a dose of her tonic, because she was full of energy, her movements quick and jerky. Her gaze darted around, not settling on any one thing, and she had difficulty sitting still at her dressing table, much to her maid's frustration as she attempted to arrange my aunt's hair. While I despaired that she'd taken her tonic again, part of me was relieved. It meant she'd be in a better mood, and not snappy as she was when the effects of the cocaine wore off.

"Aunt, do you recall a woman named Ruth Price calling on you in your hotel room in Brighton the day before we left? She wore spectacles and carried a brown leather bag."

Aunt Lilian toyed with the string of pearls that would adorn her neck when her maid finished with her hair. "Yes, my dear, I do." She put down the pearls only to pick up her earrings and stare at them. "She wanted to know how we knew the Pridhursts. I told her we'd just met them the week before. She seemed to lose interest in the conversation after that until I mentioned you occasionally worked as a private investigator, but only on cases for the right sort of people, and nothing dangerous." Her gaze met mine in the reflection of the dressing table mirror. Although my aunt knew I'd solved murder cases in the past, like my uncle she must hope that I'd put that behind me and only solved cases of a genteel nature now.

I tried following her train of thought, but failed to see the connection. "I'm sorry, I don't follow. Why did you tell Miss Price I was a private investigator?"

"Because she was one, too. Well, I assume she was, with all the questions she asked me about the Pridhursts." She flicked the pearl-drop earring with her finger, smiling at the way it swung back and forth like a pendulum.

Then she suddenly turned to face me, catching the maid unawares. The hairpiece she'd been pinning to Aunt Lilian's hair detached, pulling out a few strands of my aunt's hair along with the pins. The maid gasped in horror, but when my aunt didn't react, she bit her lip and quickly removed the hair from the pins.

"Did I do the wrong thing, Cleopatra?" Aunt Lilian asked. "That young woman wasn't one of us, you see, so I didn't see the harm. Who would she tell your secret to? No one from our circle." She shrugged as she turned back to face the mirror. "It didn't matter if she knew about your detecting." Her theory was born from snobbery, and was also faulty, but I didn't want to get into a discussion about it with her.

My gaze connected with the maid's in the mirror's reflection. The poor woman seemed frustrated by the lack of progress with Aunt Lilian's hair. I was a distraction, so I got up to leave.

Aunt Lilian's hand whipped out and caught mine. "My sweet, sweet niece. You've become like a daughter to me. To Ronald, too." She patted my hand. "But we worry about you, just as much as we worry about Florence and Floyd."

"There's no need to worry. I'm perfectly content."

"Of course you're content, my dear. You're twenty-three. No! Twenty-four now. What possible problems can you have at your age? But if you don't marry, you will be alone, and I don't want that for you. You're so *pretty*, Cleopatra, you *will* find a man to marry you."

"Aunt—"

"But you must stop making it so difficult for them."

"For who?"

"Suitors." She gripped my hand, hard, but I doubted she was aware she was hurting me. "You spent an entire day at museums today, and while I do agree that a lady should improve her mind so she can hold a conversation with gentlemen, there is a point at which they lose interest. That point comes when she is smarter than they, and when she loses her looks. Both will happen to you one day, my darling girl. Mark my words." She let me go and turned back to the mirror. She stretched out her neck and pushed up the softening skin at her jawline before releasing it. She repeated the move, over and over, as if to undo what time and gravity had inflicted. "You will wake up one day to find your looks have faded, and the gentlemen who once flirted with you have moved on. Where will you be then?"

Although I knew disagreeing with her would get me nowhere, I responded anyway. "I'll be having conversations about the knowledge I've learned over the years from books and museums." I bent and kissed her cheek. "I won't be alone, Aunt. I will always have my family."

"I am glad. For Florence and Floyd's sakes, as much your own." She picked up the string of pearls again and passed them through her fingers. "Have you finished yet?" she snapped at the maid.

I left them and returned to my suite, where I added more notes to the ones I'd jotted down at the beach. Ruth Price hadn't been following me specifically from the West Pier that day. She'd not known I was a private detective until my aunt mentioned it. Deciding then and there to enlist my services, but being unable to pay me, Ruth had scrawled a note blackmailing me into meeting her.

That was one mystery solved. Now I needed to solve the bigger one. Who killed her?

* * *

HARRY TELEPHONED the hotel the following morning and left a message with his uncle to let me know he couldn't join me. "Apparently a new case came across his desk," Mr. Hobart said when he waylaid me in the foyer. "He says you don't require assistance for what you plan to do today, anyway."

"Oh. Right." I put on a smile for the manager. "Enjoy your day, Mr. Hobart."

He glanced toward the hotel exit. "I'll try, but the reporters are getting smarter. Yesterday, Frank let one in, thinking he was a guest. The fellow then almost made it inside the ballroom. Luckily the footman on guard duty realized and sent him on his way."

"Only three more days, then it will all be over."

As I strode toward the exit, I wondered if Harry truly did have a new case, or whether something I'd said on the train had made him want to avoid me. I was determined not to think about it, however. I would only think about the next stage of the investigation.

Frank opened the door for me. "You should take an umbrella, Miss Fox. It looks like it'll rain."

The clouds were light gray, not dark, and there were patches of blue sky. "Always the pessimist, Frank. I think it'll stay clear."

"I'm not a pessimist, I'm a realist. Unlike some," he added in mutter.

I shot him a smile. "Do be careful not to let any reporters in today."

He grunted then settled his feet apart, his hands clasped loosely in front of him. He looked ready to turn away anyone who looked slightly gossipy. I hoped he didn't get too zealous and refuse entry to an important guest.

Gossip reporters were firmly on my mind, and my agenda, on the omnibus ride to Fleet Street. Harry and I were both sure that Ruth Price had telephoned Mrs. Scoop on the day before her death from the Brighton pharmacy, and I was determined to find out what Ruth had said, and why Mrs. Scoop failed to mention it to me when I questioned her.

The clerk at the front desk went to fetch Mrs. Scoop when I announced myself, but he returned with Mr. Finlayson. The editor charged into the reception area, his heavy brow plunged into a deep furrow. I wasn't sure whether the editor always looked annoyed or whether I'd just happened to see him at his worst every time I'd been here. I suspected he looked pink with rage even while he forked his favorite meal into his mouth.

I greeted him cordially.

He greeted me with a barked question. "Has her notebook been found?"

"Pardon?"

"Scoop's assistant, the dead girl. You found the body, and I'm asking if you also found her notebook. It belongs to the newspaper. You are legally required to hand it over."

I wasn't sure if he was trying to pull the wool over my eyes, but the point was moot. "I don't have it, nor have I seen it."

"If you do come across it, you must return it."

Mrs. Scoop spotted us through the window from the newsroom and made directly for us.

The editor had his back to the newsroom door, so didn't see Mrs. Scoop emerge. "What evidence do you have that she was murdered?" he asked me.

"I, er, am not at liberty to say."

"If you do uncover evidence of foul play, I ought to be the first to know."

"Actually, I believe the police should be told first, then her family—"

"I'll pay you."

Mrs. Scoop strode to us, her arms crossed over her chest.

"We have an agreement, Finlayson." Her voice was quiet, as if she didn't want anyone else to hear.

He didn't seem to care, or perhaps he wasn't capable of speaking in a tone lower than a bellow. "Your agreement is irrelevant in this situation." He turned to her fully, his brow even more furrowed. "Or is it?"

"We'll discuss it later."

He grunted, then pushed open the newsroom door. Once it closed behind him, Mrs. Scoop indicated I should move to the side where no one could overhear us talk.

"What is it this time, Miss Fox?" she asked on a sigh. She was clearly fed up with seeing me. I wasn't too enthusiastic about being at the office of *The Evening Bulletin* myself, but it was a necessary evil.

"Ruth made a telephone call from Brighton last Wednesday, the day before she died."

"And?"

"She telephoned you, didn't she?"

"No, Miss Fox. Whoever told you that is lying."

"A witness overheard her urging you to go to print with a particular story. What was it?"

Mrs. Scoop flicked her fingers in a wave, dismissing my question. "I don't recall."

"Then allow me to refresh your memory. Ruth overheard Clement Beecroft on the telephone organizing to meet someone. She followed him and saw or heard something newsworthy. She thought it important enough to telephone you immediately."

Mrs. Scoop's fingers made a flicking motion again. I suspected she wished she was holding a cigarette. "Very well. You have forced my hand, Miss Fox. I'll tell you the truth. You're right. Ruth telephoned me from Brighton. She told me she'd seen Clement Beecroft with Geraldine Lacroix, the lead actress from his latest production. They were...intimate."

"No. Ruth called you about something else, something more. Everyone knows Beecroft has liaisons with his leading ladies. That's not newsworthy enough for her to telephone you, or to urge you to go to print. Why are you lying, Mrs. Scoop?"

"I'm not," she bit off. "You don't know everything, Miss

Fox. I told Ruth I wouldn't print the story about Beecroft because I *can't* print a story like that. I even have it written into my contract here."

"Is that what Finlayson was referring to just now when he said your agreement is irrelevant in this situation?"

She nodded. "It *is* relevant, by the way, and I will remind him of why in the most vehement terms. You see, my contract states that while I work for *The Evening Bulletin*, this paper can't print anything about Beecroft's relationships. If Ruth *was* murdered, and Finlayson prints an article about it, it will need to mention details about her visit to Brighton. Details that will reveal Beecroft's relationship with Geraldine Lacroix. When Ruth called me from Brighton to tell me she'd seen them together, I refused to print it. She became a little cross because she didn't understand why."

"Will you tell me why you have that clause in your contract?"

She glanced through the window behind the reception desk at the bustling newsroom beyond. "It's an agreement Beecroft and I came to years ago. You see, he knows something about me. Something I'd like to keep private. If I mention his affairs in my column, he'll break his silence. It will ruin my career."

"It must be something terrible if Finlayson would dismiss an anonymous gossip columnist."

"In case you haven't noticed, he employs very few women here, and none as journalists. I am the closest thing to a female reporter in this office, and I had to claw my way up from the typing floor. Finlayson would happily dismiss me if even a whiff of scandal was attached to my name. Writing about Beecroft's liaisons simply isn't worth the repercussions."

"May I ask what he knows about you that is so dangerous to your career?"

She simply narrowed her gaze at me.

I tried a different angle. "If you've known Beecroft a long time, do you know how he got his start as an impresario? It requires a substantial amount of money to put on theatrical performances."

"I believe he was financed by his family."

"But he has a Cockney accent. I assumed he wasn't born into wealth."

"Perhaps it wasn't a family member, then. Perhaps it was a lover. I have known him a number of years, Miss Fox, but not long enough to know the details of his origins."

"Could the money have come from his wife or her family? Was she wealthy when she married him?"

"I don't know."

A reporter hurried in from the street and pushed open the door to the newsroom. Mrs. Scoop's gaze followed him. "If you'll excuse me, I have work to do."

I watched her enter the newsroom, too, then I left.

I walked back to the hotel via the Laneway Theater. A printed sign next to the box office stated that Beecroft's production had begun. The next performance was a matinee that afternoon, with no performance that evening.

I stepped out from the covered portico into the rain. Frank was going to enjoy gloating about being right. I considered avoiding him and calling on Harry at his office, but decided against it. I didn't want to disturb him if he was busy, and I'd not learned much from Mrs. Scoop anyway. What I had learned didn't need discussing further with a colleague to understand it. It was very clear. Ruth had telephoned her to tell her about Beecroft's affair with Geraldine Lacroix, but Mrs. Scoop couldn't print the story because of her agreement with Beecroft.

The rain was light, so I continued on my way. A theory had begun forming when I spoke to Mrs. Scoop, but the walk solidified it in my mind. My next move was clear. First, I had to change out of my damp clothes.

Frank had never looked so smug. "I won't say I told you so, Miss Fox, but..." He pointed at my hat. "Your silk flowers are drooping."

"They'll recover. Like me, my hats are English and quite used to a little drizzle."

Frank's mouth moved in what I suspected was his attempt at a smile.

I had some time before I needed to enact the next part of my plan, so I gathered as many prior editions of *The Evening Bulletin* as I could find. Terence kept several older copies at the post desk, and I found the previous night's edition in the smoking room. I'd just settled on my sofa when there was a knock at the door.

Harmony entered before I had a chance to rise. "Good, you're here." She flopped onto the sofa beside me with a sigh.

"Is something the matter?"

She undid the laces of her boots and kicked them off. She wiggled her toes. "I needed to sit for a few minutes, somewhere Mr. Bainbridge or Mrs. Hessing won't look for me."

"Floyd will know you're here, but you probably have a little while before he realizes."

"Have you got any tea?"

"No, but I wouldn't mind a cup myself. Don't get up," I said as she started to rise. I ordered a pot of tea and two cups through the speaking tube that connected to the kitchen, then sat again. "Has Mrs. Hessing paid the suppliers?"

She sighed again. "Not yet. The suppliers are upset and guess who receives the brunt of their frustration."

I squeezed her arm. "I know it doesn't seem like it now, but it will be a marvelous reception, I'm sure of it. Miss Hessing and Mr. Liddicoat will be thrilled."

"I think they'd prefer an elopement and no fuss whatsoever. They just want to be together." Harmony tipped her head back to rest on the sofa, a wistful smile touching her lips. "I've never seen Miss Hessing so happy, Cleo. She has made an excellent choice in Mr. Liddicoat. They are perfect together. It makes one wonder, doesn't it?"

"Wonder about what?"

"Marriage, and if some couples really can be happy forever. I've not seen much evidence of it, myself."

Nor had I. "Is this about you and Victor?"

She picked up the stack of newspapers and sifted through them. "Why do you only have editions of *The Evening Bulletin*?"

I took the top one and flipped to the gossip column. "Mrs. Scoop told me she never writes about Clement Beecroft's affairs, and I wanted to see if that is true. But I only have a week's worth here. I'd need to go further back to know for sure."

"It is true. I read this paper most nights. The following

morning, if the maids have any gossip about Beecroft, I can't join in because I've not read about it. In fact, not only does *The Evening Bulletin* not report about his relationships, it doesn't mention a single thing about him. Not even his productions are reviewed, good or bad."

Now that was curious, but it didn't affect my theory or what I'd do next to prove it. "It's a shame you're not free this afternoon, Harmony. You could keep me company."

"What about Harry? Isn't he helping you?"

"Apparently he has another case now."

"Oh, I almost forgot. How was Brighton?"

"We learned a lot." I started to tell her what we'd discovered about Ruth's movements, but Harmony interrupted me.

"I meant how was your time with Harry. Did you two… get along?"

Taking a leaf out of her book, instead of answering, I continued to tell her what we'd learned in Brighton.

* * *

I WAITED where I could see the door used by cast and crew to enter and exit the Laneway Theater. After a long hour, my patience was rewarded with the appearance of Clement Beecroft. Fortunately, he was alone. If he'd left with Geraldine Lacroix, I probably would've had to abandon my plan to follow him. He would most likely have gone to her flat, whereas I needed him to go home to find out where he lived.

He didn't get into one of the cabs that had been waiting since the matinee finished an hour ago, and instead he set off on foot. He walked quickly, and I had to trot to keep up and not lose sight of him. We'd almost reached Bloomsbury Square Garden when he removed a key from his pocket and unlocked the blue door of one of the handsome houses. It wasn't as large as most townhouses in the more exclusive area near the Mayfair Hotel, but it wasn't small either. Clement Beecroft was doing very well. As lead actor and impresario, he would benefit financially when his shows were successful, but I was still curious about how a man with a humble background got started in such a cutthroat business.

I didn't knock on the blue door. If enough time passed and

no one else arrived, I would, but I decided to wait. It turned out to be the right course of action, and my patience was once again rewarded.

A woman strode up to the blue door, her face obscured by a large hat that she'd drawn down low. She removed a key from her bag and inserted it into the lock. Although I couldn't see her face, I was familiar with the thin frame and clawlike hand that turned the doorknob.

I stepped out from the shadows. "Good afternoon, Mrs. Blaine. May I have a word?"

CHAPTER 11

$\mathcal{M}$rs. Scoop spun around. Her eyes flared wide upon seeing me and hearing me call her by her real name, but she quickly schooled her features. Her gaze turned cool. "Congratulations, Miss Fox. Or should that be Miss Ferret, since you have a knack for sniffing things out?"

The neighbor's door opened, and a couple emerged. Mrs. Blaine quickly turned her face away from them. It would seem she didn't even want her neighbors knowing she was married to Mr. Beecroft. Or, rather, Mr. Blaine.

I made a point of greeting the couple, even going so far as to mention the weather. I wanted them to remember me. I wanted Mrs. Scoop to realize they would remember me, too, just in case she or her husband posed a threat.

"Shall we discuss this inside, or do you want your neighbors to overhear?" I asked her. "But before we do, I should warn you that several friends know I am here, and one of them is even watching this house now."

She glanced along the street then pushed open the front door.

I brushed past her and entered the dark entrance hall.

She stood at the base of the stairs. "Clem! Down here! Now!"

"Why?" he shouted back.

"Because you've been a fool." She flicked her hand in the direction of the front reception room then followed me in.

The room was decorated with solid, ornately carved furniture popular in the mid-eighties, with heavy brocade curtains in rust-red to match the floral wallpaper. The lighter fabrics in pastel shades and delicate furniture favored by modern tastes were nowhere in sight. Mrs. Scoop was a practical woman, not a fashionable one.

I opened the curtains to make my ruse that I was being watched more believable.

Clement Beecroft—Blaine—stopped in the doorway and stared at me.

"Close your mouth, Clem, and come in," his wife snapped. "Miss Fox requires a satisfactory explanation, or she'll blame one of us for Ruth's death."

"I didn't kill her!"

"Sit."

He swore under his breath as he dutifully sat. "I didn't kill her," he said again. "I never left my compartment. Ask that thug who was in there with me. He'll tell you. Unless he's lying, which he might do to save his own skin. *He* left the compartment, you see. Have you found him?"

"Stop prattling," Mrs. Scoop said with a roll of her eyes.

"Be quiet, you ugly crone."

Mrs. Scoop pressed her lips together and removed the cigarette case from her bag. She didn't open it and retrieve a cigarette, however. Perhaps they didn't smoke in the house. The smoking room at the hotel smelled like the tobacco had seeped into the very walls, no matter how much the maids cleaned, but the Blaines' parlor smelled only of furniture polish.

"Ruth didn't know you were married to Clement Beecroft," I said to Mrs. Scoop. When she didn't answer, I continued. "You sent her to Brighton to learn more about the Pridhursts, just as you told me that first day I met you. But she happened to see a famous actor staying in the same hotel as her. That was a coincidence I'm sure you didn't anticipate when you made the reservation."

Mrs. Scoop's jaw firmed as she nodded at her husband. "We holidayed in Brighton years ago and stayed near Rutherford House. We couldn't afford a room there at the time, but we admired it so much that we planned to return when we could."

"Happy times," he sneered.

"I can't believe you took your whore there."

"It is one of the nicest. It's also discreet."

"Not that discreet," I told him. "Ruth overheard you speaking on the telephone and reluctantly arranging to meet someone. She followed you and discovered something rather scandalous." I waited, hoping one or both would react and tell me what that scandal entailed. They were smarter than that, however. "Ruth then telephoned her employer, but Mrs. Scoop refused to print it. She has a clause in her contract that states she won't print anything about Beecroft." I fixed my gaze on her. "You told me you had the clause written into your contract because Beecroft knows something about your past that would hurt you if made public. I presume that secret is your marriage. Why is it so awful if the public knew?"

"Would you want the world to know you're married to a man who has a new mistress every time he puts on a new play? Not to mention he is ridiculous. I have a reputation to uphold, Miss Fox. Being married to him is embarrassing."

He made a sound of disgust in his throat. "She has a reputation as a gossip, snoop, and thoroughly mean witch to uphold."

Mrs. Scoop rolled her eyes again. "Pathetic."

"Your name is really Blaine," I said to Mr. Beecroft before their conversation became even pettier. "Is that what Ruth uncovered in Brighton? That you had humble origins?"

Mr. Beecroft shrugged. "I don't know. I didn't even know who she was until after she died." He looked to his wife.

She nodded. "You're right, Miss Fox. That's what Ruth told me over the telephone. She said she heard Clem's cockney accent when he spoke to that man."

"Who was he?"

"Someone who knew Clem when he was younger, demanding money to keep quiet. They grew up together, you see, and he knew Clem worked as a laborer and lived in the slums before he became famous."

Mr. Beecroft tugged on his cuffs. "I have an image to protect. My audience adore me, because they believe I'm a debonair and cultured gentleman. They'd stop coming to my plays if I talked like I crawled my way out of a gutter."

"Stop throwing themselves at you, too," Mrs. Scoop snarled. "What a tragedy."

"I paid the man money to keep him quiet."

"Why did he approach you now and not years ago?" I asked.

"I suppose he's not much of a theatergoer and only just discovered who I became. I didn't ask. It wasn't an amiable chat over a pint between old friends. He demanded money and I paid him."

"Was he on the same train that day Ruth died?"

"If he was, he didn't travel first class. Nor have I had any contact with him before or since."

Mrs. Scoop glanced at the clock on the mantelpiece. "Is that all? I have work to do."

Mr. Beecroft rose and did up his jacket button. "And I have someone waiting for me."

His wife's lips twisted with disgust. "You must wonder how we got together, Miss Fox."

I was actually wondering why they didn't get a divorce, but nodded. "Did he charm you?"

"Why would I charm *her*?" Mr. Beecroft snorted. "You've seen the sort of woman I like, Miss Fox. Beautiful, elegant, vivacious." He wrinkled his nose at his wife.

I expected one or both of them to tell me he charmed her because of her money, but they did not.

Mrs. Scoop simply said, "Don't," in a waspish whisper. She led the way out of the parlor.

Her husband ignored her. Indeed, he looked rather triumphant as he told me the story. "We've known each other since we were children. Anyway, one night I was drunk and got her with child. We were eighteen. Her father forced me to marry her." He rubbed his jaw. "A month after the wedding, she lost the baby."

I'd assumed she'd come from a wealthy family, but it seemed her origins were as humble as his. She was better at hiding the cockney accent.

"It's quite a feat to rise from nothing to become one of

London's leading impresarios," I said. "How did you get started?"

"The usual way. I was a popular actor in successful shows. I quickly built a reputation and was able to borrow money to put on my first production. It was extremely well received, and the rest is history." He stretched out his arms, as if inviting accolades. "My wife's assistant discovered the truth about my upbringing, but I didn't kill her. I never left my compartment, and if anyone says I did, they're lying. Find that man with the flat nose. He'll confirm it."

Mrs. Scoop stood by the open front door, her fingernail tapping on the frame. Her flinty gaze followed me as I stepped outside. "Yes, Miss Ferret will suit nicely when I write about you in my column."

"Are you threatening to expose me, Mrs. Blaine?"

"Are you threatening to expose us, Miss Fox?"

"If one or both of you are guilty of Ruth's murder, I'm afraid I have no choice but to go to the police." I descended the steps to the pavement. "Print what you want about me. My family are aware of my occupation."

Her thin lips stretched with her smile. "But are their friends and the hotel guests?"

I walked away, my heart hammering in my chest. They were a thoroughly nasty couple, not only to me, but to each other. I'd seen some unhappy marriages, but that one went beyond unhappy. Their dislike had turned to hatred over the years, and that had made them cruel. Surely the scandal of a divorce was better than their current miserable existence.

* * *

DETECTIVE SERGEANT FANNING'S shift had already ended. I was told to return to Scotland Yard the following morning. I considered contacting Harry's father, but decided against it. Although he and Harry would be worthy sounding boards for my theories, I still didn't know who murdered Ruth. I simply wanted to pass on what I'd learned to the detective who'd been assigned to the case.

I returned to the hotel to find a rather contrite Frank. It

was an unusual emotion for him to display, so I stopped to ask what was wrong.

"I let in a reporter," he muttered. "Sir Ronald just finished scolding me. But it's not my fault, Miss Fox. They're tricky. They dress like guests."

"But you usually know the faces of all the guests currently staying with us, which I must say, is quite a feat."

"I do, but it's the ones who come just for afternoon tea that trip me up. A lady can come with her friends just once and never be seen again. If she dresses appropriately and speaks like a toff, how am I supposed to know she's not one?"

"It's a dilemma for you. I'll speak to my uncle on your behalf."

"Will you?"

"Of course, if you want me to. Now, put on that lovely smile you're famous for and end your shift in good humor."

If he realized I was teasing, he didn't show it. He didn't smile, either, but I hadn't expected him to. At least he didn't look quite so downcast.

Inside, Mr. Hobart saw me from across the foyer where he was chatting to a guest. He excused himself and approached.

My spirits lifted. "Do you have a message for me?"

"How did you know? Lady Pridhurst telephoned."

"Oh."

"You were hoping someone else called?"

"No, not at all. What did she have to say?"

"She asked to have afternoon tea with you tomorrow, here. Just you and her daughter. If you can't make it, you're to let her know. She's staying at the Coburg Hotel."

"Thank you, Mr. Hobart." I saw him glance at the clock on the wall behind the front desk. "Are you about to head home?"

"I am. Mrs. Hobart will have my dinner ready at seven, as usual. I don't like to be late when she's gone to all that effort."

"You're a good husband."

"If I am, then it's because she makes it easy for me."

It was such a simple statement, said in rather an offhanded manner, yet it resonated with me. Being married to the right person ought to make life easy, even when times were difficult. *Especially* when times were difficult. Mr. Hobart was fortunate in that he'd found someone who did that for him.

Perhaps some couples didn't work because they were mismatched in too many ways. Perhaps those couples were doomed from the start. Marrying someone because she fell pregnant after a drunken night together wasn't the sturdiest foundation for a long, loving relationship.

* * *

I RECOUNTED my findings to D.S. Fanning the following morning at his desk. He didn't have his own office, but sat with the other policemen in a crowded, noisy room. In many ways, it was much like the office of *The Evening Bulletin*, with its hum of activity and people coming and going, squeezing past desks and talking over the top of each other. Unlike the newspaper, however, Scotland Yard didn't employ typists. I was the only woman in the room.

Detective Fanning didn't make any notes. He listened with his arms crossed, if he was indeed listening at all. He probably wouldn't have agreed to meet me if it hadn't been for Monty taking me through from the front desk when I arrived. Monty wasn't his superior—they were both sergeants—but Fanning seemed to respect him enough to humor me.

Unfortunately, Monty was called away and Fanning was growing more disinterested by the minute.

I wrapped up my account by summarizing what I wanted from him. "You have to find the man who shared Beecroft's compartment. Have the press put out a description of him. He's very distinctive. Perhaps an illustrator could speak to the other travelers on that train, including Beecroft, and make a sketch to pass around."

"So, Beecroft's real name is Blaine?"

"Yes. Clement Blaine. His wife called him Clem, so I assume he only changed his surname, not his first."

"And he's no better than me, you say?" He huffed a humorless laugh. "The lads will like that."

"Secondly, an autopsy needs to be conducted to find Ruth's cause of death." I put up my hands to ward off the argument I knew was coming. "I know you think it was suicide, but in light of new evidence, the possibility of murder must be considered."

"What evidence? You've presented me with nothing substantial, just theories. The family have buried the body, Miss Fox. It would be ungodly to dig it up now. You and that other fellow need to leave this alone. There's no definitive evidence to suggest she was murdered."

"Other fellow? Do you mean Harry Armitage?"

He shook his head. "The one who came here telling me the girl would never have killed herself, and that she was probably murdered. Real insistent, he was. He had to be removed by three constables."

"Was it her brother, Enoch Price?"

"Big brute of a fellow. Looked like he'd gone ten rounds with Ruby Robert. The boxer, Bob Fitzsimmons," he added when I stared back, open-mouthed.

"That's him! That's the fellow who shared the compartment with Beecroft, the one the conductor said entered Ruth's compartment. Geraldine Lacroix also saw him pass her compartment. He's the one whose likeness you should have distributed to the press."

Detective Fanning scratched his sideburns. "You think he murdered her?"

"It's a strong possibility. I place him at the top of my suspect list."

Fanning shook his head. "It doesn't make sense. If he murdered the girl, why would he come here and tell me to reopen the investigation? Wouldn't he be relieved I concluded it was suicide?"

His point took the wind out of my sails. He was right. The man probably wasn't the murderer. But he was an important witness. "Do you know where I can find him?"

"Sorry, Miss Fox. I only have a name." He removed a file from his drawer and flipped through the pages until he came to the one he wanted. "Here it is. Thomas Salter. Ring any bells?"

"Ye-es," I said as I tried to recall it from the depths of my memory. I couldn't quite grasp it, however. "Is there anything you can tell me about him? Anything at all that might help me locate him?"

He slotted the file back into his drawer. "He had a cockney accent. Does that help?"

"Not really." I stood. "Sergeant, that's three people who don't believe Ruth killed herself. Thomas Salter, Enoch Price, and me. Please, consider reopening your investigation."

He lifted a stack of papers off his desk and released them. The resounding thud drew the attention of several of his colleagues. "I have too much to do. I don't have time to reopen closed cases."

I shot to my feet. "If the murderer strikes again, it will be your fault, Sergeant."

Fanning swallowed heavily as he looked around at his colleagues, who were staring at him. I strode away without a backward glance, my head high. Sometimes, with the right people and at the right moment, a little histrionics can achieve the desired result.

I'd have to wait and see if it worked on D.S. Fanning.

* * *

It was time to call on Harry. The name Thomas Salter was vaguely familiar, yet I still couldn't remember where I'd heard it. Perhaps Harry's memory would prove better than mine.

Fortunately, I found him in his office. I'd worried he might be out investigating his own case, and I'd have to wait in the Roma Café for his return. He did appear to be working when I entered without knocking. There were several pieces of paper strewn over his desk, but he had his eye to a microscope, peering at something under the lens.

"Cleo, take a look at this," he said without looking up.

Once upon a time, I would have asked him how he knew it was me, but these days he expected me to enter without knocking. He finally sat back when I joined him on that side of the desk.

I bent to look through the microscope. My vision filled with a thick horizontal line bordered top and bottom by a dark center that lightened at the edges. "What is it?"

"A short hair. It proves that my client's dog is innocent, as it can't possibly belong to him."

"Innocent of what crime?"

"Theft of some apples left unattended in a basket outside a coach house in Belgravia. My client lives with his dog above one of the neighboring coach houses in the mews." Harry removed the slide containing the hair and placed it alongside two paper bags, each labeled in his neat handwriting. I could hardly see the hair, it was so short. "Several strands like this were found at the crime scene. I can tell the victim that his apples were stolen by his own horse." He tapped the paper bag labeled HORSE. "Not the dog." He indicated the other bag, labeled DOG.

I sat on one of the guest chairs on the other side of his desk. "Well done. London is safer now."

His lips twitched. "I agree it's hardly riveting stuff, and I wasn't paid much, but I took it on because I knew it would be fast to solve. Also, I wanted to use my new microscope on a real case." He placed the lens inside the small drawer of a wooden box then slotted the brass microscope into the box before closing it. He looked immensely satisfied with himself. The microscope and the possibilities of its uses appealed to Harry's curious mind.

"Did you buy it from that scientific instrument shop in Regent Street?"

"My father bought it from a deceased estate. It's an early birthday gift from my parents."

"Very early. Your birthday is in October."

He placed the microscope box in a cupboard and locked it. "You remembered."

"I have an excellent memory. Usually. That's why I'm here, actually. D.S. Fanning accidentally found out the name of the thug who shared Beecroft's compartment."

"Accidentally?"

"He showed up at Scotland Yard, demanding Fanning reopen the case because he didn't believe Ruth killed herself."

"Ah. So, he's not the murderer."

"It would seem he isn't, but I still need to speak to him. His name is Thomas Salter. It rings a bell, but I can't for the life of me remember where I've heard it."

"You wouldn't have heard it, you would have seen it." Harry reached for a newspaper placed to one side of his desk and flipped through the pages. When he found the article he wanted, he showed it to me. "Look at the byline."

The report about an automobile driver cheating in an endurance event was written by Thomas Salter. I'd noticed others taking a keen interest in the story over the last few days, but had merely skimmed the articles about it. I must have seen Salter's name attached to one of them. I checked the masthead.

The London Tattler.

I gasped. The man seen entering Ruth's compartment by multiple witnesses worked for the closest rival newspaper to *The Evening Bulletin* where Ruth worked. It couldn't be a coincidence that they were both on the same train.

CHAPTER 12

"*H*e's a journalist." My voice held a touch of wonder in it, which Harry picked up.

"You shouldn't judge a man by his face," he said with an admonishing arch of his brows. It was an echo from the days when I'd pegged him to be too handsome to be clever.

"It was our other witnesses who called him a thuggish type with his flattened nose and workingman's clothes." I stood and picked up the newspaper. "May I hold onto this?"

"Only if I can come with you."

"I wouldn't want to keep you from your important work of solving dastardly crimes."

He collected his hat and jacket from the coat stand by the door. He seemed to assume I would let him accompany me to question Thomas Salter. "I'm sure justice can wait a little longer. I doubt the horse in question will form a criminal gang over the next few hours."

As we walked to Fleet Street, I told Harry about my discovery that Mrs. Scoop was in fact Mrs. Blaine, and was married to Clement Blaine, also known as Beecroft. He was surprised by the revelation, but not surprised at the cruel nature of their relationship.

"He treats her abominably by carrying on with other women right under her nose," he said. "It's a surprise they haven't divorced if their marriage is so bitter."

I'd wondered about that, too. What did either of them

gain by staying together? "They have a long history, having met when they were both living in the slums as children. Perhaps they know too many secrets about each other to trust they could separate amicably, without those secrets coming to light."

* * *

THE LONDON TATTLER had an office just off Fleet Street, not far from its larger rival, *The Evening Bulletin*. The smaller newspaper felt like a calmer place to work, with more space between the desks, and fewer typists and journalists rushing about. It also didn't have a stentorian editor like Finlayson.

We spoke to Thomas Salter at his desk, tucked away in the corner. Just as the witnesses had described him, he wore ill-fitting clothes over a bullish frame. His jacket and cap hung on a coat stand nearby, and he'd rolled his shirtsleeves to his elbows, revealing forearms more typical of a navvy than a journalist. His wide, flat nose suited the rest of his blunt features, although I doubted it was like that from birth.

I introduced Harry and myself as private detectives. "We're investigating the death of Ruth Price." I'd been prepared to launch into the reasons why I'd taken on the case, but he didn't give me an opportunity.

A look of relief came over him. "I'm pleased someone is taking her death seriously. Scotland Yard aren't interested. I've tried to investigate, but I'm not getting anywhere." He grabbed spare chairs and moved them to his desk. "Please, sit. Tell me what you know."

If he'd killed Ruth, he was a better actor than Clement Beecroft. He seemed like a concerned friend, eager to find her killer.

"First of all," I began, "why did you go to Scotland Yard and try to encourage them to change their verdict? You and Ruth work for different newspapers. Wasn't she a rival?"

"We were friends." Mr. Salter rubbed a hand over his face and jaw. When it came away, he looked like a changed man with all the vitality gone. I suspected he hadn't slept properly for days.

I felt awkward confronting this man about his relationship

with Ruth, but fortunately Harry had no such qualms. "You were more than friends, weren't you? You were lovers."

"Ruth and I were courting. We were going to be married, but hadn't told anyone yet. We needed to think of a diplomatic way to announce it. She introduced me to her brother when we first started courting, you see, but he reacted badly so she told him she ended it."

"What do you mean by badly?" I asked.

"He lost his temper and ordered her to never see me again. Enoch didn't like me, because I'm not particularly religious. I don't go to church. I don't even think I believe in God." He shrugged boulder-sized shoulders. "Enoch wanted Ruth to marry someone from their church community, someone of deep faith, like him."

"Ruth didn't want that, too? It's my understanding she was very religious herself."

"More than me, yes, but not as devout as her brother. She pretended to be, to keep the peace at home. Enoch could be a bully to her. That's why she told him she'd ended our courtship. She was worried he'd spy on her if he thought we were still together."

"Spying is a little drastic, isn't it?"

"Have you met their housekeeper, Miss Fox? Ruth was certain she'd seen that woman follow her one day." He cracked his knuckles. His fingers were gnarled, as if they'd been broken and not healed properly. "Enoch Price didn't deserve such a kind, thoughtful sister."

Would Enoch do something terrible if he discovered Ruth lied and was still being courted by Salter? Would rage fueled by religious zealotry drive him to end the life of the sister who'd strayed from her beliefs?

Enoch hadn't been on that train, however, so my theory didn't hold water.

Mr. Salter continued. "We didn't tell her employer at *The Evening Bulletin* either. Mrs. Scoop would have dismissed her. She would accuse Ruth of feeding information to me, even if she wasn't."

"Did she ever feed information to you?" I asked.

"Sometimes, usually only when Mrs. Scoop wasn't interested in what Ruth uncovered."

That would be anything about Clement Beecroft, including the latest scandal of his visit to Brighton at the same time as Geraldine Lacroix.

Harry nodded at the bulging joints of Mr. Salter's hands. "You were a boxer?"

"What gave it away?" Mr. Salter's voice was thick with sarcasm. He instantly regretted his tone. "I'm sorry. That was unnecessary. Yes, I was a boxer in my youth. After one knock too many, I threw it in. I'd noticed reporters attending the fights then writing up an account for their newspapers, so I decided to try my hand at journalism. I specialized in boxing tournaments, and given I knew many of the contenders, I gained access where others couldn't. I started at *The Evening Bulletin*, which is where I met Ruth. I moved to *The London Tattler* after they offered me a job writing about all sports, not just boxing."

"Including scandals that happen in sports," I said. "You've got a nose for them, it seems. Pardon the pun," I added when I realized he might be sensitive about his most distinguishing feature.

"This face is why I find the scandals that others don't. People underestimate me. They think I'm just another former boxer with mashed potato for brains. They don't hold their tongues in my presence, and they don't worry about hiding evidence when I stroll in. It's impossible for them to believe that I'm capable of *saying* a grammatically correct sentence, let alone writing one. As ugly as it is, this face has opened up possibilities for me. I'm just fortunate it didn't disgust Ruth." He closed his eyes and drew in a deep breath before opening them again. "I *was* fortunate. She loved me despite my appearance."

"People underestimated her, too," I said gently.

He nodded. "She looked as though a harsh word would reduce her to tears, but she was strong, tenacious. More tenacious than me."

"Did you go to Brighton to be with her? It would be the perfect escape for you both, outside of London and away from Enoch and Mrs. Scoop. You could be together, and no one would care." I already knew he hadn't stayed at the same hotel as Ruth, but I wanted to test him. If he lied and said he was with her, I'd have to doubt everything he said.

"I went to Brighton to speak to someone who works with Alastair McAllister, the driver and part-owner of an automobile company who a source claims cheated in the Thousand Mile Trial back in April. I'd made contact with one of the other engineers and organized to meet him. I decided to take the opportunity to also watch McAllister. It just so happened that Ruth needed to go to Brighton for work, too. We didn't meet each other, but I saw her when McAllister met with the man she was following. She saw me, too, but didn't approach. We just nodded in acknowledgment and left it at that. We would have discussed their meeting when we were both back in London, but…" He lowered his gaze.

"Lord Pridhurst and McAllister were in cahoots?" Harry asked.

"It's likely Pridhurst invested in McAllister's motorcar company. Given he's a gambling man in heavy debt, he probably knew about the cheating scheme."

"Did McAllister see Ruth?" I asked.

"I don't know. If he has anything to do with her death…" He passed a hand down his face. "Ruth left a message at the inn where I was staying to meet me on the night before we were due to leave, but I didn't return until very late and was only given the message the following morning. I assume she wanted to discuss Pridhurst and McAllister meeting." He studied his brutalized hands, then closed them into fists. "If I had met her, perhaps she wouldn't have died."

"Or perhaps you would have died, too," Harry told him.

Mr. Salter continued to stare at his hands.

"Where did you stay?" I asked.

"The Horse and Cart Inn. I chose it because it's located closer to McAllister's team's workshop than most of the hotels. It was also cheap. I'm sure the staff will remember me if you want to ask them."

I wrote the name down in my notebook. "We know Ruth was in Brighton to watch the Pridhursts, and we know she saw Clement Beecroft and Geraldine Lacroix there, too. We also know she telephoned Mrs. Scoop on her last day in Brighton, telling her to print a story she'd uncovered. A witness says she was very insistent, so it seems it was a big story. Do you think it was about McAllister and Pridhurst meeting?"

He thought about it a moment then shook his head. "McAllister was my story. She wouldn't have told Mrs. Scoop about the connection without first asking me how much to share, and how much to withhold so I could use it."

I wasn't sure an ambitious woman would be so generous as to simply hand over information, but I didn't know how ambitious Ruth was, or how much she cared for Mr. Salter.

Something just occurred to me. Something that, if I was correct, could give us the identity of the last remaining mystery passenger. "What does McAllister look like?"

Mr. Salter sifted through the newspapers stacked on the floor beside his desk and opened one to an article he'd written about Alastair McAllister cheating. The illustration showed a smiling man standing beside a vehicle. His face was side-on. It was the same article as the one in my bag.

"Are there any photographs of him, rather than sketches?"

"Not in our paper, I'm afraid. The budget doesn't extend to photographs. Not that the photographs would tell the full story. McAllister makes sure they're all taken of his right side, not his left."

I turned to Harry, but he'd already realized the same thing as me.

"Is that because of a burn scar on his left side?" Harry asked.

Mr. Salter nodded. "He's sensitive about it."

So much so, that when he dressed as a woman to catch the train from Brighton, he lowered the large hat over the left side of his face to cover as much of the scar as possible.

I tried to contain my excitement, but Mr. Salter was too observant.

He sat up straighter. "What is it? How is McAllister connected to Ruth's death?"

"He was on the express from Brighton that morning," I said. "He sat in the compartment next to Ruth's."

Mr. Salter cracked his knuckles again.

Harry suddenly rose, as if he expected Mr. Salter to become violently angry.

But Mr. Salter proved he wasn't ruled by his emotions. He shook his head and calmly explained why he didn't think McAllister had anything to do with Ruth's death. "Even if McAllister saw Ruth, he would assume she was just a young woman. He wouldn't know she worked for a newspaper, or that she was spying on his associate, Pridhurst."

I had further thoughts, but I didn't express them. There was a problem with his entire account, and it was time to put it to him. "You said you didn't speak to Ruth at all while you were away."

"That's right."

"You sat in the third compartment of the first-class car with Clement Beecroft on the way home."

"Yes."

"Did he leave at any point on the journey?"

"No."

"Did you see anyone pass your compartment?"

Mr. Salter shook his head. "I've been asking myself the same questions, trying to recall who I saw on the train. I can assure you, I saw no one pass, but that doesn't mean they didn't bob down, or that the murderer wasn't in her compartment all along, or in the one between hers and mine."

My heart sank. I'd wanted him to admit that he'd gone to her cabin for a lover's tryst where he'd left her alive and unharmed before the Ouse Valley Viaduct. But my questions hadn't led him to correct himself, meaning the absence of an admission wasn't simply a mistake. It was a deliberate omission, and it went against three witnesses who'd seen him.

Three was too many to dismiss as a mistake.

If Mr. Salter sensed I suspected him, he didn't show it. He seemed distracted by his thoughts. "That moronic detective from Scotland Yard wouldn't tell me anything. I have so many questions. Were any of her injuries inconsistent with a terrible fall? Was there poison in her system that would have rendered her incapable of screaming as she fell? What had she written in the final pages of her notebook?"

"Did she have her notebook with her in Brighton?" I asked.

"She took it everywhere. She kept it in her bag and

guarded the bag as if it were her most prized possession." He sighed. "I suppose it was."

"Can you please write down where we can find Alastair McAllister?"

"Of course. You'll want to question him and see if the woman in his compartment got up and left at any point on the journey." He tore a page out of his notebook and scribbled down an address.

Harry and I thanked him and left.

"He's lying," I said.

Harry wasn't so sure, however. "I think he's genuinely upset about her death."

"*Three* people saw him leave his compartment, Harry."

"I agree that it's an overwhelming condemnation on the face of it, but think about *who* claims they saw him. Beecroft and Geraldine are lovers. He could ask her to lie for him and she'd probably do it without question."

It was a valid point. "Or vice versa—*she* could ask *him* to lie for her. But the conductor?"

"Bribery."

"All right. We need to know for certain. We'll confront the conductor with the allegation. We also need to return to Brighton to speak to Alistair McAllister." I patted my bag where I'd slipped the piece of paper with his address. "Even if he had nothing to do with Ruth, as Salter thinks, and didn't kill her, he's still a witness. If he says he saw no one pass his compartment, then it means Salter is telling the truth and the other three lied. If they lied, then any one of them could have done it, as well as Odette Pridhurst who the conductor claims he saw. But I'm not sure we can believe anything he says now."

"Leave that to me. I'll get the truth from him."

"How?"

Harry merely smiled.

* * *

FORTUNATELY, the conductor was still at Victoria Station after arriving on the latest train from Brighton. If we'd missed him, we would have had to wait several hours, and even then, I'd probably miss him again as I was due to meet one of our main suspects and her mother for afternoon tea.

There were fewer travelers on the platform than during our last visit, as it had been several minutes since the Brighton train arrived and it wasn't due to depart again for several more. Jack West was taking advantage of the break by chatting to the sweaty, sooty fireman whose job it was to keep the engine's firebox fed with a constant supply of coal.

Jack West stepped away when Harry told him we wanted to speak to him privately. He'd greeted us with a friendly smile, but Harry's somber tone wiped it away.

Mr. West scratched his beard. "How can I help you this time?"

"I think you know why we're here." Harry said in that same ominous tone.

The conductor shifted his weight to his other foot, and in doing so, moved a little away from Harry.

Harry stepped closer, within reach of Mr. West. He closed his fists at his sides. "Don't attempt to run. I will catch you, and I don't care if it causes a scene."

Mr. West glanced around. Realizing escape was impossible, he heaved a sigh. "All right, I admit it. I took money from that actor and lied about seeing that passenger moving about."

"Go on."

"I needed the money. My girl is sick, and doctors are expensive. The good ones, anyway." He paused, perhaps waiting for a sympathetic response from us. We didn't fill the silence and he continued unprompted. "That actor came to me and offered me a few quid to tell anyone who asked that I saw the flat-nosed fellow go into compartment one. I don't know why he wanted me to lie."

"When did Beecroft approach you?" I asked.

"Late last Sunday."

That was the same day we'd spoken to Beecroft at the theater, when he'd run off upon seeing us, only to calmly answer our questions in his office when we caught up to him. He must have realized then that he needed a false witness.

"Tell us who you *did* see," I said. "Be honest, this time."

"The posh girl and the mannish woman with the big hat

both entered the dead woman's compartment. The girl made sure she wasn't seen by passengers in the compartments she passed by ducking down, and the woman just walked in, but she only came from the next compartment along so no one would have seen her except me."

It was the same passengers he'd told us about last time, minus Thomas Salter. The problem was, if the mannish woman—who we now suspected was Alastair McAllister—had left the compartment he shared with Geraldine Lacroix, why hadn't *she* told us? She'd clearly lied about seeing Thomas Salter, but why had it been necessary to omit seeing her compartment companion leave?

"What about Beecroft?" I asked. "Did he move compartments?"

"No."

"Geraldine Lacroix? The beautiful actress?"

He shook his head. "She was in the same compartment as the ugly woman but unlike her, the beauty didn't leave."

"Are you sure?" I pressed. "You didn't see either Clement Beecroft or Geraldine Lacroix leave their compartments?"

"I didn't." He scratched his beard. "But I think I nodded off for a while."

It was a sentence that set our investigation in a backward direction. A number of passengers could have slipped out of their compartment, bobbed down below the windows, as they moved along the corridor, and entered Ruth's compartment. We had to rely on the statements of each passenger as to whether their companion got up and left or not, if we couldn't rely on the conductor.

Considering the passengers in compartments two and three were strangers to their fellow passenger and therefore unlikely to lie for them, it left the Pridhursts firmly in the frame.

"What do you think?" I asked Harry as we crossed the road.

He tossed a coin to the street sweeper who'd swept aside the horse deposits to make a clean path for us. "I think Beecroft bribed the conductor to frame Thomas Salter for Ruth's murder. But why, when Beecroft didn't get up and move about?"

"That we know of. Perhaps the conductor is continuing to lie for him, or he did fall asleep and didn't notice."

"I don't think West is lying anymore. He must realize it's not worth continuing."

I agreed. So that left us with one of our suspects taking advantage of the conductor napping. "Given Beecroft bribed him to lie about Salter, it must be either he or Geraldine who killed Ruth. We should question them again."

"We will. But I want to speak to McAllister first. He was in the same compartment as Geraldine. If we believe his version of events, and he didn't kill Ruth, he might have seen the murderer pass his compartment."

"Or leave it," I added, "if the murderer was Geraldine."

CHAPTER 13

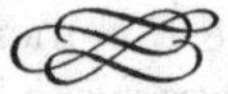

$\mathcal{A}$fter making arrangements with Harry to meet the following morning, I returned to the Mayfair Hotel in time to change for afternoon tea. I arrived early and sat at one of the tables at the far side, neither near the door nor the windows. I was somewhat obscured by a potted palm.

Mr. Chapman didn't like my choice of tables. He left his position at the reservations desk and charged toward me with his nose in the air like a bloodhound catching the scent of its prey on the wind. "You must sit at the Bainbridge table, Miss Fox. It's reserved for the family's exclusive use, and neither Lady Bainbridge nor Miss Bainbridge are in attendance today."

"I'd like to sit here, this once." I waited, but he didn't leave, so I looked past him toward the door. "Guests are starting to arrive."

He spun around. "There's no one there."

"They walked out again, when they saw the desk unattended."

He hurried away, his steps even quicker than before.

Mr. Chapman wasn't the only one upset by my choice of a different table. The waiters got confused. Richard, the head waiter, always served the family, but I was seated in Gregory's area. After whispering to one another and shooting odd looks at me, I called them both over.

"Don't worry, Richard. Gregory may serve me today."

"But it's highly irregular, Miss Fox," the head waiter said.

"I don't mind. Truly."

Richard glanced at Mr. Chapman, standing in the entrance greeting the first guests. "But if Sir Ronald finds out..."

"He won't."

Lady Pridhurst and Odette arrived, putting an end to the conversation. I greeted them with smiles.

They greeted me with scowls. In Odette's case, it was accompanied by watery eyes and a handkerchief to her nose. When she lowered her hand, I could see that her nose was red and swollen from crying.

It wasn't polite to point it out, so I did what all well brought up ladies do in such situations. I lied. "What a pleasant surprise it was to receive your invitation. You both look well."

"Thank you, Miss Fox." Lady Pridhurst glanced pointedly at her daughter when she didn't respond.

"Thank you," Odette repeated, her voice so soft I barely heard it.

Lady Pridhurst made a great show of admiring the sitting room with its crisp white tablecloths, shiny silverware, and dozens of potted palm trees. "This is a lovely room. The Coburg Hotel doesn't have a sitting room quite as elegant as this one, or as large. Oh look, Odette, there's a reading room and library tucked into the corner over there. Odette enjoys reading," she told me. "Do you like to read, Miss Fox?"

We chatted like familiar acquaintances meeting again after happy times, but Odette's miserable silence blanketed the first half hour with a sense of foreboding. It was a relief when Lady Pridhurst finally steered the conversation to the reason for their visit.

"My husband saw you in Hyde Park recently, Miss Fox. He thinks you overheard an interesting conversation he had with your friend about the journey home from Brighton."

It would seem Lord Pridhurst had put two and two together and realized I'd been with Harry at Hyde Park. Whether he also realized I was a private detective remained to be seen.

"I was on the same train as you," I said. "A young lady

died on the journey, and Mr. Armitage and I are trying to get to the bottom of the mystery of how she died."

Odette emitted a small sob into her handkerchief.

Her mother picked up her teacup. "What a terrible tragedy. To end one's life like that… Most unfortunate."

She sipped her tea before replacing the cup in the saucer. Watching her, it was as though nothing were amiss in her life. Yet her daughter was upset, her husband on the verge of losing his fortune and reputation, and she must know they were suspects in Ruth's murder. I wondered if she was truly unaffected, or if it was merely a facade for the sake of appearances.

I was tired of politeness and circling the truth, so I got to the point. "Several people, including myself, don't believe it was suicide. I'm sure Lord Pridhurst mentioned that to you, too."

Her lips pinched into a grimace. "He seems to have misunderstood, Miss Fox. He thinks you blame Odette for pushing that girl out of the carriage."

Odette's attempt at smothering her sob failed. Several ladies at neighboring tables glanced at us. Lady Pridhurst hissed at her daughter, ordering her to be quiet.

"If that's what he told you, then he has indeed misunderstood," I said. "My friend was merely trying to discover everyone's movements. You were in the fourth compartment, next to ours. A witness saw Odette sneak past the other compartments and enter the victim's."

Lady Pridhurst's nostrils flared. "A lady doesn't *sneak*, Miss Fox. It's true that Odette went to that woman's compartment, but it was done openly and without guile. If anyone says otherwise, they're lying. Please pass that on to your investigator friend."

I'd expected a flat denial. Her admission that Odette had indeed gone to Ruth's compartment made my task a lot easier. I would let her win the argument over the way Odette had moved about the carriage. There were more important truths to be uncovered.

But they were Odette's truths, not her mother's. I wanted to hear what *she* had to say. Considering she'd come along, it would seem she intended to speak for herself. That was a point in the girl's favor.

I gave her a sympathetic smile. "This has been a most trying situation for you, hasn't it?"

Odette lowered the handkerchief to her lap and nodded.

"The woman who fell from the train was named Ruth Price. I believe she didn't jump or fall by accident. I believe she was rendered unconscious in her compartment then bundled out through the window." I paused to let her take that in. "It's very important you tell me the truth, Odette. I know this is difficult for you, and you're worried about Mr. Holland discovering your father's...difficulties, but I won't be the one to tell him."

Odette finally lifted her gaze to mine. "Thank you, Miss Fox. It has been my greatest fear that he won't propose. I very much want to marry him." She glanced at her mother who encouraged her with a nod. "What do you want to know?"

"Was Ruth alive when you went into her compartment?"

"Yes. She was alive when I left, too."

"Why did you go?"

"My father noticed her following us late on the last day of our holiday. Father confronted her and she admitted she worked for a gossip columnist who goes by the name Mrs. Scoop."

"She just admitted it?" I asked.

"My husband can be persuasive," Lady Pridhurst said. We locked gazes for a long moment before she looked away.

"He followed her to the hotel where she was staying," Odette added.

No wonder Ruth had given up enough information to satisfy Lord Pridhurst. She must have been concerned that he knew where to find her. She may not have felt safe anymore.

Neither Odette nor Lady Pridhurst seemed to realize they'd just given Lord Pridhurst a strong motive for murdering Ruth.

"My father told us on the journey back to London that his misfortune was about to be splashed over the gossip pages of *The Evening Bulletin* thanks to Miss Price. He told me that Mr. Holland would feel deceived when he read about it. I was very upset. I blamed him, but he told me to direct blame to the person responsible for our imminent downfall."

"That woman," Lady Pridhurst bit off.

Odette pressed her lips together and lowered her head.

I bit my tongue. Pointing out that the family's downfall was solely the fault of Lord Pridhurst wouldn't keep Odette talking.

"I went to her compartment," Odette went on. "I didn't want anyone to see me and wonder why I was speaking to a stranger, so I was careful not to be seen." She glanced at her mother, but Lady Pridhurst sat quite still. She looked like a classical marble statue, all pale and elegant and cold.

"And you confronted Ruth Price," I prompted.

Odette nodded. "She told me she couldn't stop the newspaper printing salacious details. She was merely the assistant to Mrs. Scoop, and it was up to her as to whether she wrote the article or not. Then I left and returned to my compartment."

Lady Pridhurst patted her daughter's hand in the first sign of affection since their arrival. "That woman was alive when Odette left her. She didn't harm her."

"Does the name Alastair McAllister mean anything to you?" I asked.

Both ladies shook their heads. Lord Pridhust must have met the driver alone when his wife and daughter were otherwise occupied. It was quite possible he noticed Ruth following him to that meeting and warned McAllister. Perhaps McAllister had panicked and decided to confront Ruth. He'd somehow found out when she was leaving Brighton and dressed in a disguise to follow her unobtrusively. Then he'd slipped into her compartment, according to the conductor, although Geraldine Lacroix hadn't seen him leave the compartment they shared. Someone was lying to me.

"Thank you for coming here and talking to me," I said. "I'm sure it wasn't easy."

"This has been most upsetting for Odette. For me, too."

I waited for them to rise and leave, but both remained seated.

"We have a proposition for you, Miss Fox," Lady Pridhurst went on. "Could you ask your investigator friend to act as a go-between for us?" Lady Pridhurst opened her reticule and removed a banknote. She palmed it and, like Harry paying a bribe to the hotel porter, slipped it across the table to me. "Have him give this to Mrs. Scoop. Tell her it's for her continued silence."

I stared at her gloved hand and blew out a breath. "I doubt she would accept it. I'm not sure why she hasn't printed the story yet, but it will appear soon, I'm sure."

"When my husband confronted her, she told him she was verifying some details. No doubt *The Evening Bulletin* doesn't want to be sued." She tapped her finger on the tablecloth. "Take it, Miss Fox."

I did. "I'll use this to tempt her to forget the story, and return it if I can't. I mean, I'll ask Mr. Armitage to do it."

That seemed to satisfy her. She rose. "Come along, Odette."

Odette and I both stood. We bobbed small curtsies in farewell. But I couldn't let them walk away without offering the poor girl some advice. Advice that her parents ought to give her, but I wasn't sure they would. Denial seemed to be their response to a crisis. "You should tell Mr. Holland your situation as soon as possible. Marriages should be based on honesty. Beginning your marriage with a lie that is exposed later will destroy any chance of happiness."

"And if he ends our courtship?" Odette asked in a trembling voice.

"Then you will know that he never loved you. He only wanted to marry you for what your father's business could offer."

Odette's eyes filled with tears again. She bit her lower lip as it began to quiver.

Lady Pridhurst took her daughter's arm. "Thank you for your assistance, Miss Fox, but my husband and I can manage the situation with Mr. Holland, if you and your friend manage Mrs. Scoop."

As they walked away, Lady Pridhurst bent her head to her daughter's. I could just make out her quietly telling Odette that marriages for people like them were undertaken for different reasons than for ordinary people, and the sooner she understood that the more content she'd be.

With a sigh, I followed some distance behind. Odette's shoulders slumped as they passed a smiling Mr. Chapman. I believed her when she claimed she left Ruth alive in her compartment. For one thing, Odette didn't look strong enough to bundle anyone out of a window.

I tucked the banknote up my sleeve. I doubted Mrs. Scoop would drop the story about Lord Pridhurst, no matter how much anyone offered her, or pleaded for mercy. She'd shown no sorrow over the death of her assistant, so it was unlikely she'd have any sympathy for a stranger.

* * *

It was difficult to keep secrets in the hotel, so it wasn't surprising when Flossy asked me why I'd had afternoon tea with Lady Pridhurst and Odette without her. She was rather put out not to be invited. I assumed Mr. Chapman tattled.

Fortunately, I didn't have to completely lie to her. "They discovered I'm a private detective and hired me to run an errand for them. I'm afraid I can't divulge its nature to you, Flossy. I must maintain discretion."

"Can you give me a hint?"

"No."

She sank into the corner of the sofa with a pout. "Let's talk about our outfits for the wedding."

We sat in her suite, waiting for the meals we'd ordered to be sent up from the kitchen. With no social engagements scheduled, we were able to enjoy a peaceful night at home. I was relieved, but Flossy seemed bored.

"We've already told each other what we're wearing," I said. "And we've discussed hairstyles and jewelry."

She plucked at the piping on the sofa cushion. "Then we'll talk about gentlemen. That blond guest with the gold-topped walking stick checked out yesterday and didn't even say goodbye."

"Had you been introduced?"

"No, but according to the fortune-telling machine at the Palace Pier's arcade, he could be my husband one day."

"Perhaps the machine was wrong."

"Then my future husband could be anyone! How will I identify the man I'm supposed to marry if I don't know what he looks like?"

She sank even further into the sofa. She didn't rise to answer the knock on the door, so I got up, preparing to let in the waiter with our meals.

Instead, Floyd greeted me. "I've been looking for you, Cleo."

I stepped aside to let him in, but he remained in the corridor. "Why have you been looking for me?"

"I'm about to go out and expect to be home very late." He wore evening wear of a tailcoat with silk lapels and a top hat, but the black tie and waistcoat, instead of white, meant he wasn't going somewhere too formal. Most likely he was meeting his chums at a party or club, rather than attending a ball or dinner.

"Is that wise, this close to the wedding? It's only two days away."

"That's why I'm looking for you. When Harmony joins you for breakfast tomorrow morning, can you tell her not to wake me until midday. I'll need my beauty sleep."

Flossy proved she could hear us from the sitting room. "You need more than sleep, Brother!"

"I wouldn't throw stones if I were you, Sister!"

I grabbed Floyd by the jacket lapel and dragged him inside. "Pipe down, both of you. The other guests will hear."

Flossy appeared, arms crossed beneath her bosom. "What does that mean?" she asked Floyd.

He ignored her. "So will you tell Harmony for me, Cleo?"

"I won't see her in the morning. I sent her a message to say I'm having an early breakfast and will be leaving the hotel before she starts work."

"Where are you going?"

"None of your business." I smoothed the wrinkle I'd left in his lapel when I'd grabbed it. "I don't think you should have a late night. Tomorrow is the last chance to perfect all the last-minute details for the wedding. You'll need to be alert and prepared, particularly with Mrs. Hessing still refusing to agree to the suppliers' prices. What if they decide not to fulfill the orders until someone pays? Your father won't be impressed if he's left to pick up the bill."

"Harmony will take care of it. That's why I hired her."

"It's not her job to force Mrs. Hessing to pay. It's yours. *You* are the liaison between the hotel and the client."

"Stop worrying, Cleo. Everything will come together on the day." He removed his watch by its chain from his waist-coat pocket. "I have to go."

"Can I come?" Flossy asked.

"No. It's not a place for young ladies."

"Where are you going?" I asked.

"None of your business." He seemed pleased to be able to throw my response back at me. He tempered it by chucking me under the chin. "Enjoy your outing tomorrow, Cousin. Don't get into too much trouble."

"You too, Floyd," I said with a resigned sigh.

* * *

HARRY and I changed trains in Brighton and caught the service to Portslade on the western edge of Hove. The journey gave Harry plenty of time to tell me everything he knew about the Thousand Mile Trial, the event in which Alistair McAllister reportedly cheated. The Automobile Club of Great Britain & Ireland had organized the endurance trial to show-case the prowess of automobiles over a long distance. It wasn't a race, but was designed to put to bed the notion that horseless carriages—as some still called motorized vehicles—were unreliable.

Held in April and May, the event had been a resounding success for the companies who'd managed to design and manufacture a vehicle that finished. Out of the sixty-five who took part, only thirty-five completed the course. The Brighton-Hove Automobile Company had been one of them. Interest in the company boomed. They couldn't keep up with orders for new vehicles. Investors saw the potential and laid down large sums to encourage the company to expand.

The vehicle they'd entered had been driven by one of their founders and the head engineer, Alistair McAllister. According to the article written by Thomas Salter, a farmhand had claimed McAllister swapped his vehicle with another along the route. He'd hidden a spare vehicle in a barn on a farm outside Edinburgh. It looked identical to the one in which he'd started the Trial days earlier in London. By swapping the vehicle with older parts worn by constant driving on rough roads with the fresher one, he'd returned to London triumphant. McAllister was lauded as a hero of British auto manufacturing.

But his success was apparently based on a lie, and that lie had come unstuck when the farmhand told his story to Thomas Salter. Mr. Salter traveled to Brighton to speak to an employee at the Brighton-Hove Automobile Company. That fellow must have confirmed the story, because Mr. Salter's article appeared in *The London Tattler*.

Everything Harry told me gave McAllister a motive for killing Thomas Salter, not Ruth. Yet, if we were correct, he'd dressed in a disguise and entered her compartment on the express to London. Even if he didn't murder her, I wanted to know why he was interested in her.

We found the factory in Portslade easily enough. Everyone we asked for directions knew of it. The single building with all six of its chimneys spewing smoke was smaller than I expected, which explained why the Brighton-Hove Automobile Company had plans to move to a larger site, according to Harry. Those plans might be on hold now, if investors pulled out due to the cheating scandal.

We asked to speak to Alistair McAllister, but were directed to a stiff-lipped man in an office whose upper lip became even stiffer when we repeated our request to speak to McAllister.

"Your kind are not welcome here!" he bellowed.

"Our kind?" Harry echoed.

"Gutter press."

"We're private detectives from London."

His demeanor instantly changed. He tugged his shirt collar away from his neck and cleared his throat. "Please inform your client that the Brighton-Hove Automobile Company did not cheat in the Thousand Mile Trial." He stood and rounded the desk, approaching us cautiously, as if worried he'd frighten us away and therefore the client he imagined we represented. "He's welcome to speak to us in person at any time. Please, let us have a chance to allay his fears before he makes any rash decisions."

"You misunderstand," Harry said. "We have no interest in the Trial and our client isn't one of your investors. We want to speak to McAllister in relation to the death of Ruth Price." He kept his voice even, but I detected a little tightness in the consonants. If the man didn't give up the whereabouts to McAllister soon, Harry might lose his temper. It happened so rarely that I sometimes forgot it even existed.

I had little interest in seeing it again. It would probably have the opposite effect anyway and get us thrown out of the office. "What my colleague should have said is, we wish to speak to McAllister about the *murder* of a gossip columnist's assistant on the express train from Brighton to London. If he doesn't want to speak to us, then I'm afraid it will look very bad for him. Scotland Yard won't like it."

The man's gaze shifted to peer past me. It was the only warning, but it didn't come early enough.

"Turn around with your hands in the air," came the growl from behind us. "Don't do anything foolish or I *will* shoot."

CHAPTER 14

$\mathcal{H}$arry moved to step between me and Alistair McAllister, but the click of the gun cocking stopped him in his tracks. My heart stopped, too, only to restart with a frenzied pounding.

McAllister bared his teeth. "I said, don't move." I knew it was McAllister by the crumpled skin on the left side of his face. His left hand also bore burn scars, but they would have been hidden beneath a glove on the train. His right hand, the one that gripped the gun, was steady, the knuckles white. His gaze was equally steady as it fixed on Harry.

Harry raised his hands. His movements were slow so as not to startle the gunman. Despite his initial reaction to protect me, he was now at ease. The tension had left his body, and his face softened as much as it ever could with those strong cheekbones of his. Even his stance seemed less threatening somehow. I suspected he planned to disarm McAllister by lulling him into a false sense of security.

My nerves were already on edge, but realizing Harry was going to bear the brunt of McAllister's ire shredded them completely. "Don't shoot." My quavering voice made it sound more like a plea than a demand.

It was so weak, I hadn't even attracted McAllister's attention. Harry, however, swallowed heavily. He wasn't used to me being so tentative.

"If this is a hostage situation, then I ask you, as a gentleman, to let Miss Fox go."

Behind us, McAllister's colleague murmured an agreement. "Good God, man. What are you doing?"

McAllister continued to glare at Harry. "I didn't murder that woman. She killed herself."

"The cause of death is being questioned by several parties," Harry said. "No one is accusing you of murdering her, however. You're a potential witness, that's all. We merely want to ask you the same questions we've asked all of the other passengers who were on that train."

McAllister's gaze flicked from Harry to me to his colleague then back to Harry. "I know how it seems, with my disguise, but I did not kill anyone. Do you understand?"

"We do," Harry assured him. "Lower the weapon and let's have a productive conversation to get to the bottom of a few things. The only way you can truly exonerate yourself is by helping us find the real killer."

It was that final statement that got through to McAllister. He lowered the gun to his side.

The sound of pent-up breaths being released filled the office. McAllister's colleague approached him cautiously and put out his hand for the weapon. McAllister placed the gun on his palm, and the colleague headed for the door.

"I'll give you some privacy."

"Leave the door open," Harry said.

The man nodded, then disappeared into the outer office. Harry, McAllister and I remained standing, even though there were enough chairs. I gripped the edge of the desk behind me to steady myself. My legs felt a little weak from relief.

Thankfully, Harry conducted the interview. If I spoke, my voice might tremble, and I'd already shown enough weakness in front of our suspect. "You boarded the express from Brighton to London that day specifically to speak to Ruth Price. Did you wear a disguise so you wouldn't be recognized?"

Mr. McAllister angled himself so that the smooth right side of his face was presented to me. Thomas Salter had told us the engineer didn't like to be photographed from his left because he was sensitive about the scar. It seemed that sensitivity extended to in-person meetings, too. "I became a well-known figure locally after the Thousand Mile Trial. I wanted to speak to that woman privately, without anyone speculating about the reason."

"Can you tell us why?"

"I wanted to find out what she knew about me, and what she was going to do with the information. Even if she'd lived, it was for nothing," he added bitterly. "The article was printed anyway."

"Not by her paper. It was printed in *The London Tattler*, but Ruth Price worked as assistant to a gossip columnist at *The Evening Bulletin*. Another journalist was investigating you, not Ruth."

McAllister pulled out a chair and sat down heavily. He rubbed a hand over his scarred cheek and jaw. "When I heard about the article, I presumed she sent her information back to London before boarding so it reached the paper despite her death. Are you telling me there was another journalist spying on me?" He blinked up at Harry. "I didn't see anyone."

Thomas Salter truly had learned to blend in. He was probably right in that his distinctive appearance fooled everyone into thinking he was a moronic thug, not a capable journalist.

McAllister lowered his head. "She was telling the truth," he murmured.

"What do you mean?" Harry asked.

"I confronted her in her compartment. I demanded to know what she knew about me and why she'd been spying on me. She said she hadn't; that she'd been following someone else."

Jack West had told us he'd seen the 'mannish woman' entering Ruth's compartment, but Geraldine Lacroix claimed she'd only seen Thomas Salter moving about the carriage. After confronting the conductor about his evidence, we now knew he'd lied and that Salter *hadn't* got up, which meant Geraldine had also lied. It seemed she'd lied about the movements of her compartment companion, McAllister, too. She'd claimed he hadn't left, but he'd just admitted he had. Was she trying to protect him? If so, how were they connected?

"Ruth was following Lord Pridhurst," Harry said. "You

met him in Brighton, and I assume it was he who pointed Ruth out to you."

McAllister nodded.

"Did you see anyone else moving about the carriage on that journey to London?"

"No."

"Did Geraldine Lacroix leave the compartment?"

"Who?"

"The woman who shared your compartment. She's an actress. She works with one of the other passengers, Clement Beecroft, but they didn't travel together."

McAllister pointed a finger to his chest. "And you think *I'm* guilty? That sounds like a guilty act to me, not traveling together when they know each other. But no, she didn't get up until we arrived at Victoria Station."

"Are you sure?" Harry pressed. "You didn't fall asleep at any point?"

"I was awake the entire time." McAllister stood. "Are you finished?"

"Sit down," Harry growled. McAllister sat. He was a slender man and not very tall. He knew he was no match for Harry. "We weren't entirely honest with you. Ruth Price didn't write that article exposing you as a cheat, but she was being courted by the man who did."

McAllister's eyes widened. "So, she *was* spying on me on his behalf?"

"He was acting alone. As I said, she was there to spy on Pridhurst. What can you tell us about him?"

"He's an investor in the company. He's wealthy and well-connected."

"Why did he meet you while he was holidaying in Brighton with his family?"

"He wanted to check on his investment." McAllister shrugged. "I showed him around the factory. We discussed expansion plans."

"Did he know that you'd cheated in the Thousand Mile Trial at that point?"

McAllister shot to his feet. "I did *not* cheat. I'm going to sue *The London Tattler* for slander. They've ruined my reputation."

Harry straightened and McAllister took a step back. "If Pridhurst didn't know about the scandal then, he must have been very upset to learn about it a few days later when he read that article. His investment is now worthless."

"We'll survive and he'll get a good return." McAllister folded his arms over his chest, tucking away his scarred left hand. "What does any of this have to do with that woman's death?"

"You confronted her on the train because you thought she was about to expose you. Perhaps you weren't the only one."

"You think Pridhurst confronted her, too? I didn't see him pass my compartment." He frowned. "I suppose he could have ducked down, or crawled past. Very undignified, but he was desperate for the company to succeed. I got the impression he was relying on a quick return on his investment. When I showed him around the factory that day, he kept asking how soon we could move to bigger premises and increase production. Reading that slanderous rubbish about me in the *Tattler* must have come as a shock to him as much as it did me."

Harry had no further questions and thanked him.

I'd found my voice, however, and had one more. "How did Ruth Price seem to you when you confronted her in her compartment?"

"A little on edge," McAllister said. "She jumped when I entered but looked relieved to see me and not someone else. Relieved then surprised when she realized I was a man."

So, Ruth was worried. She had an inkling she'd upset someone and expected a confrontation. The question was, who?

"That woman was alive when I left her. You must believe me." McAllister removed a handkerchief from his pocket and dabbed at the droplets of sweat on his brow. "Everything is falling to pieces. My reputation is in the gutter. Investors are pulling out. My wife will leave me if she finds out I borrowed her clothes. I can't have murder pinned on me, too."

He was a broken man, all because of one poor decision. I hadn't expected to feel sympathy for him after he threatened us with the gun. He was also still a suspect and had lied and cheated in the race, so there was reason to believe he would lie again to save himself. Even so, I didn't want to pile more problems on top of the ones he already had.

"Mr. Armitage and I will find the killer, Mr. McAllister. You can be certain justice will be done."

My words had no effect, and we left him in the office, the picture of misery.

As we ate haddock pies purchased from a cart at the market on our walk back to the station, we tried to untangle truth from lies. Harry and I both came to the same conclusion. Clement Beecroft and Geraldine Lacroix were in the thick of it. Almost every line of inquiry led back to them.

"McAllister admits he left his compartment to speak to Ruth," I said. "So why didn't Geraldine Lacroix notice him leave? Why did she lie about seeing Thomas Salter, yet not mention McAllister moving about?"

Harry agreed she was guilty of one lie, at the very least. "It's time we have another chat to both her and Beecroft."

* * *

THE DOOR TO Geraldine Lacroix's dressing room was slightly ajar, and her voice could be clearly heard through the gap. The accent was a cockney one, not cultured as it had been the first time we met her.

Harry and I glanced at one another, then I barged inside. He stayed in the corridor, in case she wasn't decent. She was fully clothed, however, a dressmaker kneeling beside her, adjusting the hem of her gown. I called Harry in.

Geraldine's spine stiffened. "How dare you enter without knocking!" Her accent was all plummy vowels and prim indignation. "Get out!"

I ignored her and began the interrogation with a question that I'd wanted to know the answer to ever since meeting her. "What is your real name?"

"I beg your pardon!"

"Where are you from?"

She tossed her head. "Fetch someone," she ordered the dressmaker.

The dressmaker quickly tied the end of her thread and snipped off the excess. "I'll get Mr. Beecroft." She slammed the lid on her sewing kit closed and glared at me as she passed.

"He's not here," I told her. "We already checked."

Harry closed the door behind her. "You were born within the sound of the Bow Bells, if I'm not mistaken."

I'd heard about the cockney dialect only being spoken in the areas of London where residents could hear the bells of St Mary-le-Bow church in Cheapside. Outside of that five-mile radius, the accent was slightly different. As a non-Londoner, I couldn't detect the nuances. I doubted most people could, and that's why the word cockney had come to encompass the accent of the entire East End. But a true cockney speaker knew the difference.

Geraldine looked surprised that Harry identified her accent so precisely, but I wasn't. He had lived in all sorts of areas and knew the slums equally as well as he knew Mayfair.

"I lied about my origins," she finally admitted. "If that's against the law now, the police will have to arrest almost everyone on the stage."

"Including Beecroft," I added. "We know his name is Clement Blaine and he was brought up in Bethnal Green. We know he's married. We also know you and he both lied about seeing Thomas Salter moving about the first-class carriage the day Ruth Price died."

Geraldine pressed a hand to her stomach and drew in a deep breath. She let it out slowly then lifted her gaze to Harry's. She blinked long lashes at him. "If you can pick a Bethnal Green accent, then you too must have humble origins, Mr. Armitage. You understand why I lied, don't you?"

"I understand the need to reinvent yourself." Harry invited her to sit at her dressing table. "But lying to us only makes you look guilty. I don't think you want anyone to accuse you of murdering Ruth Price."

Her flirtatious blinks turned to startled ones. "I didn't do it!"

"Did Ruth know about your past?" I asked.

She looked irritated that I'd resumed the interrogation, instead of Harry. "I don't know." She reached for his hand. "I never met that woman, and I certainly didn't kill her. You must believe me, Mr. Armitage."

Harry patted her hand before letting go. "Tell us why you claimed you saw Thomas Salter passing your compartment on that fateful trip." At her blank look, he added, "The man with the flat nose sharing Beecroft's compartment."

"Clem told me to say it. He said if we don't blame someone else, then you'll blame us because that woman was spying on us in Brighton."

"Did you see her watching you?"

"I didn't. I assume Clem did."

"Why blame Salter specifically?" Harry asked.

"Of all the passengers in that carriage, he looked likely."

"You blamed him because he looked like a murderer?" I asked, incredulous.

She shrugged a shoulder. "He certainly looked like a ne'er-do-well."

"Do you not see the irony, Miss Lacroix? Or whatever your name is?" Perhaps my tone was harsh, but I was astounded someone from the slums would judge someone else by the way they looked. Not to mention I was a little tired of her flirting with Harry while being curt with me.

She sniffed and turned back to Harry. "Clem and I have reputations to uphold. He thought the best way to deflect your attention from us was to point the finger at someone else. I think he chose wisely. I'm sorry we lied, and I'm sorry that woman is dead, even though she was assistant to a gossip columnist and probably deserved it. You ought to look at other people she was spying on for her employer. I'm famous enough, and loved enough by my audience, that I could weather my past being exposed, as well as my dalliance with Clem." With another sniff, she studied her reflection in the mirror. "Perhaps someone else couldn't."

"Do you know she worked for Beecroft's wife?" Harry's words had her whipping around in her chair to stare at him. "Her professional name is Mrs. Scoop, and she's the gossip columnist at *The Evening Bulletin*. Have you noticed she never writes about her husband in her column?"

"He kept that secret well hidden." She frowned. "There you are then. If what you say is true, *Clem* didn't have a reason to kill that woman, because the paper she worked for would never print anything about him, and therefore I have no reason to kill her either."

"Unless Beecroft discovered she knew something else about him," Harry pointed out. "Or you did."

"Now you're just grasping at straws, Mr. Armitage." Her flirtatious tone was back, and a smile, too. "I'm sure you can do better."

Something that had niggled at me since our first outing to Brighton together snapped into sharp focus. "A witness told us that Beecroft arrived at the hotel looking worried. He thought someone had followed him, presumably from the station. As you say, he wouldn't be worried about Ruth. Do you know who made him anxious? Did he talk to you about it?"

Part of me expected her to snap at me and tell me to mind my own business. But she turned thoughtful. "He was fine when he left London. We caught the same train to Brighton, although we didn't sit together, and he looked cheerful. But when I saw him again at the hotel, he did seem anxious."

"Was anyone on that train who was also on it coming home?"

"I don't think so. No one seemed familiar, but I don't know if I saw every passenger, on either journey."

There was someone who might remember. Someone who was on every express train that ran between Brighton and London.

Harry must have had the same idea. He checked his watch and gave me a brief nod. We had thirty minutes to make the arrival of the last express from Brighton.

* * *

THE CONDUCTOR who farewelled passengers alighting from the first-class carriage of the express from Brighton wasn't Jack West. We asked the fellow if Mr. West had the day off, but he shook his head.

"West doesn't usually work the express. His shifts cover the regular service."

Harry and I exchanged glances. "But he was on the

express a few times recently," Harry pointed out. "Most notably when Ruth Price died over the Ouse Valley Viaduct."

The conductor touched the brim of his cap as a passenger arrived. "I was ill, and he filled in for me. Then he asked another time or two because he said he liked the express. I reckon one of those times was when the woman threw herself off. Now he's back to the regular stopping all stations service."

Again, Harry and I exchanged glances.

"What can you tell us about him?" I asked the conductor. At his shrug, I added, "How long has he worked for the London, Brighton and South Coast Railway company?"

"Not long. About a month."

"And before that?"

"He worked for another company. I don't know which one. I reckon it was years ago, though, not recent."

"Why do you say that?"

The conductor checked his watch then tucked it back into his waistcoat pocket. "He was experienced, but was surprised at how fast the journey is. There've been improvements in the tracks and locomotives these last couple of decades, you see. It means we can get to Brighton in just over an hour on the express. Real surprised by that at first, was West." The conductor touched the brim of his cap again and greeted a couple who climbed on board. "Strange thing is, West denied being out of the railways for years when I pointed out that the improvements weren't new or limited to the Brighton line. Denied it strongly, I might add. He seemed offended that I doubted him. I suppose he needed the work and didn't want our superiors to find out he lied about having recent experience. Poor cove must have been desperate if he had to lie."

Desperate for work? Or desperate to work on the Brighton line? Something wasn't right about Jack West.

Harry knew it, too. "Do you know where we can find him? Does he live in London or Brighton?"

"London. I don't know where he lives, but he drinks at The George in Lambeth."

Lambeth wasn't far, but we caught an omnibus anyway. The afternoon heat made any kind of exertion uncomfortable work, and it had already been a long day that was likely to feel even longer by the time we finished questioning Jack West. Harry agreed with me that there was something very suspicious about him, but we couldn't agree whether he was guilty, an accessory to another's guilt, or merely unlucky.

While I leaned toward guilty, Harry was at the other end of the spectrum. "He doesn't have a motive for killing Ruth," he pointed out.

"That we know of, yet."

"He also covered the express shift because the regular conductor was ill. West couldn't orchestrate that."

"Not the first one, that's true. But he *did* orchestrate the other shifts, including the one during which Ruth died. I don't believe in coincidences, Harry."

The George Inn was the sort of place where generations of local men had gathered after long shifts in neighboring factories. Its black and white Tudor facade was a little crooked, and the wooden bar inside bore scratches that no one had bothered to polish away. Harry had to duck to enter and keep his hat in his hand. Even so, the low ceiling beams were mere inches from the top of his head.

We couldn't see Jack West. Harry asked the landlord where we could find him, but he wouldn't answer. He slammed a tankard of ale down in front of a patron, all the while glaring at Harry.

Once the landlord's back was turned, the patron signaled to Harry that he'd talk in exchange for money. Harry settled some coins on the bar. The patron gave us an address for Jack West. He laughed as he pocketed his earnings.

Harry had been about to walk off, but stopped. "Is something amusing?"

The man chuckled into his tankard. "West cleared off this morning. You won't find him. He's long gone."

If Harry doubted West's guilt before, he didn't anymore. We left the inn and headed for the address the man had given us. Perhaps a neighbor could tell us more about him, including where he may have gone. I wasn't hopeful, however. The residents in places like Lambeth didn't trust strangers. We had to rely on bribery, but without a client to pay our fee, we were reluctant to spend more.

Harry came up with a solution once he saw that West's

lodgings were located in a quiet court in a building where no one locked their doors, probably because they had nothing worth stealing. "I'll sneak in. You keep watch outside."

I didn't want to wait outside, and I knew just what to say to make Harry change his mind without making it seem like I was refusing to cooperate. "You think it's safe for me out here?"

He looked around. The houses were old and tired, with peeling paint and broken windows. A rat darted out from beneath a pile of broken crates, splintered pieces of wood, and books that must be there for the residents to use to fuel their stoves. My stomach tied into a small knot at the sight of the books, some with their spines bent, and others missing their covers altogether. While the court was currently empty, if a resident returned and saw me unaccompanied, they might think me fair game. I wore a nice day dress that marked me as someone worth robbing.

"We'll go in together," Harry conceded.

He pushed open the door while I looked up at the windows of the buildings surrounding us on three sides. Nobody watched on.

We slipped inside. Women's voices came from the depths of the building. A baby cried and another took up the same tune in response. The noise covered the sound of the creaking steps as we climbed the stairs.

If the patron in The George was telling the truth, West had rented the first room off the landing on the second floor. The door was unlocked. Harry checked inside before ushering me through.

The man at the pub hadn't lied about Jack West leaving. The room was empty, except for a stained mattress on a rickety bed, a dirty washbasin on a stand, and a dented kettle sitting on a portable gas stove. The acrid smell of smoke filled the small room, and perhaps explained why the wall near the bed was stained brown. A chipped bowl on the windowsill overflowed with cigarette butts. It was the only evidence that someone had lived there until recently.

Or so I thought.

Harry spotted something on the floor under the bed. He reached under and drew out a photograph. It must have fallen out of a pocket and been left behind. The photograph was taken at the beach, and all six men in it wore trousers and shirts with their sleeves and trouser legs rolled up. Their feet were bare, as if they'd just dipped their toes into the water. All the men, aged in their early twenties, scowled at the photographer.

Harry pointed to the man standing in the middle. "West."

Closer inspection proved him right. It was Jack West, without his beard. The photograph must have been taken years ago. I didn't recognize any of the other men, but something struck me about their forearms.

"They all have the same markings on their skin," I said, pointing to West's forearm. "Is it a rash? Scars?"

"A tattoo. Five dots arranged in a cross, one dot for each point and one in the center."

"You seem quite familiar with it. You've seen it before?"

"I have," he said, sounding ominous. "There was an infamous criminal gang from the East End where every member got a tattoo like this on their forearm. I was young then, but I knew to steer clear of them."

"What happened to them?"

"I think they disbanded. Some members probably died, others went to prison. That's most likely what happened to West. The conductor told us he suspected West hadn't worked on the railways for years. What if the reason for that was because he'd been in jail?"

"And just came out," I murmured.

Harry tucked the photograph into his pocket. "I don't see how this relates to the murder of Ruth. Even if she somehow learned about his past, she wouldn't care. It's hardly newsworthy. Neither she nor Mrs. Scoop would bother writing about the criminal past of a railway employee."

I looked past him to the windowsill and the bowl filled with the used ends of cigarettes. "You're right. Ruth wouldn't care. But she *would* be interested in his associate who *did* have a reputation to lose."

"You know who it is, don't you?"

"Not for certain, but I have a strong inkling. Come on. It's getting late and we still have a lot of work to do."

CHAPTER 15

$\mathscr{H}$arry and I made it outside without being spotted by any of the tenement's occupants. The moment we set foot in the court, however, he peppered me with questions.

"Did West kill Ruth?"

"I think so, but he didn't act alone."

"Who helped him? And why?"

Movement in the pile of firewood caught my eye. A rat darted out before disappearing among the broken crates and books. There was one piece of evidence that, if found, would be damning enough for prosecutors to use against Jack West. And I suspected it was hiding in the rat-infested pile.

Harry was growing impatient. "Are you going to tell me, or do I have to guess?"

"I'll tell you. But first, you have to fish out all the journals and notebooks you can find in there."

He looked at the pile. He looked back at me. "You're not going to help?"

"I would, but I have a mortal fear of vermin."

"Mortal?"

I gave him a little shove toward the pile. "I will cheer you on from the sidelines."

"And if I get bitten by something and catch a disease?"

"You're wearing gloves. Besides, this is your chance to impress me with your bravery."

He looked at the pile again. Then he sighed. "You modern women are hard to please. I remember when ladies preferred flowers."

"I doubt you've ever bothered with flowers, Harry. A smile and a wink would have most women swooning."

He tilted his head to the side and regarded me. "Do you want me to do this or not?" He didn't wait for an answer but strode up to the pile with all the determination of a knight charging into battle. He didn't ask me what he was looking for. He already knew.

He picked up some books only to discard them again after reading the first page. There were more books poking out from beneath some rags. He took a piece of wood and used it to remove the rags one by one. Something scurried out near his foot only to disappear again.

If it had happened to me, I would have screamed. Harry simply worked faster.

At last, he brandished a soft leather-bound volume.

"My hero," I said, accepting it from him.

He threw the piece of wood back on the pile. The noise startled an entire family of rats that scurried out before returning to their home. "I deserve a kiss for that."

"I'm not going anywhere near you, Harry. You've been inches from rat-infested rubbish."

I flipped open the journal, thankful that I also wore gloves. Ruth Price's name appeared in neat writing on the inside front cover above the address for *The Evening Bulletin*. She'd written the date at the top of each page and noted times down the side followed by an observation.

I continued to turn the pages. "It's a timeline of her days and what she saw or heard in relation to her various investigations." I stopped at the last written page. It was dated the day she arrived in Brighton, which was the same day Beecroft arrived. The following pages had been torn out.

I swore under my breath. "This was supposed to prove West's guilt."

Harry looked back at the tenement building. "West would have destroyed any pages with his name on them. Finding this here proves *he* took it from her. He's guilty. Well done, Cleo."

"Thank you." I held the book out to him. When he didn't take it, I added, "It was very sweet of you to look through the rubbish for me."

He accepted the book with an arch look to say he saw through my attempt to charm him into holding on to the filthy journal.

A hard-faced woman with no teeth emerged from the tenement carrying a broom. She shook it at us. "Who're you and what do you want?"

"Do you know where we can find Jack West?"

"I do not, but if you find 'im, tell 'im I want what he owes me for the room." She shouted a colorful string of names for West, some of which were new to me.

We headed out of the court, and I finally told Harry my theory as we walked to the main road to catch an omnibus. "I think Jack West killed Ruth after she learned he'd been in jail. I think he did it because she learned he and Beecroft were in the same gang. If there's a tattoo with five dots forming a cross on Beecroft's forearm, we can prove it."

"If there is, then Scotland Yard just need witnesses who saw Beecroft and West together on the train from London to Brighton to prove they met."

Harry was following along without me having to explain that Beecroft must have caught the train to Brighton on which West worked as a conductor. "They may not have spoken on the train or at the station. It may have happened later. The hotel porter said Beecroft was worried someone was watching him. It must have been Jack West, having followed him from Brighton Station. Ruth saw and grew curious, so she investigated and overheard them talking like old acquaintances. Beecroft probably used his Cockney accent. Ruth probably saw West's tattoo then and there, but only saw Beecroft's when he went swimming. She knew it meant they were in a gang together, and telephoned Mrs. Scoop from the pharmacy to inform her."

"Either Beecroft or West realized she was spying on them," Harry went on. "Beecroft became anxious, since he has far more to lose. He knew his wife, Mrs. Scoop, wouldn't print anything incriminating about him, but he probably worried Ruth would feed the information to another paper."

Harry lengthened his strides, only to slow them when he realized I couldn't keep up. "It doesn't quite explain everything, however. Having this journal in his possession proves West took it from Ruth, probably before pushing her out of the window. He likely strangled her until she lost consciousness beforehand, hence the mark on her neck."

"But?"

"But why would West kill for Beecroft?"

"Money. Beecroft hired him as some sort of assassin."

"It's a risk."

"Gang members can have a strong code of loyalty. Perhaps West wanted to protect his friend."

"I agree he wanted to protect someone," Harry said. "But I'm not convinced it's Beecroft. It could be Geraldine. Or Mrs. Scoop. Perhaps he knew her well, too. Perhaps she was also in the gang. He might even have been in love with her."

I shook my head. While I couldn't imagine Mrs. Scoop loving anyone, that wasn't the reason I dismissed her as West's co-conspirator. "I think it's Beecroft. He doesn't smoke."

"Pardon?"

"When I found out Beecroft was in fact Blaine, and married to Mrs. Scoop, I noticed she didn't smoke around him, even though I could tell she wanted to. There was also no smell of cigarette smoke in their sitting room."

"Ah. Now I see." Harry shook his head and huffed a disbelieving laugh. "Jack West smokes. The day we first went to the Laneway Theater, Beecroft ran from the stage to his office when he saw us. When we caught up to him, he made up an excuse about believing us to be debt collectors. He started smoking. Correction. He was holding a cigarette. I don't recall him actually taking a puff."

"I don't think he did either. He wanted us to believe it was his cigarette tin, because it was evidence that Jack West was in that office, waiting for him, and he knew it. He fled when he saw us, told West to hide in his closet because he knew we were on his heels, but West left the tin on the desk, so Beecroft took a cigarette from it to make us believe it was his."

"West was hiding in there the entire time," Harry added with a shake of his head.

An omnibus rumbled down the road. Harry took my hand and set off at a run to catch it. Once on board, we took our seats.

I flapped a hand in front of my hot face. "Is this even going in the right direction? I didn't notice the sign."

"I did." Harry smiled. "It goes past the Laneway Theater."

I smiled, too. "Excellent."

* * *

THE STAFF WOULDN'T LET us into the theater. It was a little over two hours before the actors were due on stage and they were adamant that we couldn't enter without a ticket. Neither bribery nor charm worked, and the box office had sold out. There were no seats available for the evening's production.

Harry tried to convince me it was for the best. "If we go charging in, Beecroft might flee. West certainly would if he was hiding here. We'll contact Scotland Yard and tell Fanning everything we know. There's enough evidence to encourage him to reopen the case."

"You have more faith in Fanning than I do. Besides, it's late. He has probably gone home for the day. We have to strike tonight. If West is still in the city, he won't be for long."

Harry indicated the two men guarding the closed theater doors. "And how do you propose we get inside?"

I sighed. He was right. It was hopeless. We had no choice but to rely on D.S. Fanning.

We found a public silence cabinet at a nearby pharmacy. Harry telephoned Scotland Yard, only to hang up the receiver without speaking to Fanning. "He has left for the day." He picked up the receiver again and asked the operator to put him through to Ealing. Few homes were equipped with telephones, but Harry's father, a former detective inspector, had wanted to be contactable at all hours so had one installed. It was very convenient.

I listened as Harry told D.I. Hobart why we wanted to speak to Fanning. After he hung up, he said his father didn't know where we could find the sergeant. "But some of his former colleagues might," Harry added. "He's going to make some inquiries. My mother wants me to join them for dinner, so I'll go there now and he should have an address for Fanning by the time I arrive."

It was the best we could do, but felt woefully inadequate given our main suspect could already be beyond reach.

We parted, with Harry heading for a railway station to catch a train to Ealing, and me walking back to the Mayfair Hotel. I couldn't stop thinking about Harry's theory that something was amiss. West had no reason to kill Ruth. *Beecroft* did. Yet we'd found the journal at West's place. Was Beecroft trying to implicate West? If so, he must have assumed we would find out about West's past and look there.

I was so distracted by my thoughts that I barely registered that Frank wasn't manning the door until it closed behind me. His shift must have finished. Goliath's, too, as he was nowhere in sight. Peter was still on duty, however, as was Mr. Hobart. The manager handed something to a couple I recognized as having arrived the day before from Russia. They thanked Mr. Hobart for finding them tickets to a popular play. The lady even called him a miracle-worker considering the production was due to start soon.

I smiled to myself. Harry and I had overlooked one of our greatest assets.

When the guests departed, I approached Mr. Hobart. "Please, please tell me you can get tickets for tonight's production at the Laneway Theater."

"Beecroft's latest? Of course. How many do you need?"

I could have hugged him. "Two."

His lips curved into a slow smile. "Is the second ticket for Harry?"

Oh dear. He was making an assumption that everyone who saw Harry and I together at the theater would make. It wasn't an assumption I wanted made. "Can you get me four tickets?"

Mr. Hobart's smile slipped a little. "Of course, Miss Fox."

"Are my cousins in the hotel, do you know?"

"I believe so. Shall I send the tickets up to your suite?"

"Thank you. Oh, and can you also telephone your brother? Harry is heading there now. If you could pass on a message, telling him I'll leave his ticket at the box office."

Mr. Hobart performed a shallow bow.

"You're a marvel," I said.

I took the stairs to the fourth floor and knocked on Flossy's door. When she answered, I told her to dress for the theater.

"But I've sent my maid away," she whined.

"I'll help you dress and you can help me. I'll return in a few minutes. I have to find Floyd."

She pulled a face. "Is he coming with us?"

"We need a chaperone, and I don't think your mother is up to it."

"Can't you be my chaperone? You're old enough and..." She waved off what she was about to say.

"No one is interested in a bluestocking who has been on the shelf as long as I have?"

Flossy bit the inside of her lip and gave a little shrug.

If I wanted to find a husband, I would have been offended. Instead, I laughed. "You need a chaperone because I might not be with you the entire time. Floyd will do nicely."

"Why?"

"Because he—" I cut myself off before I blurted out that he would keep my secret if I kept his. Flossy would insist on knowing what those secrets were. "Because he's family," I said instead.

I found Floyd in his suite with Harmony. She sat at the desk, a ledger open in front of her. Floyd lounged on the sofa, yawning. Harmony looked relieved to see me.

"I'm sorry for interrupting your meeting," I said.

Floyd sat up, swinging his feet to the floor. "You haven't."

"She has," Harmony corrected him. "But you might be able to help us, Cleo. Mr. Bainbridge is refusing to speak to Mrs. Hessing about the supplier problem, and the wedding is tomorrow!"

Floyd sighed. "The suppliers have all supplied, Harmony. Everything is in place. They won't back out now. I don't see the problem."

"The problem is, they're furious their prices haven't been agreed upon by Mrs. Hessing. They know she won't pay. I know it, too. She'll leave the country, and we'll have to foot the bill or see the hotel's reputation ruined. They won't work with us again if we don't."

"There are always other suppliers who will."

Harmony looked like she wanted to say more, but I suspected she held herself back. She appealed to me with a flash of her eyes.

It was time to pull out all the stops, and I knew something that might convince Floyd to act. Something Harmony would never dare say to him. "Your father won't trust you to take on another event again, Floyd. Is that what you want?" For one sickening moment, I thought that might be his plan.

But he flinched as if the notion pained him. He rubbed his jaw. "All right. I'll pay the suppliers from the hotel's account first thing in the morning. That will tide them over and ensure they don't speak ill of the hotel."

"And then you'll convince Mrs. Hessing to pay back the hotel?" I prompted.

"I'll try." He did not sound confident.

I checked the time on my watch. I needed to get ready. "Floyd, you're coming to the theater with Flossy and me tonight."

"Is something good showing, or is it a musical comedy?"

"I've heard it's excellent."

He pushed himself to his feet. "All right, then. I'll order something to eat and meet you in the foyer in an hour."

* * *

HARRY DIDN'T SLIP into the spare seat beside me until after the curtain had risen.

"You made it," I whispered.

"It was a scramble. Luckily my mother kept some of my old clothes or I would have had to come in what I've been wearing all day. They still fit although there's a small moth hole in the jacket sleeve." He removed his top hat so the person behind him could see. "I borrowed this from my father."

Seated on my other side, Floyd cleared his throat.

Harry leaned forward to peer past me and nodded a greeting. Floyd responded in kind. While Harry had helped Floyd escape a difficult situation that started Floyd on the road to cleaning himself up, he still didn't like Harry overmuch. The employer-employee divide was too wide. Harry had worked at the hotel for so long that Floyd couldn't take the leap across the divide and accept him as an equal. They probably wouldn't get along anyway. Floyd oozed privilege from every pore. He was lazy and irresponsible. Harry was his opposite in almost every way.

"I see you brought the cavalry," Harry whispered to me. "Worried about being alone with me in a dark theater?"

"That is not appropriate talk from a gentleman. And shhh. I want to watch the show."

Harry settled into his seat and remained silent, but Floyd did not. "You shouldn't have invited him, Cleo."

"We're working," I whispered.

"I don't care. It's sending out a certain signal."

"To whom? I don't recognize anyone in the vicinity."

"Not to anyone in the audience. To Armitage."

"He knows where I stand on that particular matter."

"That won't stop him from trying. We'll swap seats at interval. I'll sit between you."

We didn't swap seats because I didn't return to my seat after the interval and neither did Harry. While Flossy and I took care of the necessaries in the lady's room, I informed her that I was meeting one of the actresses backstage to discuss my investigation, and Harry was helping me. She was tasked with telling Floyd. I suggested she wait until the curtain rose on the second act to give him as little opportunity as possible to protest.

It was remarkably easy to enter the backstage area. The crew were too busy to notice us, and the cast were either on stage or in the wings. The locked door of Beecroft's office gave Harry no difficulty. He had it unlocked in moments.

Inside, he wordlessly indicated I should stay back. He then opened the door to the closet. It was empty except for costumes. There was no sign of Jack West. There was no sign of cigarettes, either, not even a lingering smell. If West had been there recently, he hadn't smoked.

We sat and waited. When we heard the audience applause, Harry took his position against the wall near the door, so that when Beecroft entered, he didn't see Harry until Harry had blocked the exit.

Beecroft was trapped. "What is the meaning of this?" he bellowed.

Before I could answer, Geraldine Lacroix appeared. She was breathing heavily after her exertions on the stage, but smiled, too. Performing made her happy. Her smile disappeared when she saw Beecroft looking so anxious.

Before Harry could send her away, I invited her inside. I had a notion that she might prove useful.

"Is everything all right, Clem?" she asked.

"No, it bloody well isn't. Go and fetch a couple of toughs to get rid of these two."

"You'll want to stay," I told her. "You'll want to hear how your lover is an accessory to murder."

She gasped and clutched her throat. "Clem?"

"I didn't murder that woman!" Beecroft cried. "She jumped off the train."

Harry closed the door. "Miss Fox said you're an accessory."

Beecroft removed a handkerchief from his pocket and dabbed at his sweating forehead. He smeared the stage makeup in the process, getting some of it in his hair. "It's nothing to do with me."

"You were involved," I said. "We can prove it."

He snorted, but the flicker of fear in his eyes gave him away. "This is absurd. I want a solicitor."

"You can have one when you talk to the police. They'll be here soon."

"You have nothing on me. Nothing!"

I turned to his lover. "Geraldine, I once told you that his name is really Clement Blaine, not Beecroft."

She lifted a bare shoulder. She still wore the costume of a rather scantily clad temptress that revealed quite a lot of décolletage. "What of it?"

"Clement didn't change his name and accent to start a new career. He changed his name because of a criminal past."

Geraldine's eyes flared, before she shrugged again. "I know he's not a saint, but he never hurt me. He's been a thorough gentleman."

I finally turned to Beecroft, who was now sweating

profusely in the warm office. "You know Jack West. You recognized each other on the London to Brighton express."

"Who?" Geraldine asked.

"The conductor who threw Ruth Price out of her compartment after rendering her unconscious."

Geraldine paled as a shiver racked her.

Harry removed his jacket and placed it around her shoulders.

Beecroft lifted his chin. With his nose in the air, he sniffed. The confident, aloof pose was put on for our benefit, but the sweating betrayed him. "I don't know anyone by that name. I don't recall the conductor."

I ignored his denials. I'd expected them. My explanation was partly for Geraldine's benefit, anyway. I suspected she had information that would prove useful. It was also partly to stall until the police arrived. If, in fact, Harry's father had convinced D.S. Fanning to come.

"Jack West followed you to your hotel in Brighton," I went on. "Ruth Price happened to be staying there, too. That was most unfortunate for you, because she had a nose for a good story. She recognized you upon your arrival, and noticed you anxiously glancing around. She then spotted Jack West and became curious as to why he followed you, and why you were worried about him."

"This is absurd," Beecroft muttered. "You have no way of knowing any of that."

"That's because you know Jack West destroyed the evidence in her journal. But I'll get to that in a moment. Ruth discovered you and West knew each other by listening in to your conversation over the telephone and when you met him."

Beecroft scoffed. "You have nothing on me."

"After discovering the truth about your past and your connection to a convicted felon, Ruth telephoned Mrs. Scoop in London to tell her she had an incredible story for her to print. But when Mrs. Scoop heard it involved her husband, she wasn't interested."

Geraldine flinched ever so slightly at the mention of her married lover's wife.

"Mrs. Scoop couldn't expose your past in her column," I

went on. "She told Ruth to forget what she'd seen and heard, but Ruth knew the story was too big to simply let go."

"What story? That I came from an East End slum and once knew a convicted felon named Jack West?" Beecroft dabbed his handkerchief across his forehead. "There's nothing in that, Miss Fox."

"I agree. It's not enough. Not for Ruth Price to say she had an incredible story that must be printed, nor for Jack West to murder her on your behalf. That's why we believe there's more."

He laughed, loudly. Too loudly. I must have been on the right path.

"You hid Jack West in here." I indicated the closet. "He was hiding in here that first day we spoke to you. You pretended to smoke, but it was *his* cigarette. *You* don't smoke."

Geraldine didn't correct me, so I assumed I was right.

"Why would I hide him?" Beecroft cried. "I wouldn't hide someone simply because we knew each other years ago."

"Perhaps he told you that you owed him," I went on. "He'd murdered her for you, after all, to stop her selling the story of your shadowy past to another paper."

Beecroft merely scoffed again, but Geraldine's attention was now riveted. "What past? Clem, what did you do?"

"He was in the same gang as Jack West." It was a leap, but not a very large one. Beecroft confirmed it with the slight pinching of his lips, followed by a vehement albeit belated denial.

I was prepared to let him rant, but Harry wasn't.

"Enough," he growled. "If you weren't in West's gang, roll up your sleeves."

Beecroft spluttered an excessive refusal. He had a tendency to overact when he was trying to hide something.

Geraldine clutched Harry's jacket tightly closed at her throat. "Why do you want him to roll up his sleeves?"

"Members of a particular gang have a tattoo on their forearm," Harry said. "Five dots, arranged in the shape of a cross."

She gasped, only to slap a hand over her mouth to smother it.

Beecroft gave a quick shake of his head at her. He tried to be subtle, but I saw it. If she saw it, too, she chose to ignore him. Geraldine was no longer his ally. She realized his downfall was imminent and it would be spectacular. She didn't want to be dragged down with him. "He has the same tattoo on his left arm. My god, Clem. You lied to me. You told me you had nothing to do with her death, and that the police were simply overreacting to her suicide." She sidled closer to Harry. "He asked me to lie for him and tell you I saw that thug pass my compartment window. I didn't! I didn't see anyone."

"Because you fell asleep," I said. She'd not even noticed Alistair McAllister leave.

She nodded. "Clem told me people would try to blame either him or me, because we're famous, and the press would love knocking us off our perch. We couldn't vouch for each other, because we weren't in the same compartment, but we could throw suspicion onto someone else."

"An innocent man," Harry growled.

She edged away from him, blinking in surprise at his harsh tone. "He looked the most likely," she muttered.

Beecroft folded his arms, as if he expected Harry to force his sleeves up to expose the tattoo. "You're making all this up. If the conductor is guilty, it's nothing to do with me. You can't prove anything."

"Perhaps not yet," I said. "But when West is found, he'll talk. He won't want to take the entire blame for you."

"For me! Ha!" He snapped his jaw shut and turned away.

Had he been about to tell us that West had murdered Ruth for more selfish reasons, perhaps to protect himself, not Beecroft?

That niggling feeling that we were missing something grew stronger.

Someone pounded on the door. "Scotland Yard! Open up!"

Harry opened the door. "It was unlocked," he told D.S. Fanning.

Fanning threw back his shoulders and marched inside. "Armitage, isn't it? Hobart's son? He telephoned me and told me to come here and arrest a suspect." He glanced between

Geraldine and Beecroft. "You'd better tell me what's going on."

Fifteen minutes later, the constables D.S. Fanning had brought with him locked Clement Beecroft in their vehicle.

Fanning tucked the journal Harry had given him into his pocket and asked us to join him the following morning at Scotland Yard. "There's something I want to tell you."

"Tell us now," Harry said.

"My wife will murder me. It's our anniversary. Besides, it can wait until tomorrow."

"It has to be early," I told them. "I have a wedding to attend."

Speaking of being metaphorically murdered by one's family, Floyd glared daggers at me while Flossy sat in one of the chairs lining the wall, studying her fingernails. Except for two cleaners sweeping the floor, the foyer was otherwise empty. The show had finished some time ago and the audience had vacated the theater.

Floyd approached us, frowning. "Cobbit is waiting."

"Don't be frosty," I said. "We're coming."

Floyd pointed at me. "Just you." He pointed at Harry. "Not him."

"Don't be childish. We're giving Harry a ride home."

Harry put his jacket on, having accepted it when Geraldine returned to her dressing room. "It's a pleasant evening. I'll walk."

Floyd continued to scowl all the way to the carriage, where he assisted Flossy then me up the step to the cabin. "You should have told me the reason for coming tonight, Cleo."

"You wouldn't have approved. In fact, you probably would have tried to stop me."

"I'm not my father. If you want to investigate a murder, go ahead. Just be careful."

"It's not the investigation you wouldn't have approved of. It's Harry's presence."

He climbed in after me and closed the door. "He's not suitable for you."

I lurched with the forward momentum of the carriage.

"Would you rather come with me when I confront a potential murderer? Or shall I do it alone?"

He turned to the window, ending the conversation.

I turned to the other window and released a long breath. My part in the investigation was over. Now that Scotland Yard were involved, they could search for Jack West. First thing tomorrow morning, I'd hear what Fanning had to say. Then I'd enjoy the wedding. It was going to be a marvelous day.

CHAPTER 16

Detective Sergeant Fanning looked tired. He told Harry and me that he'd arrived before dawn to work on the investigation. I felt little sympathy for him. If he'd started investigating when I'd first suggested Ruth may have been murdered, maybe he wouldn't be scrambling now.

We sat at his desk, a file opened between us and him. He shuffled through the papers until he found a series of photographs. "First things first. I asked for the body to be exhumed and for an autopsy to be carried out."

I reached for the photographs. "You did? When?"

"After Miss Price's beau came to see me. He was very convincing when he explained why he didn't think she would kill herself." He looked at the photographs still in his hand and passed them to Harry. "A lady shouldn't see these."

I didn't bother to argue with him. I simply moved my chair closer to Harry and studied the photographs, too. All three clearly showed the ligature mark and bruising around Ruth's neck.

"The coroner says she was strangled," Fanning went on. "Her neck was fractured. The injury wasn't fatal, however. The amount of blood at the site where the body was recovered suggests the fall killed her."

"Strangulation cut off her airway and rendered her unconscious," Harry murmured as he handed back the photographs.

"Correct. That's why she didn't scream as she fell." Fanning returned the photographs to the file. "I wanted to tell you myself, in person, since you helped me capture West's accomplice."

"We didn't *help* you," I said. "We did the entire thing."

Fanning glanced around to see who'd overheard, but I'd made sure to keep my voice low. Most of the policemen would already know that we'd driven this investigation, not Fanning, but it wouldn't help us in the future if we publicly rubbed his nose in his incompetence.

"Speaking of Blaine, there's a development on that front, too." Fanning looked pleased with himself. "I did some research in our old files early this morning and found out that Clement Blaine was convicted of a robbery fifteen years ago, along with another member of his gang."

"Jack West," I said.

"Jack *Wilson*." He sifted through the papers again and removed a photograph of a prisoner. It was a beardless Jack West. "He changed his name when he was released a few months ago, probably to hide his identity in case a potential employer dug too deeply into his past. He got a job as a conductor easily since he knew what to do. He was working as a conductor at the time of his arrest, you see. The Manchester police got him after a tip-off from Scotland Yard. Guess who told our boys where to find him."

"Clement Blaine," Harry said with a wry smile. "He grassed up his former friend. No wonder he was afraid of West when he saw him again after all these years. He suspected West would retaliate."

"He's lucky to be alive," I added.

Fanning pointed at me. "I reckon there's a reason why West didn't kill him. You see, Blaine got a much shorter sentence from the judge after laying the blame for the robbery on his more senior partner, Wilson. But the stolen property was never recovered."

He showed us a report on the original robbery, where a large sum of money had been stolen from a train. It was being transported to the Manchester branch of a London-based bank, but had never made it. Evidence led them to arrest Clement Blaine, but the police had always suspected he had the help of an insider from the railway. Blaine gave them Jack Wilson's name during an interrogation.

"I've spent some time questioning Blaine this morning," Fanning said. "He hasn't told me where to find either the money or Wilson. I'll keep trying."

Harry told him it would do no good. "I doubt he knows where Wilson is. As to the money, it's probably all spent."

"It is," I said. "The missing money is the key to everything. It's why Jack West killed Ruth. He murdered her to protect Beecroft's—Blaine's—reputation, just as we suspected, Harry. But not out of a sense of loyalty or because Beecroft is, or was, his friend. He did it because Beecroft is the one who has all the money now. Beecroft spent what they stole after he got out of jail to reinvent himself as an actor and impresario."

Fanning sat forward. "You mean he used it to put on plays?"

"It's a costly endeavor. I'd never quite believed him when he said he simply worked hard as an actor and saved enough to convince the bank to give him a loan."

"Banks want proof of identity," Harry agreed. "If there's any doubt, they hire private detectives to investigate. They also want collateral and a solid foundation already in place in which to grow their investment. They don't loan money to just anybody." It sounded like he was speaking from experience.

Fanning glanced over his shoulder to the corridor that led to the interview rooms. I suspected Beecroft was in one of them, or had been, earlier. "Wilson was blackmailing him?"

"In a way, yes," I said. "He must have demanded money in some form or other from Beecroft. Either an outright payment, or proceeds from his plays, perhaps."

Fanning nodded slowly. "So, if the story about Beecroft's past got into the newspapers, his reputation would be ruined. Theater managers would refuse to house his plays, no one would work for him, and Wilson's source of funds would vanish."

"Precisely." I removed my watch from my waistcoat pocket and checked the time. "I'm afraid I must go. Thank you for inviting us to hear your side of the investigation, Detective."

Fanning stood and tugged on his jacket hem to straighten it. "My pleasure, Miss Fox. And may I say, good work." This last part he said to Harry.

Harry pointed his hat at me. "It was all Miss Fox." He placed his hat on his head. "And you know it, Detective. It's time you admit she's brilliant."

Fanning turned pink as he peered along the corridor. "I believe I'm wanted in the interrogation room."

We saw ourselves out.

It was a perfect day for a wedding, but I needed to get back to the hotel quickly to change my outfit. Harry signaled for a cab to wait as its passengers alighted onto the pavement. We climbed on board, and Harry gave the driver the name of the hotel.

I settled on the seat. "Thank you for defending me, but we both know it wasn't all me. I couldn't have done it without you, Harry."

He nodded sagely. "True."

I laughed.

"Does this mean you're going to continue to work with me?" he asked. "There'll be no more little tantrums in which you attempt to keep your distance?"

He could be very direct when he wanted to be. He knew me well enough to know it wouldn't upset me. "If you want to work with me again, calling my very reasonable doubts tantrums won't work."

"Your doubts weren't based on reason, Cleo. They were based on fear."

"I'm not afraid of you, nor of my reputation as a detective being overshadowed by yours."

"I know."

It was best if I didn't press him for his opinion further. I knew that he knew I was afraid of getting too close to him. If he told me as much, I could no longer pretend my feelings for him had nothing to do with my fear.

"No more keeping our distance *if* we work on an investigation together that satisfies my uncle's requirements," I clarified. "We got away with it this time because he believes we're still looking for Mrs. Hessing's gossip columnist."

"I'm not afraid of Sir Ronald."

"Nor am I. But I am aware that I live under his roof. I have to respect his wishes until such time as I can afford to move out of the hotel."

His hand had been resting on his thigh, which was almost touching mine. It now curled into a fist. "Cleo—"

"Don't, Harry. Let's just enjoy the glow that comes with successfully solving a case."

Neither of us spoke for the rest of the journey.

****

THE MAYFAIR HOTEL'S foyer was almost too calm, considering the wedding reception was mere hours away. I'd expected frantic staff running hither and thither, arguments with suppliers, and the mother-of-the-bride making demands in a shrill voice. But everyone was smiling as they went about their business. Mr. Hobart and Peter were absent, however. Goliath informed me that all the senior staff were in a meeting.

Not only was the foyer calm, but so was the fourth floor where the bride was getting ready. I changed my outfit with Jane's help. The pastel blue trimmed with white lace and beads arranged in a wavy pattern at the hem and across my décolletage flattered my figure. It wasn't too frilly, and the beading gave it a summery seaside effect. Jane used tongs to turn the loose strands of my hair into curls. She was pleased with how they looked and declared me ready with a clap of her hands. I asked her to inform Flossy that I'd wait for the family in the foyer, then I took the lift down.

The foyer was no longer calm.

There was some confusion over who was using the hotel carriages—the Bainbridge family or the bridal party. Peter tried to sort that out, while Mrs. Short and Mr. Chapman directed delivery men wheeling carts filled with flowers into the ballroom. Mr. Chapman looked rattled, probably because the delivery was late, and Mrs. Short looked annoyed. That could have been because the men should have taken the service entrance, not the front door, although annoyance was an expression never far from her face, so she may have been perfectly fine. Frank, holding the door open, merely shook his head.

Harmony and Mr. Hobart were in rather terse discussions with some men. A few guests not involved in the wedding stood idly by, looking somewhat confused. The poor clerk was attempting to check new arrivals in, but there was quite a queue at the desk, many of whom had no luggage. They were most likely already checked in and simply had the sort of questions that Mr. Hobart or Peter usually dealt with.

I introduced myself to the line of guests and asked if I could assist anyone. I fielded some questions about the routine of the hotel and gave directions to attractions. I handed out maps of the city and railway timetables, freeing up the check-in clerk to perform his main duty more efficiently.

I'd just finished noting down a name for dinner reservations that evening to pass on to Mr. Chapman when I spotted Mrs. Scoop enter the hotel. She paused beneath the central chandelier and looked around. Our gazes met.

I hurried toward her before she took too much notice of the chaos. "The press isn't welcome," I told her. "You'll receive official reports after the wedding to print as you see fit."

"I'm not interested in the wedding." Her gaze betrayed her, however. It darted about, taking in the harried staff and last-minute deliveries. It settled on the lift door. In a few moments, Miss Hessing would emerge through it wearing her wedding dress and clutching a bouquet of white roses.

"Then why are you here?" I asked.

"I visited my fool of a husband in the holding cell at the Yard. He told me all about his involvement with Jack Wilson, and the part he played in Ruth's death. I'd like to point out that he in no way encouraged Wilson to murder her."

"You knew your husband met Wilson in Brighton. Ruth telephoned you and urged you to print a story about them being in a gang together. Yet you said nothing to me about it."

"I didn't know he was the conductor on that train, and I certainly didn't know he murdered Ruth. Like you, I believed Clem when he told me that the man Ruth saw him speaking to was simply someone he knew years ago."

I scoffed. "Do you expect me to believe you didn't know your husband was in a criminal gang? Or that he was arrested and questioned over a train robbery?"

"I only became aware after the arrest. I'd just lost my baby and I wasn't particularly interested in his life. But I didn't connect that incident to the man Ruth saw him speaking to in Brighton."

If she was lying, she was a very good actress. "Have you come here to convince me of your innocence?"

She studied me coolly. "Why do I need to convince *you*, Miss Fox? I'm here because I think I know where Wilson is hiding."

"Where?"

"My husband keeps a flat in Pimlico. He takes his mistresses there. He thinks I don't know about it, but of course I do. I can't be absolutely sure, but I think you'll find Wilson hiding there."

"You do realize if he is, that means your husband helped him by giving him the key. It won't look good for him in court."

Her brittle laugh held no humor. "I no longer care. I'll be filing for divorce soon. I've had enough of Clem's behavior. This is merely the icing on the cake. I've known for a long time that we ought to part, but like most unpleasant things, I put it off. Now...well, I simply have no interest in protecting him anymore. I won't fall with him, Miss Fox. I've worked too hard to watch him burn it all down."

"You won't be able to escape this scandal entirely. Everyone will find out about your marriage."

"They will find out that Mrs. Blaine is divorcing her no-good husband. Mrs. Scoop will be safe. It's why I've never given anyone at the paper my real name, other than the solicitor who drew up my contract. Not even Finlayson knows." She withdrew a piece of paper from her bag and held it out to me. "This is the address of the flat."

"Why not give it to the police?"

"Because I think you want the accolades. Why let an idiot of a detective get all the glory when you did the work?" She shook the paper. "Take it. And take the glory that comes your way when the world finds out you solved Ruth's murder."

"If you're implying that the *Bulletin* will print my name in an article about the case, please ensure that doesn't happen. My family are aware of my investigations, but they would prefer I kept that part of my life private."

"Very well, if that's what you want." She must have realized I didn't quite trust her, because she tried to reassure me. "I give you my word, Miss Fox. That ought to be enough when you consider that I never told the police about you."

"Pardon?"

"Your name was on Ruth's list of people associated with this hotel who could potentially be swayed to talk about the wedding."

"Ruth was wrong. I wouldn't have talked."

"Didn't you say she also blackmailed you in Brighton, or was about to? Some would call that motive." She glanced at the lift again as the door opened, but lost interest when a couple of guests emerged, not Miss Hessing. "There will be an article about Ruth's murder in tonight's paper. Finlayson insists on it, now that there has been a development. I'll make sure your name is not mentioned."

I breathed a sigh of relief. "Thank you. You may print the name of Armitage and Associates instead. Harry Armitage worked with me every step of the way."

The columnist shook her head in disappointment. "You'll never get ahead if you give others credit. Particularly a man. Unless you own your investigations, you will never make a name for yourself, never attract clients or make any money. Take some advice from someone who had to fight in a man's world and won—take credit for your accomplishments, Miss Fox. Don't let your family's wish for a polite, discreet niece smother your dream. I didn't let my husband's wishes smother mine. Now I have my name on my own office door."

I'd once wanted my name alongside Harry's on his office door. I'd also wanted to have my own agency. I still did. But I didn't want to distance myself from my family in the process. Mrs. Blaine's relationship with her husband was probably in dire straits before she became Mrs. Scoop, but I didn't want to model my life on hers. Not a single part of it.

I read the address on the piece of paper. "I'll telephone Scotland Yard immediately."

She didn't leave, however. Her continuous glances at the lift told me why. I had an idea, but first, there was one more item of business to attend to.

"I noticed you haven't printed the story about Lord Pridhurst yet," I said.

"Finlayson won't allow it to run without further proof. I'd planned to get that proof from Ruth's journal, but it has disappeared."

I didn't tell her the police had it. She would find that out eventually, but not from me. "I have a proposal for you." I opened my bag and showed her the money Lady Pridhurst had slipped to me at afternoon tea. "I was tasked with giving you this in exchange for your paper dropping the story."

Mrs. Scoop hesitated. Then she reached for the money.

I drew the bag away and closed the clasp. "Instead, I have another idea. I'll allow you exclusive access to the wedding reception. You may observe discreetly. You may not speak to any guests."

Her breath hitched in excitement. "No other journalist will be allowed in?"

"Only you. Beginning from the moment Miss Hessing walks out of that lift."

Her sharp gaze shifted to the lift. "You have the authority to make this promise?"

"I do. However, there are some conditions, but I don't think you'll disagree to them. Firstly, you can only write favorable things."

She stiffened. "I write what I observe, Miss Fox. I won't be compromised."

I looked to Harmony and Mr. Hobart, just finishing tense discussions with suppliers. Harmony tucked her clipboard against her chest, a look of sheer determination on her face. Mr. Chapman hurried past on his way to the ballroom, his tie impeccably straight, a fresh rosebud pinned to his lapel, his hair perfect. He was the personification of a dapper gentleman with better taste than most women. Together with Mrs. Poole's cooking and management of the kitchen, I knew this team would ensure the wedding reception was a spectacular success.

"All right. You can write what you like, but I insist you

mention every single supplier by name, from the designer of Miss Hessing's dress to the florist and other decorations. I will provide you with a list before the end of the evening. And the *entire* column must be dedicated to the wedding. Those are the final conditions."

Mrs. Scoop thrust out her hand. I shook it.

She settled into one of the armchairs where she could see the lift door, and I approached Mr. Hobart and Harmony.

"Is that the gossip columnist, Mrs. Scoop?" Harmony asked, peering past me. "She shouldn't be here."

"I've allowed her exclusive access in exchange for a glowing report on the event in which she will mention every supplier."

Mr. Hobart pumped his fist in triumph. "Well done, Miss Fox. Mrs. Hessing will be glad to hear it. She has wanted to control what was written about the wedding all along, but knows how cruel the British press can be. You can reassure her now. Meanwhile, I'll inform Frank to be very careful about not letting in any more journalists. If Mrs. Scoop wants an exclusive, she'll get it."

I turned to Harmony to give her advice, but she had already realized the implications for her role. "I should be able to catch the suppliers before they leave. I'm sure they'll agree to a renegotiation if their businesses are mentioned in glowing terms in the city's most popular society pages."

"When you've done that, pass a list of suppliers to Mrs. Scoop," I told her.

Harmony smiled. "You look beautiful, by the way."

I clasped her hand. "Thank you."

Before Mr. Hobart departed, I asked if I could use his telephone. I placed a call to D.S. Fanning and gave him the address of the flat in Pimlico. On a whim, I tried Harry's office, too, but he wasn't there.

* * *

THE CHURCH CEREMONY WAS LOVELY. The happy couple stared into one another's eyes as they exchanged vows, then beamed as they left the church. I'd been one of the first guests to arrive at the church, so I didn't notice those who arrived after me.

Seeing Harry on the church steps as I left stopped me in my tracks. He always looked handsome, but there was something particularly alluring when he dressed in a tailcoat. He touched the brim of his hat in greeting but didn't approach. I kept my distance, too. My uncle would not approve of me chatting to his former employee at a social function. He hadn't seen Harry yet, but he would if Harry was returning to the hotel for the reception.

Mr. Liddicoat's polo-playing cousin joined Harry and the two men fell into conversation. Harry must be a guest of Mr. Liddicoat's, out of gratitude for clearing his cousin's name recently. I couldn't imagine Mrs. Hessing inviting a private detective she'd hired to her daughter's wedding. She was too much of a snob.

Some guests walked back to the hotel, but I climbed into one of the Mayfair's carriages along with my aunt, uncle and Flossy. Floyd had already returned to the hotel to be there to welcome the wedding guests when they arrived. The journey was short, but everyone was in a good mood. Even my aunt smiled, although it was wan and thin, like her figure. When we alighted from the carriage outside the hotel, she told us she needed to return briefly to her suite. I suspected she would take a dose of her tonic before joining us in the ballroom for the reception.

Uncle Ronald supported her through the front door, held open by Frank. Flossy followed close behind. I smiled at the doorman and was about to engage him in a chat about his favorite topic, the weather, when a figure rushed out of the shadows.

He grabbed my arm and shoved my back against the wall. The breath *whooshed* from my body, but thankfully I didn't hit my head.

The face of Jack Wilson filled my vision, lips twisted in a grimace within his unkempt beard. But it was his eyes that frightened me. The pupils were huge, making him look like a wild animal in the grip of a murderous fever. I'd seen eyes like that before, and knew it wasn't a fever that gripped him. It was cocaine.

CHAPTER 17

$\mathcal{J}$ack Wilson pressed himself against me. Trapped between him and the wall, I doubted anyone even noticed I was there. Had Frank seen him accost me? I didn't know. All I knew was that Wilson's hot, stinking breath made me want to throw up.

"Bloody meddling woman. If only you'd leave me be, I could have got what Blaine owed me and disappeared." He spoke rapidly, his words tumbling over themselves. It only confirmed what I suspected. He was under the control of cocaine, just like Aunt Lilian.

I tried to use my body to push him away, but he didn't budge. I tried to hit him, but he was too close, and my arms were pinned to my sides. I opened my mouth to scream.

I never got the chance to utter a sound.

Suddenly Wilson was gone, ripped away from me by Harry. Harry swung his fist, but Wilson tore free and ducked. The cocaine gave him unnatural speed and alertness. He punched Harry in the gut before Harry even knew what was coming. He grunted but remained upright and stepped out of Wilson's reach in case another punch came his way.

Harry realized he couldn't stop a cocaine-fueled man the size of Jack Wilson. He needed help. But Frank had disappeared, and the other gentlemen in the vicinity were reluctant to assist. Most crossed the street to avoid the scene.

I darted toward the hotel door to get help. Discretion be

damned. Mrs. Scoop, waiting inside for the reception to begin, would witness the dreadful scene and write about it in her column, but I didn't care. I couldn't let Harry battle Wilson alone.

The door was pushed open from the other side before I reached it. Goliath barreled out. Between the two of them, he and Harry subdued Wilson and marched him away from the hotel. Wilson struggled and shouted, only to suddenly quieten. I suspected either Harry or Goliath had punched him.

As quickly as the scene had erupted into chaos, it was calm again. The timing couldn't have been more perfect. The carriages carrying Mrs. Hessing and her friends, and Mr. Liddicoat and his bride, were arriving.

Frank had emerged from the hotel behind Goliath, holding Harry's hat. He must have fetched Goliath when Wilson appeared. He handed the hat to me, blew out a rallying breath, and opened the carriage door for the bride and groom.

Following his lead, I drew in a deep breath, too, and let it out slowly, releasing my tension along with it. I tucked the hat behind me and took the hand Mrs. Liddicoat offered.

"Oh, Miss Fox, you do look so lovely in that dress."

I laughed. "I believe you stole my line."

I took a step back to admire her in the cream satin wedding gown. It was demure and understated, like the bride herself, with pearls trimming the high chiffon neckline, the ruched sleeves and the edges of her long veil. The skirt and train were embroidered in a leafy pattern I'd not seen before. Perhaps it was from an American plant or was something the dressmaker invented. It looked so elegant, with incredibly fine stitching. Mrs. Scoop's readership would enjoy learning about this new trend, and the statuesque American who'd captured the heart of an Englishman.

"You are perfection, my dearest Mrs. Liddicoat."

She giggled. "The name sounds so strange."

Mrs. Hessing stamped the end of her walking stick on the pavement. "Hurry along, Clare. Your guests are waiting."

Mr. Liddicoat offered his arm to his bride. He smiled at me as I congratulated them and escorted her through to the hotel.

I looked in the direction Harry and Goliath had gone, but I didn't see them returning. Inside, I gave Harry's hat to the attendant in the luggage room, which doubled as a cloakroom, and made my way to the ballroom where the reception was being held. It used to be the hotel's restaurant before the new one had been built next door. It was an excellent space for grand functions to be held without forgoing the regular dinner service.

I paused just inside the ballroom entrance to take it all in. I'd been right. Mr. Chapman's eye, coupled with Harmony's management, had resulted in a display that made the guests gasp with wonder. The theme of a winter fairyland was unexpected yet delightful, given the August heat. Strings of small lights hung in swathes across the ceiling and wrapped around what appeared to be stalactites. I couldn't tell how they were made from where I stood, or how they managed not to fall off. There were dozens of trees and shrubs in white pots positioned close to the walls, their leaves dusted with artificial snow. More snow had been arranged in drifts, as if the wind had pushed it against the pots. Paths had been created between the drifts and led to the area set aside for dancing. All of the tables were covered in white tablecloths with the hotel's best silverware set out. The centerpieces were slender leafless white trees, each surrounded by a skirt of dozens of white roses. More strings of tiny bulbs dripped from the tree branches, like a bright wintry willow.

Where the wedding dress suited the bride's taste, the ballroom was decorated in her mother's, yet it wasn't loud. I suspected Mr. Chapman considered such an untraditional reception vulgar, but I found it to be ostentatious without being excessive. I spotted him speaking to the waiters before they entered the room with their trays laden with champagne glasses. In keeping with the theme, they all wore white jackets, except for Mr. Chapman.

Harmony appeared from the service area, too. She wore a blouse and skirt to differentiate her from the guests, but she'd done her hair in an elegant arrangement, and wore a pair of pearl-drop earrings that I'd loaned her. She saw me watching her and nodded. I nodded back, and would have joined her, but all the guests suddenly turned as the doors opened.

Mr. and Mrs. Liddicoat entered to rapturous applause.

When Harry arrived a while later, the last vestiges of the anxiety I'd felt since being accosted by Jack Wilson faded. He'd been placed at a table with Mr. Liddicoat's cousin. My family didn't notice him, until he came to our table when the dancing began. He greeted them politely.

Aunt Lilian and Flossy responded in kind, but Floyd scowled and Uncle Ronald seemed confused as to why Harry was there. Harry explained the connection.

"Broadman?" Floyd swiped up his wine glass. "I should've known you two would get along."

Uncle Ronald remained silent. It would seem he'd decided to live by the rule often touted by parents to their young children—if you don't have anything nice to say, don't say anything. He wasn't going to make a scene at the wedding. He'd probably store it up for later.

Harry arched a brow at me in question, asking if I was all right. I nodded. He didn't ask me to dance. The frosty reception from the Bainbridge men probably had something to do with that. It was a wise decision. I would have done the same thing in his shoes. It was quite all right with me. I enjoyed dancing with a variety of other gentlemen, and Harry wasn't short of partners either. If our glances happened to connect from time to time, it was purely coincidental. It meant nothing.

It was after a particularly vigorous polka that I resumed my seat next to my uncle. I picked up my fan and flapped it in front of my warm face.

"Look at him," my uncle said. "He belongs here."

I followed his gaze to Harry, dancing with a middle-aged American friend of Mrs. Hessing's. Uncle Ronald's statement rendered me quite speechless.

"Armitage is a natural with the guests," he went on. "He would have made a better manager than Hobart one day, if only he'd stayed."

It was something he'd said before, having conveniently forgotten the reason why Harry no longer worked at the hotel. This time, I didn't bother reminding him that he'd dismissed Harry from his position as assistant manager.

As the dance came to an end, I spotted Mrs. Hessing on

her own. Since I wanted to have a word with her, I excused myself.

Uncle Ronald caught my hand. "You're not going to dance with him, are you?"

"He hasn't asked me."

"Good." He frowned. "Did he come with the woman he's courting?" He looked around. "Have you met her? What does she look like? A tall beauty, I'd wager."

Miss Morris was a tall beauty, indeed, and very elegant. She'd also been wrong for Harry, or so he'd told me when he ended their relationship. None of which I was going to tell my uncle.

"I see Mrs. Hessing on her own. We can't have that."

He let me go to speak to one of his best guests.

I sat on the empty seat beside her. "May I talk to you for a moment, Mrs. Hessing?"

"It appears that you already are."

I nodded at Mr. and Mrs. Liddicoat, gazing into one another's eyes as they danced not far away. "I wish to congratulate you on the marriage of your daughter. They look very happy."

"They are young. They have no problems. But problems always arise."

Her poor attitude toward her daughter had been evident from the day I met them, but this time her bitterness astounded me. It was Clare's wedding day. She'd married a man who complemented her in every way. Could she not just be happy for her?

"You're right," I said. "Problems do always arise. But I think she has found someone who will help her through those problems, not make them worse."

She murmured a noncommittal, "Hmmm."

"When are you returning home, Mrs. Hessing?"

"Can't wait to get rid of me, Miss Fox?"

"Not at all," I lied. "I'm counting the days until you visit us again."

She narrowed her gaze at me, but there was a small uplift of her lips at the corners. Could it be that my caustic response amused her?

"I'm simply asking in the hope you'll be here long enough

to read about the wedding in the society pages." I'd seen Mrs. Scoop standing off to the side earlier, scratching notes in her journal. She must have left some time ago, however, as I hadn't seen her since.

"There won't be any reports," Mrs. Hessing said. "I scared the press away. I didn't want any negativity."

"In my experience, it's foolish to try to control journalists. Some are very clever. They blend in. Perhaps one got in here, despite our best efforts to keep uninvited guests out." I lifted a shoulder in a casual shrug. "We won't know until tomorrow. Or perhaps something will appear in tonight's evening editions."

She narrowed her gaze at me. "Is there something you wish to tell me, Miss Fox?"

"I'd like to request that you pay the suppliers before you leave, if their fees are lower than they originally quoted."

"How much lower?"

I smiled. "Mr. Bainbridge will discuss it with you tomorrow. He has been working very hard to make this a success. Miss Cotton, too, and the rest of the staff." I indicated the room. "I'm not sure what I was expecting, but this has exceeded anything I could imagine. Well done, Mrs. Hessing. The reception deserves an entire column in the city's leading society pages. Let's hope a journalist snuck in, despite our best efforts."

She hesitated. She seemed unsure whether I'd orchestrated something or not. She picked up her glass of wine and saluted me with it. "We shall see, won't we?"

I stood. "May I say, on behalf of my family, how much we have enjoyed having you and your daughter stay with us. I've made a new friend in Clare, and for that, I am grateful."

She lowered her glass, suddenly deflated, as if the fighting spirit she was famous for had suddenly vanished. Perhaps she was only now becoming aware that without her daughter, she would be returning home to an empty house, her only family half a world away.

After the bride and groom were farewelled to rousing applause, I fancied another dance. I looked around for a partner, only to realize Harry must have left. I decided to save my feet and not dance, after all.

My uncle insisted we stay until the end and all the guests had left. When Mrs. Hessing and her companions finally departed, we waited until the staff had gathered under Harmony's instruction. Floyd made a brief speech, praising his assistant, the cook and steward, and Uncle Ronald led a round of more applause.

As the waiters began cleaning up, my uncle escorted my aunt from the ballroom. I followed with my cousins either side of me. We made our way up the stairs while Aunt Lilian and Uncle Ronald took the lift. Flossy giggled for no particular reason, proving she was a little tipsy. Floyd was beyond tipsy and had reached the drunk phase. He tripped over a step, but instead of getting up, he sat down.

Flossy kicked off her shoes and sat down beside him. "How do you think they made the snow? It looked so real."

"Borax, water and soap," I said. "Castile soap, if I'm not mistaken. It's milder and makes a better consistency."

"How do you know?"

Floyd shushed her before I could answer. "She's a detective, and a bloody good one."

I sat on the step below them. "I scooped up some on my finger and tasted it."

Flossy fell about, giggling.

Floyd pushed himself to his feet and reached a hand down to each of us. "Come on, girls. Almost there."

We each took one of his hands and together the three of us continued up the stairs, slowly and carefully. I was still smiling when we reached the third-floor landing. Floyd wiped it away with what he said next, however.

"I'm glad to see you didn't dance with Armitage, Cleo. It wouldn't have been appropriate."

Flossy's objection saved me from voicing mine. "Don't be silly. He was there as a guest. It would have been perfectly acceptable for one of us to dance with him. It's a pity he didn't ask. Didn't he look dashing, Cleo?" She sighed dramatically.

It was time to change the subject. "Something has been on my mind ever since we returned from Brighton, and I want a proper answer this time."

They both looked at me, intrigued.

"Why don't you like sea bathing, Flossy? Is it because you don't want to get your hair wet? You can wear a cap, you know."

She released Floyd's arm and stormed up the stairs to the fourth floor where she spun around, hand on hip. "I don't know what you mean."

Floyd's chuckle began low in his chest, growing louder until it finally bubbled out of him. "She doesn't like it because when she was little and waded in up to her knees, something brushed against her leg. She screamed until her voice gave out. Everyone came running to rescue her. Father had to carry her out of the water like a baby. It turned out to be seaweed."

"Something *did* brush against my leg, and it *wasn't* seaweed. It swam away." She sniffed. "I don't see the point of sea bathing anyway. If I want to get wet, I can have a bath."

I told her I would make her go in with me next time. "The best way to get over your fear is to tackle it head-on."

"I am quite happy to live with my fear, if it means I get to keep all of my toes."

Floyd and I burst out laughing. After pouting for a few moments, Flossy joined in.

* * *

Mrs. Scoop's report on the wedding was everything I'd hoped it would be. She was effusive in her praise of every detail, from the suppliers to the venue and its decorations. Uncle Ronald was particularly pleased with the lines that said the event was 'beyond compare', and that the Mayfair Hotel was 'worthy of its reputation for faultless luxury'. He was so pleased that he even praised Floyd. The bonus he gave Harmony was very welcome, but it was his promise to let her manage future events that left her smiling for days afterward.

As I sat in the staff parlor with Harmony, Victor, Goliath and Frank, I had to explain how I'd manipulated Mrs. Scoop into giving her glowing review. I made a point of telling them that I'd simply *requested* she be favorable in exchange for exclusivity. I hadn't demanded it.

"She wanted to maintain her integrity and print the truth

as she saw it. Although I did stipulate that she had to mention each of the suppliers by name."

"A stipulation that paid off," Harmony said. "They agreed to lower their prices and Mrs. Hessing paid them this morning."

"Just in time before she checks out," Goliath added.

Frank grunted. "Good riddance. She smacked my leg with her walking stick the other day when I didn't open the door fast enough for her."

It wasn't just Mrs. Scoop's social pages that had us poring over the latest edition of *The Evening Bulletin*. Ruth Price's picture on the front page had been a little confronting when I first saw it, but the full-page article that accompanied it had me riveted. It gave the facts surrounding her murder, and the solving of it, mentioning Armitage and Associates on several occasions. My name was not in it, as I'd requested. The publicity should be good for Harry.

The remainder of the article was a heartfelt tribute to Ruth, the smart, vibrant young woman robbed of a bright future. The article read as though it had been written by someone who admired her greatly and knew her well. I didn't recognize the name in the byline, however.

Also left out of the article were the names of the other suspects. The Pridhursts would be relieved. Earlier that day, I'd met with Lady Pridhurst and Odette with the intention of returning the money they'd given me to bribe Mrs. Scoop. I'd informed them that I'd used other means to ensure their secret was safe, at least from Mrs. Scoop's pages. Lady Pridhurst insisted I keep the money.

Odette also informed me that she'd spoken to Mr. Holland and admitted everything. Mr. Holland was still considering his options, which I didn't think boded well for a happy future together, but I refrained from commenting.

Peter poked his head around the parlor door. "Miss Fox, you have a visitor. Shall I send him in?"

"I'll come out," I said rising.

I filed out of the parlor along with the other staff, who headed off to their respective areas of the hotel after their short break. I signed to Victor to wait a moment, however.

Once the others had left, I asked him how everything was with Harmony.

"I haven't seen much of her lately," he said. "She's been busy."

"Has that caused problems between you?"

"No. I just miss her."

I smiled. "You should tell her that."

"Regarding our discussion at the Ouse Valley Viaduct, I want you to know I've decided not to say anything to Harmony about the next stage of our relationship. I like things the way they are, and I think she does, too. Talking about next stages will ruin everything."

"If it makes you both happy, then you should maintain your own pace."

We parted ways, he heading to the kitchen and me to the foyer where I wasn't surprised to see Harry waiting for me. He had a copy of the latest edition of *The Evening Bulletin* under his arm. He showed me the front page and pointed to one of the lines that mentioned his agency.

"I believe I have you to thank for this." His gaze softened and he leaned in. For a breath-stealing moment, I thought he would kiss me right there in the foyer. "So, thank you, Cleo," he murmured. "The publicity has already led to inquiries."

I drew in a steadying breath to help gather my wits. "You did play a major part in solving the murder, Harry, so you deserve it. Anyway, I asked Mrs. Scoop to mention you, not this person." I looked closer at the byline. "C.E. Meyers."

"I had an inkling who it might be, so I telephoned *The Evening Bulletin* and spoke to Mrs. Scoop. She confirmed my suspicion."

"Who is it?"

"Catherine Elizabeth Meyers, the maiden name of Mrs. Blaine. Or Scoop, if you prefer. Apparently, she plans on using that name for any feature articles Finlayson allows her to write. This one is her first."

"It's superbly written. Thomas Salter and Enoch Price should be pleased Ruth has been recognized like this."

"Enoch wasn't all that pleased when I saw him this morning." Harry dug into his inside jacket pocket. "He called on me after reading my name and paid me a fee." He held out an envelope. "He was relieved that the police were changing their verdict to murder. It's not a lot, but he said I deserved something for my efforts. But it's *you* who deserve it, Cleo. I did tell Enoch, by the way, but..." He shrugged.

He didn't need to say more. I could well imagine Enoch Price refusing to accept that a woman solved his sister's murder.

Instinct and manners almost made me refuse the money, but in the end, I accepted half and slipped the other half into his jacket pocket. I *did* deserve some payment.

"Thank you, Harry. Not just for this, but for stepping in when Wilson attacked. You were marvelous."

He looked down at the floor, his cheeks turning a little pink with embarrassment. "Goliath helped."

"And I have already thanked him."

Harry shuffled his feet. For a man who was always so sure of himself, he seemed out of sorts. "You looked like you enjoyed yourself at the wedding."

"I did. Did you?"

With his head still bent forward, he lifted his gaze, peering at me through his long lashes. The effect was both vulnerable and dashing. My heart fluttered. "I would have enjoyed it more if I'd danced with you."

"You never asked," I pointed out.

"I didn't dare."

"You've never been scared of my uncle or cousin before. You've always stood your ground."

His lips tilted with his intriguing smile. "I wasn't scared of them. I was scared of the other men waiting to dance with you. If I'd tried to jump the queue, there would have been a riot."

I laughed as I shook my head. "You're a devil, Harry. There weren't that many men wanting to dance with me. Besides, who said I would have let you jump the queue?"

He leaned down again and murmured in my ear. "You would have let me. I guarantee it."

He was close enough to hear the hitch in my breath, and perhaps even to hear the blood rushing through my veins. It certainly sounded loud enough to me.

I scrambled to think of something amusing to say that

would settle my frayed nerves, but he walked away before I could.

He turned back when he reached the exit, doffed his hat, and tossed me a self-satisfied smile that left me in no doubt that he knew the effect he had on me.

Available 3rd June 2025 :
MURDER AT HAMBLEDON HALL
The 10th Cleopatra Fox Mystery

Who killed the gamekeeper, and why? Read on for a description of MURDER AT HAMBLEDON HALL by C.J. Archer.

ABOUT: MURDER AT HAMBLEDON HALL

The genteel tranquility of a country house party is shattered when the gamekeeper is shot. Was his death the result of his recent indiscretions, or long-buried secrets?

The weekend was supposed to be an enjoyable time with her family at the neo-Gothic manor of Lord and Lady Kershaw, but when the gamekeeper is murdered, Cleo can't rest until the killer is caught. As a witness herself, she's frustrated with the incompetence of the local police who lay the blame on a man who conveniently disappeared. When she realizes their ineptitude is a result of Lord Kershaw's influence, she focuses her investigation on the earl and his family, against the wishes of her uncle.

The arrival of her suspects at the Mayfair Hotel allows Cleo to continue the investigation after the country house party ends, but what she discovers unnerves her. The gamekeeper's reputation for seducing young women has left a trail of broken hearts, from the lowest maid to the highest lady. But could there be another reason for his murder?

Meanwhile, the hotel staff have secrets of their own to hide. As loyalties are tested on several fronts, Cleo needs her friends more than ever if she is to unravel the mysteries, both old and new.

Available June 2025 :
MURDER AT HAMBLEDON HALL
The 10th Cleopatra Fox Mystery

A MESSAGE FROM THE AUTHOR

I hope you enjoyed reading MURDER ON THE BRIGHTON EXPRESS as much as I enjoyed writing it. As an independent author, getting the word out about my book is vital to its success, so if you liked this book please consider telling your friends and writing a review at the store where you purchased it. If you would like to be contacted when I release a new book, subscribe to my newsletter at http://cjarcher. com/contact-cj/newsletter/. You will only be contacted when I have a new book out.

ALSO BY C.J. ARCHER

SERIES WITH 2 OR MORE BOOKS

The Glass Library

Cleopatra Fox Mysteries

After The Rift

Glass and Steele

The Ministry of Curiosities Series

The Emily Chambers Spirit Medium Trilogy

The 1st Freak House Trilogy

The 2nd Freak House Trilogy

The 3rd Freak House Trilogy

The Assassins Guild Series

Lord Hawkesbury's Players Series

Witch Born

SINGLE TITLES NOT IN A SERIES

Courting His Countess

Surrender

Redemption

The Mercenary's Price

ABOUT THE AUTHOR

C.J. Archer has loved history and books for as long as she can remember and feels fortunate that she found a way to combine the two. She spent her early childhood in the dramatic beauty of outback Queensland, Australia, but now lives in suburban Melbourne with her husband, two children and a mischievous black & white cat named Coco.

Subscribe to C.J.'s newsletter through her website to be notified when she releases a new book, as well as get access to exclusive content and subscriber-only giveaways. Her website also contains up to date details on all her books: http://cjarcher.com She loves to hear from readers. You can contact her through email cj@cjarcher.com or follow her on social media to get the latest updates on her books:

facebook.com/CJArcherAuthorPage

x.com/cj_archer

instagram.com/authorcjarcher